Endorsements

Green World Gray is an intriguing adventure into the world of time travel. This story has mysteries, adventure, and a sibling team that kept me turning the page, wondering what would happen next. It was a insightful tale that left me asking myself what I would give up to make someone I love happy, and how seemingly insignificant decisions can make an impact. The characters and relationships were just as compelling as the time traveling itself. I loved this book, right up to the ending!"

– Whitnew Gutwein Ebert, Teacher at VIPKid

"Once I read the first few pages, I couldn't put it down! The story was easy to understand and had a great plot! I might be 13, but I truly mean what I said."

– Melanie Persons, Grade 7, Transit Middle School

"Besides being an exciting and intriguing read, this book was full of the whole gamut of human emotions from (near) tears and sorrow to smiles and laughter. Most of all, the suspense and anticipation made it hard to put the book down. I believe that young readers will devour this book and will eagerly await the next story to be penned by this outstanding author."

– Kathleen Marie Terragnoli, Professor Emeritus,
University of Valley Forge

To all the kids who will make the world a greener, better place,
and
To all the parents who'd like to go back in time
for just one day.

GREENWORLDGRAY

by Marianne Modica

Contents

PART I – PAST

Chapter 1

SOMETHING WEIRD

Time seemed to move differently once school was out. Some days it stretched out like a dry, hot desert road that led to nowhere. On other days, when least expected, something brilliant would fall from the sky and land smack in the middle of that long, desolate road. A tiny meteorite, a bit of carbon from a dying red giant, a silver staple from an alien space ship, or a stray particle of the time wave itself would bounce, explode, and pick up speed, winding and spinning and carrying one to places one never imagined. Chester, the Horace's cat, knew this very well, even if his charges did not.

On this particular day, when Will and Halia Horace settled in the hallway between their bedrooms, time was in its former state. Will rested on his knees, digging through a pile of Legos. He brushed his straggly brown hair out of his eyes as he constructed a vehicle that was part Tardis and part

1

USS Enterprise. Kids at school might think that a thirteen-year-old was too old for Legos, but Will figured that was their problem. He couldn't care less what they thought about him or anything else.

Across from him Hal leaned back, long legs stretched out and almost touching the opposite wall. Although she was only two years older than her brother, she was a good six inches taller. She flipped through the pictures on her phone, her facial expression changing from a slight smile to a tiny frown and back again. There were lots of other places in the house where brother and sister might have been more comfortable—the sofa in the family room, for example, was warm and soft and covered with big, plush pillows. But since Will was forced to endure family movie nights on that sofa, he didn't often settle there on his own. And since his father fell asleep there most nights while watching *Law and Order* reruns, Will tended to think of the sofa as stage one of Dad's bedtime ritual. Stage two was stumbling up the stairs, yelling, "Go to bed!" at anyone in his path, and stage three was collapsing on his actual bed, where Mom had been sleeping for hours. No, Will preferred the small, close space that connected the messy, unpredictable world of his room with the tidy, serene world of his sister's. Anyway, the upstairs hallway was Chester's favorite spot and more often than not Will and Hal plopped themselves there just to be near their sleeping cat.

"Look at this picture," Hal said, shoving her phone in Will's face. Will glanced at the selfie of Hal with Esther and Rebekah, sisters who lived two houses down.

"Yeah?" said Will. "So what?"

"Look closer," Hal answered, and Will noticed a fourth head behind the girls.

"Some dude photobombing. Again, so what?"

"That's not just any dude," Hal replied.
"That's David Rast. Which could mean he likes one of us."

"Or it could mean he had nothing better to do."

"True. But you never know." Hal's thumbs flew over the keyboard. "I'll see what Rebek thinks."

Sometimes Will wished his sister had never gotten a cell phone. Their parents had resisted, sticking to the "low technology" mandate of Go Green Academy, their charter school. But Hal begged and pleaded and they'd finally given in. Since then Hal had changed, as if the phone connected her to a power source that transformed matter. Will shook his head. Whatever.

"Coming through," said Mom as she stepped carefully over the bodies in the hallway. "You two are going to have to find something constructive to do during summer vacation." Yeah, Will thought, it had been a whole two days since school ended. Better get busy before their brains turned to mush.

"We will," Hal answered. "Don't worry, Mom."

Chester opened one eye and swiped at Mom's leg as she passed. "Silly cat," Mom muttered, almost tripping, but Chester yawned and resumed his comatose pose. Mom turned right, toward the closet at the end of the hall where she kept cleaning supplies and other useless stuff. Will crawled to the edge of the wall and peeped around the corner.

"She's doing it again," he whispered.

Hal looked up from her phone. "Doing what again? And why are you spying on Mom?" She reached to pull Will back but he brushed her away.

"Something weird is going on," he insisted. "Watch."

They watched Mom enter the closet, shut the door, and reemerge not two seconds later.

"See what I mean?" Will said. "She does that all the time—goes in for a second and comes back out. Nothing in her hands—no clothes, no boxes, no nothing." Mom practically floated down the hall to her bedroom and stood at her dresser, staring at baby pictures of Hal and Will with a dreamy, tranquil smile.

"Check out the expression on her face," said Will, still whispering.

"So what," Hal replied warily. "Mom always looks like that. She's always telling us to smile."

That was no lie. Mom possessed a perpetually sunny disposition that she often tried to inflict on Will, but unfortunately for her Will was immune to that particular affliction. Hal, however, was highly susceptible and smiled almost as often as Mom did.

"I'm telling you it's weird, even for Mom. She goes into the closet and then comes right back out, as if she forgot something, only she didn't. Then she sits around like she's on drugs."

"Are you saying Mom is taking drugs in the closet? That's ridiculous!" Hal protested, and Will had to admit it was ridiculous. His mom, sunshiny, fitness nut Alexis Horace, wannabe mother of the year, the "say no to drugs" poster child, would never, ever, do such a thing in a closet or anywhere else.

Will shook his head. "Don't you get it? She doesn't have

time to do anything in the closet. She pops in and pops out a second later. So why does she keep going in there?"

"Since when do you care what Mom does? I would've thought you'd be glad she's leaving you alone."

Will had to think about that. Hal knew him well—it wasn't like him to worry about Mom's emotional well-being (or anyone else's). And Mom wasn't so far into her dream-like trances that she'd leave the stove on and burn the house down or something stupid like that. No, there was something else nudging at Will. Mom's behavior was a puzzle that Will was determined to solve.

"Besides, you're imagining things," Hal continued. "That's what happens when you spy on people," she added while scrolling through David Rast's social media page to see who his friends were, where he'd been, and what he'd been doing for the past two weeks.

Will decided to let it go for now. But he'd find a way to prove he was right. Will went back to his Lego building and Chester, who had been listening discreetly, drifted into a troubled sleep. With so much at stake, he'd need to keep a closer watch on his humans.

○–○–○

Hal finished setting the table just before Dad stepped in the door. He always looked tired and frazzled when he came home from work and Hal knew he needed to decompress from the long subway and bus commute. She waited patiently with Mom until Dad reappeared, face washed and ready for dinner. Will, as usual, had to be called three times.

When they were finally all seated, Dad started with his

usual questions. "How was your day? Anything exciting happen?" He received the usual responses.

"Fine."

"No."

With that out of the way, he turned to Mom.

"Any progress on the junk in the basement?" he asked with a little edge to his voice. Hal stopped chewing and shifted in her seat. Mom and Dad hardly ever argued outright, but lately their dinnertime conversations had been tinged with tension. Hal looked to Will, but he was in some far away world, chomping on his organic mashed potatoes without a care.

Mom smiled. "I separated everything today and Goodwill is coming tomorrow," she said brightly.

Dad spoke evenly but without Mom's perkiness. "Separated? I thought we'd agreed to get rid of all that old junk."

Chester jumped from the floor to the counter to the top of the refrigerator in two swift, sleek movements. He sat up tall, sizing up his underlings like a king on his throne.

Mom smiled again, this time sheepishly. "Well, almost all of it. I just can't part with the baby stuff yet. The crib, the stroller, the high chair—I don't know. I'm not ready to let it go."

"Alex, we agreed our family is complete, right? There's no need to keep any of that."

Mom took an elastic tie from her wrist and gathered her hair into a businesslike ponytail. Hal liked her own thick brown mane, but part of her had always wished she'd inherited Mom's silky blond tresses. "I know, honey, you're right," Mom said. "But that stuff is full of memories for me. I'm just not ready."

Dad rubbed the top of his head, a sure sign that things were about to go sideways. Hal pushed her salad around her plate while Will attacked the last grass-fed hamburger.

Dad's voice rose slightly. "Why do you have to be *ready* to get rid of junk we're not using? It's just stuff, Alexis. It's not like I'm asking you to get rid of the kids. Or the cat." When Dad shifted from "Alex" to "Alexis," escalation was imminent. Chester pushed a box of oatmeal onto the floor, dislodging the top and scattering oatmeal everywhere. "But maybe we *should* get rid of that cat," Dad growled.

Mom jumped up to grab the broom while Chester coolly slid a half-finished package of organic trail mix to the floor next to the spilled oatmeal.

"Chester!" Dad yelled. "Get down!"

Chester maintained his regal pose.

"Stupid cat!" Dad reached up to poke Chester from behind but the cat simply moved away, knocking over a pile of papers in the process.

"Why is there so much junk on top of this refrigerator?" Dad grumbled, scooping up the scattered pages of homework, class notes, and quizzes. "Do we need all these papers? School is over." He moved to dump them into the recycling bin.

"Wait!" Mom cried. "I need to go through those! There might be something the kids want to save."

"Will," Dad asked, "is there anything in this pile you want to save?"

"Nope."

"Hal?"

Hal looked from Dad to Mom and back again. "Maybe." she answered.

"You see?" Mom said. "Just put them on the counter for now."

After glaring at his family for a few seconds, Dad did as he was told and sat down to finish his dinner. Several moments of silence passed while Dad calmed down, each bite becoming a little less forceful than the one before. Finally, he sighed, "Okay, honey, you win. We'll hold on to the baby stuff for now, but eventually it's gotta go. We need the space for future storage."

"Okay," said Mom, smiling once again. Hal smiled too, relieved by the temporary truce.

That night while Mom and Dad watched the Mets game, Hal slipped into Will's room. She'd arranged her thick brown hair into a bun on the top of her head. "How does it look?" she asked.

Will glanced up from his *Doctor Who* comic. "Like a frizzy donut. Or a bagel."

"Thanks."

Will's bed was covered with mini space craft, action figures, small tools, and some other items Hal couldn't identify. When she brushed them aside to make a place to sit, a metal clock casing fell to the floor. Out bounced an assortment of gears, wheels, sprockets, and springs. "Did you take a clock apart? I hope that wasn't Mom's," she said, although there was only one clock in the house that wasn't digital and she'd just passed it in the kitchen.

"Just some old junk from Mr. Salazar." On most days their retired neighbor could be found tinkering in his garage next door. Will visited him often and usually came home with a gadget of one kind or another that he'd take apart but could never put back together again.

"Do you think anything's going on with Mom and Dad?" Hal asked.

"I think there's something going on with Mom. I told you. Something weird is happening in that closet."

"How could anything weird happen if she's only in there for a second? You know Mom's a little flakey. She probably goes to get something and forgets what it was."

"Every day?" Will asked. "And what about that look on her face?"

"Forget about the closet. Did you notice how Mom and Dad were arguing at dinner? They've been doing that more and more."

"If they get a divorce, me and Chester are staying with Mr. Salazar."

"Not funny." Hal's dark eyebrows knit together in worry. A lot of her friends' parents were divorced. "It could happen. We need to be careful not to upset them." She looked pointedly at Will.

"You mean *I* need to be careful. You never do anything to upset anyone." Hal heard no resentment in her brother's voice. He was simply stating the truth. "I'm the troubled child of the family."

Hal softened. "You're not troubled. You just don't care what other people think." She picked up a few pieces of the disassembled clock and tried to fit them together.

"You can't fix it," Will told her. "It's too complicated. I've tried."

"Maybe you give up too easily."

"Whatever. But I'm going to find a way to prove I'm right about Mom." Will went back to reading his comic and didn't even look up when Hal tossed the broken timepiece to the side and left the room.

○─○─○

By the time Will dragged himself out of bed it was mid-morning and already eighty degrees outside, warm for late June in the Queens suburb that was home. Not a morning person, Will shuffled into the kitchen with his eyes half closed and poured himself a bowl of cereal. "When nine hundred years old you reach...yeah, yeah, you know the rest," he said to Yoda's picture on the box.

Mom and Hal entered through the back door, smelling of dirt and sweat. They'd been working in the raised bed garden Mom kept in their small, fenced-in yard.

"Whew, it's humid out there," Mom commented, wiping her face on her T-shirt sleeve. "I'm going to jump in the shower." Hal sat in the chair next to her brother, who continued to stare at Yoda and chew.

"We fed the tomatoes," she offered.

"How did you know they were hungry?" Will asked, still not looking up. "Did they knock on the door with a bowl and spoon, or did you just hear their stomachs rumbling?"

"You think you're pretty funny. We're going to the pool. Want to come?"

"Who's we, and is Mom driving?" Will liked the pool, but he hated the bus ride and mile walk it took to get there if no one was willing to drive them.

"Rebekah, Esther, and me, and Mom can drive us but we'll have to take the bus home. She's got some appointments this afternoon."

"No thanks." It made no sense to Will to cool off at the pool and get all hot and sweaty again on the way home. "I'll stick with the air conditioning. Besides, there's something I need to do." Will's brain had been formulating a plan while he slept and he needed some time to work it through. A visit to Mr. Salazar might help.

They heard the bathroom door open. "Mom's done," Hal said. "I'm going to take a shower."

Will wondered how many times in one day a person would want to get wet. When he'd finished eating, he threw on shorts and a T-shirt and headed outside, hoping to find Mr. Salazar in his garage. The garage door was open, as usual, and as Will entered he stopped to look at a glossy photo of the swimming pool at the Hacienda San Maria, where Mr. Salazar had once lived with his parents. The crisp, blue water almost looked real and Will pictured himself smacking through its cold, clear surface in a cannon ball dive. He'd almost changed his mind about going to the pool when Mr. Salazar appeared, wearing his usual short sleeve, button-down work shirt and jeans. He was followed by a bored looking Chester.

"What are you doing here?" Will asked his cat. Chester rubbed his gray fur against Will's leg.

"We were just having a little talk," Mr. Salazar answered with a wink. He sat on a stool at the worktable that stretched along the length of the garage. Will sat beside him, quietly watching Mr. Salazar tinker with one of a dozen dismantled TV remotes, using a magnifying lamp and tweezers to remove

11

and replace tiny parts. Chester settled on the cool cement under the table and nestled his head in his paws. It wasn't unusual for them to sit like that in silence. That was one of the things Will liked best about Mr. Salazar; he asked no questions and expected no answers. Just being was enough for him.

But on that day just being was not enough for Will. He had something on his mind. "What would you do if you needed to see what someone was doing without them knowing it?" he asked.

Mr. Salazar put down the screwdriver he'd been using and fished though a metal toolbox for a smaller one. He showed no sign he'd heard Will's question, but a minute later he said, "I guess that depends on who this person is and why I need to know what he or she is doing."

How could Will explain his suspicions about Mom to Mr. Salazar? Not being very good at diplomacy, he decided on the direct approach. "It's my mom. Something weird is going on with her. Every day I see her shut herself into the hall closet, just for a second. She walks in, shuts the door, stands in the dark for a second, and then walks out again. Nothing in her hands. Then she sits around with a dreamy look on her face, staring at our baby pictures."

If Mr. Salazar was surprised, he didn't show it. "I see," he said. "And have you asked your mother about this? Perhaps there's a reasonable explanation."

Will hadn't asked because he knew full well his mother would not come clean. She had a long history of looking at the bright side and wasn't likely to share information that might pollute her children's perfect world. Mom even tried to hide stupid stuff, whispering to Dad about some distant cousin's divorce, as if Will even cared. Clearly, Will had not inherited his directness from his mom.

"That won't work," he said with certainty.   "You know my mom."

"I do." Mr. Salazar and Mom were both avid gardeners and often shared tips on cultivating cucumbers and tomatoes. "I've always found her to be a trustworthy person, a person of integrity."

"It's not that I don't trust her. I don't think she's doing anything wrong, it's just...weird," he said for what seemed like the zillionth time. "And she'll never admit to it, because she doesn't trust us. She thinks that because we're kids we can't handle anything. Like the world has to be perfect for us or something."

"I understand," Mr. Salazar sighed. "Well then, I suppose you'll have to find some other way. If only you could see into that closet without actually being there." He reached for an old Polaroid camera that sat on a cluttered shelf and pried the back open.

Chester jumped into Will's lap just as an idea jumped into Will's head.

"It looks like someone wants something," Mr. Salazar said.

"Probably wants to eat." Will rose with Chester in his arms. "Thanks."

Mr. Salazar waved, head bowed over his work. He wasn't big on please and thank you—another thing Will liked about him.

Will gave Chester his afternoon snack and ran upstairs to

follow through with his idea. He reached his bedroom just in time to see Mom step out of the hall closet with that dreamy look on her face.

"Mom, we're ready to go," Hal called from her doorway, pool towel in hand. When Mom didn't respond, Hal called louder. "Mom! Did you hear me? We're ready to go!" Still no response from Mom.

"She's at it again," Will said.

"At what?" Hal stepped into the hallway.

"You know what. She's off in La-La Land."

Hal tapped on the door to Mom's room. "Mom? Are you okay?"

"Oh, yes, sure. Let's go!" Mom said, swinging the door open and breezing through the hall and down the stairs. A look of concern passed between Hal and Will, but Mom didn't notice. She didn't dump her usual instructions-for-staying-home-alone on Will, either.

That was it. Will knew what he had to do, and there was no time like the present. When he heard the car turn out of the driveway, he grabbed his webcam and approached the closet. He creaked open the door slowly, not exactly afraid, but definitely wary of what he might find inside. Nothing seemed out of the ordinary—boxes and cleaning stuff on the middle shelves, folded up blankets on top, vacuum cleaner parts along the back wall. Will stepped in and positioned the webcam carefully behind a roll of paper towels. As he turned to leave he spotted a piece of stationary on the floor. It was a letter to his parents, written on school letterhead and signed by the principal, Mrs. Bumbly. That couldn't be good. Will sank to the floor and read how sorry she was to inform them that they would need to find a different school placement for their son, William, in the fall. It seemed that their small school was not equipped to provide the emotional support he needed.

Will folded up the letter and shoved it into his pocket. So, he'd be going to the regular public school in the fall. Whatever. He'd heard it wasn't a great school, but at least they didn't wear uniforms, and maybe teachers there wouldn't be on his back all the time.

Will spent the afternoon lying around the house reading comics and trying not to think about his impending doom. Mom would want to discuss the contents of the letter at dinner and Dad would not be happy. He reviewed his usual strategy—keep quiet and wait for his parents to run out of steam. Anyway, the whole summer stretched before him and he had other, more important things on his mind. Who knows what might happen before he'd have to think about school again.

Chapter 2

EVIDENCE

Will intercepted his sister outside the bathroom just as she was about to go in for yet another shower.

"I have a plan," he whispered.

"The pool was fun. Thanks for asking."

"I figured out how to see what's going on with Mom. I set up my mini spy cam in the closet."

With a horrified look, Hal pulled her brother into his room and kicked the door shut. "First, as your sister I need to point out just how creepy that sounds. Second, you have a mini spy cam? Since when?"

"I got it online with a gift card."

"How did you get away with that?"

"I told Mom it was for school. And it's not creepy. I'm gathering evidence to prove my case. The next time Mom steps into that closet I'll be ready."

But Mom had been home for hours and had made no

move toward the closet. Instead, she busied herself in the kitchen, pulverizing basil in the blender for the pesto pasta salad they'd be expected to eat for dinner. She'd barely said two words since she'd been home, but the roar of the food processor and the clang of pots more than made up for her silence.

"Mom seems upset," Hal said. Will shrugged. He thought of the letter and almost came clean to Hal, but why bother? She'd find out soon enough.

At dinnertime Will checked the icon on his computer to be sure the spy cam was up and running, then washed up and went downstairs. As he'd expected, Mom started in as soon as she'd filled their plates with her green veggie mishmash.

"I don't want to spoil dinner," she began.

"Too late," Will muttered, looking at his plate. Dad snickered but Mom cleared her throat and continued.

"I had an interesting appointment with Mrs. Bumbly today." Mom paused, letting her words soak in like the vinaigrette on the salad. Dad and Hal both turned to Will, Dad suddenly stern and Hal sympathetic.

Will maintained a careful blankness.

"Would you prefer we talk about this later, William?" asked Mom. "It doesn't really involve your sister, but I thought you might want her here for moral support."

"Whatever," Will said.

"Are you sure? I don't want to invade your privacy."

"Alex, can you just get to the point?" Dad snapped. "What did the principal say? What's he done now?"

Mom gave Dad a chilly look, Hal squirmed, and Will lined up his zucchini in a face-off with his rotini. "He hasn't done anything wrong, exactly," Mom said. "Mrs. Bumbly is concerned about Will's attitude, that's all. She thinks Will has a problem with other people. 'Detached' is the word she used. 'Disconnected from other human beings,' she said."

Chester moseyed into the room and stretched out under the table across Will's feet, inner motor purring. All eyes fell on Will, who shrugged.

"See?" said Mom in frustration. "That's what Mrs. Bumbly meant. Will doesn't seem to care what his teachers think. He hardly talks to them or to the other kids. In fact, he spends most of his time alone."

"That's not fair," Hal exclaimed. "Will talks to me all the time. And he's friends with Esther."

Dad's gaze softened. "What do you think, buddy?" he asked Will. "Do you feel detached?"

Will couldn't think of a way to explain his feelings about his teachers. They would be okay, if only they'd stop bothering him so much. Just last week Will had politely declined his reward for top science grades, explaining that lunch with the principal was not his idea of a good time. He shrugged again and kept quiet.

Mom, in the meantime, bounced back and forth like a tennis ball on steroids. To Will: "Mrs. Bumbly showed me your five-paragraph essay, which was supposed to be about your best moments in sixth grade." To Dad: "Apparently, Will's best moments happened when people left him alone." To Hal: "You got an honorable mention for that essay, remember?" Back to Will, sadly: "Honey, are you unhappy at school?"

Will frowned, confused. Wasn't this where Mom tells Dad he got kicked out of Go Green Academy? He'd expected fury or tears, not the wimpy worry on Mom's face.

"So, he's a bit of a loner," Dad said. "When I was a kid, the teachers complained I talked too much. Now they say my kid doesn't talk enough. They're never satisfied. The school year is in the past—I say we forget it and move on to the future. What do you think, Will?"

Will shrugged again. "Whatever."

Mom closed her eyes and rubbed her forehead. "I give up," she said. "Life was so much easier when you were babies. I'd rather change diapers than meet with teachers any day."

To Will's surprise, the conversation shifted to Mom's summer agenda (as Hal called it, "Mom's Plan for a Productive Summer with No Wasted Time," or, alternately, "No Veggie Left Behind").

"That's it?" Will interrupted.

"That's what?" Dad asked.

"That's all she said, the principal?"

"What else would she say, William?" Mom asked. "She expressed her concern and plans to keep an eye on you next year."

What was going on? Had Mom managed to change Mrs. Bumbly's mind? Will felt for the letter in his pocket, but it was gone. Had he dropped it somewhere? He didn't think so, but what other explanation could there be?

O—O—O

Will had planned on a quiet evening of video games, but he'd forgotten all about family movie night. Mom loved to show them movies from when she was a kid, insisting that movies, TV shows, music, and the world in general was better

19

back then. Will couldn't argue with her this week. *Back to the Future* was one of his favorite movies, too.

By the end of the movie Dad and Hal were slumped against each other, sound asleep, but for once Mom had stayed awake. She stared at the credits for a minute, then wandered upstairs in a trance. Will sneaked after her. Bam, there she went, in and out of the storage closet in a few split seconds. By the time Will checked the spycam icon on his desktop Mom had already disappeared into her bedroom and closed the door behind her.

Will watched the recording of Mom stepping into the closet. She closed the door and reached down for something—Will couldn't see what because the angle of the camera was too high. Then Mom grabbed something from an old shoebox on the shelf to her right.

Will heard a soft knock at his door and hit the pause button.

"You awake?" Hal whispered, peeking in.

"Come in and shut the door." Will clicked play and they watched Mom hit buttons on a device about the size of a cell phone. The picture jumped for a micro second as if someone had bumped the camera, and then Mom returned the device to its hiding place and stepped out of the closet.

"Well, that didn't help," Hal said. "She didn't do anything but stand there."

"Watch from the beginning." Will replayed the footage. "What do you notice?"

"Nothing much. She goes in, messes around with an old phone, then steps out again."

"Look at her face." Sure enough, Mom's expression

changed from a sad frown to a dreamy smile in a blink.

"Hmm. Do you think that thing she's holding gives her some kind of shock? Like a drug or something?"

"Maybe, but here's something even weirder," Will answered. "Watch it again and look at the time signature." Will pointed to the timer clicking away the seconds at the bottom of the screen. "She steps in ... one, one thousand ... bends down for a minute ... two, one thousand, three, one thousand ... reaches for the device ... four, one thousand ... puts it back ... five, one thousand ... reaches down again ... six, one thousand ... and steps out of the closet for a total of seven seconds. According to this she's in the closet for seven seconds."

"So?" asked Hal.

Will's voice rose in excitement. "So, when we see her go into the closet in real time she comes out not more than two seconds later. Yet the recording shows her in there for seven seconds. How can that be?"

"What are you guys up to?" Dad called as he passed the door. "Go to bed."

They waited silently for Dad's footsteps to disappear down the hall. Hal turned back to Will. "The camera doesn't lie. We must be wrong. Maybe it just feels like she comes out in two seconds."

Will was not convinced. "You can try to explain it away, but I know what I'm seeing. Tomorrow we'll triangulate our data. You'll record Mom from the hallway and I'll record her from the webcam. And then we'll check out that phone or whatever it is she's got in there."

"Okay." Hal shook her head. "And then you'll see it's

nothing and that will be the end of it."

Will let his sister leave without a response. She could live in her perfect little never-changing bubble if she wanted, but Will knew something exciting was about to happen. He felt it in his bones. He was a scientist on the brink of discovery. That night Will dreamt that the ordinary gray house cat lying across his legs turned into a white and black bald eagle and stood at the foot of the bed, inviting Will to join him. Together they soared through the bedroom window, over the school building, and into another world.

○—○—○

The next day Hal and her brother sat on the floor in the upstairs hallway, ready to spring into action. Since they couldn't sit there doing nothing without risking Mom's "you two need to do something productive" speech, they surrounded themselves with every puzzle book they could find and were deep into a pretend game of MindTrap by the time Mom noticed them.

"Wouldn't you be more comfortable sitting at the table?" she asked as she wove through the human-feline-gameboard obstacle course.

"We like it here," Hal replied.

"Okay then. I'm going to do some cleaning. Anyone feel like giving me a hand?"

"Sure. I'll clean out the hall closet," Will said, smirking.

"Thanks, honey, but that won't be necessary. I just straightened up in there a few days ago. But you can sweep the back patio later if you feel so moved."

Will said nothing so Hal spoke up. "I will, Mom."

Once Mom had passed, Will shot Hal a dirty look. "You don't have to do that," he said.

"Do what?"

"You don't have to be the good one all the time."

"I don't know what you're talking about."

"You do. But whatever. There she goes. Get ready!" Will said.

Hal crawled after Mom with her phone in hand, but Mom only pulled the mop, bucket, and tile cleaner out of the closet and headed for the bathroom. She saw Hal on all fours a few feet away and stopped.

"What are you doing?" she asked. "Don't tell me you lost another contact in the carpet."

"Nope, just looking for my phone," Hal answered weakly.

"Your phone is in your hand."

"Oh, right! Gotta get back to the game!" Hal crawled back to Will, hoping Mom would ask no more questions, since she was not very good at keeping secrets from Mom.

"False alarm," she whispered when she got back to Will. "She's just cleaning the bathroom."

Will nodded and they waited quietly, flipping through books as Mom scrubbed away, all the while singing "Yesterday" at the top of her lungs. Mom and Dad loved the Beatles—it was one of the only things they actually agreed on. Just when Mom was really feeling it, she was interrupted by a loud knock at the back door.

"See who that is, but don't let anyone in unless you know them," Mom called from the bathroom.

"Yeah, Mom, we know," Hal replied, rolling her eyes. Mom gave the same instructions every time someone came to the door, as if kidnappers lurked behind the wrought iron fence that enclosed their small corner property. Fortunately, it was the kidnappers' day off and only Rebekah and Esther stood at the door. They followed Hal into the kitchen and plopped themselves at the table. Will joined them, dumping the game board and puzzle books down with a thud.

"Did you tell Will what happened?" Esther asked.

Hal looked at her game cards uncomfortably.

"What happened when?" Will asked.

"Yesterday at the pool. Didn't Hal tell you?"

"What happened yesterday at the pool?" Will asked, frowning.

Hal squirmed and Rebekah shot her younger sister a warning look which Esther ignored. "You know that kid, David Rast?"

"The photobomber?"

"Yeah. He's a jerk."

"Most people are," Will said.

"Okay, so we're sitting around the pool yesterday, and David Rast lays his towel down right next to us. He starts acting all friendly, making conversation, but he's only talking to Hal - totally ignores me and Rebek. Then, when we go to eat lunch, he says, 'I hope that's not kimchee. I can't stand the smell of that stuff,' holding his nose and acting all grossed out. That's when your sister, calm as anything, picks up his backpack and tosses it over his head, right into the pool! He freaks out—starts screaming, 'My phone!' Jumps up and grabs the backpack right before it's about to sink."

Will grinned. "So, what happened?" he asked. "Did his phone get ruined?"

"Nah," Esther replied. "It didn't even get wet."

"Thank goodness," Hal added. As mad as she'd been, she figured they had enough trouble at home right now.

"David Rast really hates us now," Esther continued. "But it was worth it. Kimchee my butt." She and Will laughed.

"I guess he won't be making any more Korean jokes around Hal," Will noted with pride.

"He did seem to like Hal, though. And he's cute. It's too bad he's an idiot," Rebekah said.

"Yeah," Hal sighed. "Just my luck."

"Bathroom floor is wet," Mom called from upstairs. "Hello, Rebekah. Hello, Esther."

"Hi, Mrs. Horace," the Yim sisters answered in unison.

"I'll be relaxing for a bit," Mom said. "Help yourselves to lunch."

The blood drained from Hal's face as she locked eyes with Will.

"It's happening," Will whispered.

"What's happening?" Esther asked. "What's going on?"

"Stay here," Will said. "Take your phone," he told Hal, and the two of them flew up the stairs, leaving the puzzled Rebekah and Esther behind. They reached the top as Mom stepped into the closet, and Hal just had time to record the closet door closing and opening again two seconds later. When Mom emerged she was cradling something in her hands. Hal saw a quick flash of pink before she made a mad dash into the bathroom to avoid being seen, but as Mom had warned, the floor was wet. Hal slipped and slid to the sink on her knees. Her phone flew into the air, missed the toilet by an inch, and clattered to the tile floor. Hal looked up to see Will standing in the doorway.

"Great job," he said.

"I didn't want Mom to see me."

"Lucky for us, Mom is in Dreamland." Will nodded toward her closed bedroom door. "Did you get it?" He motioned at the phone.

"I think so." Thankful she'd spent the extra money for a shatterproof case, Hal played the two-second recording of Mom stepping in and out of the closet.

"That proves it," said Will.

"What's going on?" Esther called from the bottom of the stairs. "Are you coming down, or what?"

Hal look questioningly at her brother. "Should we tell them?" She knew her brother didn't like letting people into his private world, but Hal needed her friends. "They can keep a secret," she said.

"Whatever," Will sighed. "Let's show them the videos."

A few minutes later, all four crowded in front of Will's computer, comparing the recordings of Mom on the webcam and Hal's phone. "There's a five second difference," Will stated.

"How can that be?" Rebekah asked. "It's impossible."

"Yet here it is," Will replied. He played the webcam recording again. "Watch what she's doing right here," he said, pointing to the screen. "Whatever is happening, it's got something to do with that device. We have to get our hands on it."

Chapter 3

THE IMPOSSIBLE

Will hatched a simple plan. The girls would keep Mom busy that afternoon so that he could snoop around in the closet uninterrupted. They munched impatiently on peanut butter and jelly sandwiches until Mom finally appeared.

"What's up?" she asked. "Everybody keeping busy?"

Will raised an eyebrow but Hal was all over it. "Can we go to the bookstore in Lake Success? We need to get started on our summer reading." Her voice took on that whiny-begging tone that made Will want to grind his teeth but that Mom couldn't resist. Since the store was at least a thirty-minute drive each way, they were sure to be gone for most of the afternoon. Sometimes it was almost too easy, Will thought.

As soon as the females left the house, Will pulled the box down from the shelf in the closet. It was labeled, "old pictures of the kids" in Mom's totally perfect handwriting and right there on top was the device he'd seen Mom using in the video. He studied the small black rectangle carefully. Two thirds of it consisted of a screen—blank, of course. Below that were rows of letters, numbers, and unfamiliar symbols. He turned the device over and examined the back, squinting as he held it under the weak closet light. There, scratched in barely legible print were three words: JUST ONE DAY.

Will pushed the buttons randomly but was not surprised when nothing happened. He was going to need help to hack into this contraption, whatever it was, and he knew just where to go. Ignoring Mom's "stay in the house with the door locked" directive, he sprinted to Mr. Salazar's garage, but his friend was not at work there yet. Will paced back and forth in the driveway for what seemed like an eternity until Mr. Salazar finally appeared and invited him in.

"Let's be clear," Mr. Salazar said a few minutes later, turning the device over in his hands. "You want me to help you hack into this personal possession of your mother's. You want me to do this because you think this mechanism has something to do with your mother's strange behavior. Is that correct?"

"Yes," Will answered, glancing at the dusty clock that hung over the workbench. Still plenty of time before Mom and the girls got back, but Will knew from experience that time seemed to slip away quickly in Mr. Salazar's garage.

"This is a serious thing you're asking me to do," Mr. Salazar continued. As if to punctuate the statement, Chester jumped up to the table. Cat and man faced Will squarely. "Are you sure? Once it's done, it can't be undone. You may find out more than you bargained for."

Will hesitated. It wouldn't take much to convince Hal they'd imagined a mystery that didn't exist. She'd be relieved to forget the closet and the video and dive into another long, boring summer, and Will could go back to ignoring Mom—a skill he'd perfected over the years. But enigma hung before Will like a supermoon and there was no escaping its gravitational pull.

"I'm sure," Will said. "I need to know what's going on."

"Okay then, we continue." Mr. Salazar held the device under his magnifying lamp, running his fingers over the smooth surface. "No on/off switch that I can see," he said.

"I know. But there must be some way to turn it on."

When Mr. Salazar inspected the back of the device under the lamp, Will saw a rectangular panel he hadn't noticed before.

"Maybe the controls are in there," he said. Mr. Salazar reached across the table for a plastic case of micro screwdrivers. Chester, who was watching intently, meowed.

"Yes, my friend, I know. Only the smallest tool will pry this panel open," said Mr. Salazar. After a few unsuccessful attempts, Mr. Salazar managed to remove the back panel with an extra fine width straight pin. Will gaped at the hundreds of interconnected chips, wires, crystals, gears, and wheels whirling within the small enclosure.

"This is like nothing I've seen in this world," Mr. Salazar said. "It's similar to a traditional analog clock, but so many parts. And so fine, and all working together in a circular motion, do you see?" He pointed at the shifting bits of machinery with the pin. "And here, look. I believe this is a switch of sorts. Let's see what it does." Mr. Salazar gently pushed on a small square protrusion at the edge of the open panel. Will held his breath and waited, but when nothing happened he exhaled a disappointed sigh.

"I thought you'd be able to get it working. Now I'm back to square one."

"On the contrary, we have learned a great deal," Mr. Salazar said. "We've seen that this device is clock-like in nature rather than phone-like, for example. We may not know what its function is, but I doubt it is used for communication. More likely its use has something to do with the passage of time." Chester sat up straighter and rubbed his head against Mr. Salazar's face. "It seems our friend here agrees."

Will did not share their optimism. "I gotta go," he said, looking again at the clock. Sure enough, more than an hour had passed. How had that happened? It was almost as if Mr. Salazar's garage existed in an alternate universe where time had a different agenda. Will returned home, placed the device back in the shoebox, and spent the next hour staring nervously into space until he heard Mom's keys jiggling at the door.

O—O—O

The next morning, Will and Hal stood by the back door, whispering. "You mean it's a fancy clock?" Hal asked incredulously. "Why would Mom go into the closet to look at a clock?"

"Not a clock exactly, but 'something to do with the passage of time,' Mr. Salazar said."

Propped against the door were a large cooler, a bag of

paper products, and Mom's brown and white striped canvas tote, filled with her summer-fun essentials. Will put his hands in his pockets and kicked the bag over.

"Stop," scolded Hal, scooping up frisbees and badminton racquets. "Why didn't you tell me last night?"

"You slept at Rebekah's, remember? I haven't seen you since you left for the bookstore yesterday."

Hal sighed. "I wish you had a phone."

"I don't," Will replied. He watched his sister texting their conversation to Rebekah, who was, no doubt, repeating it to Esther. A phone would mean one more way for people to bother him. No thanks.

"You guys all set?" Mom asked as she entered the kitchen. Not waiting for an answer, she went to the counter to fill the cooler. Will steeled himself for the long ride ahead to a family reunion filled with aunts, uncles, cousins, and enough organic picnic food to choke a titanosaur. Whatever. At least Gram would be there. Will hadn't seen her since the funeral.

They rode in the van in silence, Hal texting away, Mom staring out the window, and Dad's eyes fixed straight ahead (for once, Mom wasn't yelling, "Watch the road!" while she stomped her imaginary brake). Some kids Will knew filled up long drives with movies or video games, but not them, no sir. Their mom insisted that car rides were the perfect opportunity for "real face-to-face communication" or to enjoy the scenery in peace. Will sat back and watched the occasional trees, grassy splotches, and green and white highway signs roll by. Breathtaking scenery for sure.

About ten minutes in Hal slid as close as her seat belt would allow and showed Will her phone on the sly. She'd written, Notice the silence? They're not talking.

Will shrugged.

I heard them arguing this morning.

Will shrugged again and Hal sighed in exasperation.

"Everything okay back there?" Mom asked.

"Fine," Hal responded, and that was the last real face-to-face communication Will had to endure until they arrived at Blue Lake State Park an hour later.

Still grumbling about the parking fee, Dad led them through the paved walking trails, around the lake to a shaded picnic area next to a playground. "Look for something large and orange," he instructed. Will scanned the crowd until he spotted Dad's older brother, Jason, wearing an orange Syracuse University T-shirt and waving furiously from the opposite end of the picnic area. Uncle Jason looked like an older, taller, rounder version of Dad. He and Aunt Judy rushed over to greet them, kissing Hal but approaching Will with a more reserved tousle of the hair. They dragged past whining children and the adults who were ignoring them to Gram, waiting at a table covered in red checkered plastic. More kisses and tousled hair followed until Will began to wish for the genetic mutation for baldness. Only Gram grabbed him into a full-fledged hug and held him there for several seconds. He didn't resist.

Once they'd settled in, Dad went off to survey the lake with Uncle Jason, while Mom and Hal drank organic mint tea with Gram and Aunt Judy. Will wandered among the aunts, uncles, and cousins that filled the surrounding tables, drifting in and out of other people's conversations until he parked himself on a bench next to his youngest cousin, Sam, who was absorbed in a video game. Although his back was to them, Will could just hear Mom's voice above the yelps and crashes of Mario Kart. Will realized that, as usual, he was the topic of conversation.

"I just don't understand," Mom was saying. "He's so different from his sister. So quiet and detached. His teachers are concerned."

"What does Paul think?" Gram asked.

"He doesn't see it. You know your son. Always ready to move on."

Gram murmured a diplomatic "Mmm," but said no more.

"It was so much easier when they were little, before they went to school," Mom said wistfully.

"Easier in some ways, but not in others," said Aunt Judy. "All the chasing around, dirty diapers, runny noses—I wouldn't want to go back to that."

"Oh, I'd go back in a heartbeat," said Mom. "Even for just one day."

"Enjoy them at every age," Gram said sadly. "It all goes by so fast." Will knew she was thinking of Gramps, who had died last spring. He remembered the day Dad told them that Gramps was gone. He and Hal had been devastated. They hadn't even known he was sick until a few weeks before. "Your mother didn't want to overburden you with all that," Dad had explained. Right, life was supposed to be perfect until you're what, eighteen? Then they dump all the bad stuff on you at once.

Will stopped thinking about Gramps because something Mom had said was poking around in his head, annoying him. Before he had a chance to figure out what it was he felt his sister tugging at his arm.

"Come on," she said urgently. "I think I know what's going on." She half dragged Will out of his seat and pulled him along the path toward the lake until he shook her off.

"Okay, okay, I'm coming," he said. "Where are we going?"

"We need to talk–somewhere quiet, where we won't be overheard. Let's go out to the dock."

On their way they passed Dad and Uncle Jason, sitting on a bench facing the crystal blue lake. "It's like she's living in the past," Will heard Dad say. He stopped dead in his tracks. Hal took a few steps before she noticed her brother was not keeping up.

"Come on," she said impatiently, but Will didn't move.

"I know what Mom's doing, too," he said, hardly believing his own words. "She's going back in time."

Chapter 4

DISCOVERY

Hal sat on her best friend's stoop a few days later and watched Esther and Will kick a soccer ball back and forth on the narrow sidewalk. The day was humid and sticky, but, as usual, Mom insisted they "get some fresh air." They'd long since given up arguing about Mom's obsession with the great outdoors. Dad had been no help in this area – he'd answered their complaints with, "When I was your age we used to play kickball in the street."

"Didn't the dinosaurs get in the way?" asked Hal innocently.

"Nah," Will jumped in. "They got run over by the covered wagons." Dad laughed but Mom prevailed and outside they went whenever she commanded. There'd been no arguments today, though, because Hal and Will needed to be sure Mom wouldn't overhear them. Although hot and uncomfortable, the Yims' front steps were far away from Mom's listening ears.

"As crazy as it sounds, that's got to be it," Hal said.

"But time travel is impossible," Rebekah stated for the fourth time.

"Correction—time travel is impossible as far as we know," Will said, gently tapping the ball with his foot. "It would be arrogant to assume we know everything about the universe."

"That's ironic, coming from you," Esther said. She kicked the ball hard and Will barely blocked it from flying into the street.

"Out of bounds," he called.

"Fine, you win," Esther conceded. "I'm too hot to play anyway." She crumpled onto the step below her sister, fanning her face with her hand. Will scooched next to her.

"Let's go over this one more time," Esther said. "You think that somehow your mother is travelling back in time. She uses some kind of cell phone to do it."

"Not a phone," Will interrupted. "I think it's a time travel device—I'm calling it the TTD for short."

"Okay, whatever," Esther said impatiently. "So, she uses the TTD to travel back in time through a wormhole in your hall closet."

"If you don't believe us, look at the videos again," Hal said. "It's the only way to explain the five second gap between the video Will took inside the closet and the one I took from the hall."

"I never said I didn't believe you," Esther answered. "But explain that gap to me again." She popped half a piece of Bubble Yum into her mouth, and tossed the other half to Will.

"It's like this," Will replied through chews. "The spycam video, taken inside the closet, shows my mom reaching for the TTD and setting it. Then we see a minuscule blink, like a little shake, and then she puts the TTD back and steps out of the closet. In between there she reaches down like she's fixing something."

"And...?"

Just then a delivery truck pulled up alongside the parked cars. The driver jumped out and handed a small package to Esther. "You want to take this for your mom?" he asked, and was back in his truck before Esther had a chance to answer. The slogan printed on the side of the truck read: Speedy Delivery – Almost Before You Called.

Will smiled. "Imagine if that delivery truck could travel in time. The company could take your order, package it, then go back in time to deliver it at the exact instant you placed the order. You'd get the package almost before you called." His voice rose in excitement. "So, Mom goes back—that's the little blink in the video—but she returns only a second after she stepped into the closet. Inside the closet, seven seconds pass, but on the outside, where we are, only two seconds have gone by. From our perspective, Mom comes back almost before she left!"

Esther and Rebekah responded with stunned silence. Hal put her head down in her arms and hid her face under her hair.

Finally, Rebekah spoke. "It makes sense, kind of," she said quietly. "But if she returns only a second after she left, why does the camera inside the closet record the time gap?"

"Good question," Will said. "I've been wondering that

myself. The space inside the closet must be different, protected in some way. Like, maybe the TTD gives off waves or something so it affects the area right near it. That would explain why the camera inside the closet records time passing normally."

"I can't believe this is really happening," Hal said. "I wish we could just have a normal summer, like last year. The world as we know it is falling apart."

Esther rolled her eyes and stood, chomping on her gum furiously. "Look at it this way," she said, slamming the soccer ball down as she spoke. "We've discovered the existence of time travel!" Bam. "It's real!" Bam. "Think of the possibilities!" Bam.

Will lurched forward and caught the ball, grinning. "It is pretty cool," he said, hugging the ball to his chest. "Or it will be," he added, glancing at Hal, "once we know Mom is okay."

"She's obviously not okay," Hal answered. "None of this is okay."

"Speaking of the possibilities," Rebekah said, "*If* your mother really is travelling through time, *if* such a thing is possible, how do you know she's going back and not forward?"

"We don't know anything for sure. But it's the way she's acting," Will explained. "She comes back all dreamy and stares at our baby pictures."

"So what?" Esther asked.

"So, what if she's more than just reminiscing? What if she'd actually just seen us that way? It makes perfect sense."

"Okay," said Rebekah, "then how do you know she's not changing things, altering the events of the past? *If* she is, *if* such a thing is possible, you would never even know it."

"*If* you don't stop saying *if* I'm going to use your head as a goal post," Esther said, grabbing the soccer ball away from Will.

"That's a good point." Will said. "If Mom is altering the timeline we'd have no way of knowing. We'd simply transform along with the changes she makes."

"What would she possibly want to change?" Hal asked. "Everything was perfect the way it was, before all this started."

"What if everything was not perfect?" Will said quietly. "What if something bad happened, like, say, I got kicked out of school, and Mom went back in time to fix it?"

Hal tried to search her brother's face but his gaze was fixed downward.

"Huh?" said Esther. "Where did that come from?"

"I found a letter in the closet saying I couldn't go back to school in the fall. I expected a cataclysmic event at dinner, but it never came. No word of my imminent expulsion from Go Geek Academy."

"That proves nothing," Rebekah said. "Your mom could have changed Mrs. Bumbly's mind."

"Where is this letter?" Hal asked. "Why didn't you show it to me?" She wanted to be mad at her brother for keeping a secret, but she was keeping a secret of her own.

"I would have," Will said, "but it's gone. It disappeared."

"You mean you lost it," said Esther.

"No. I mean it disappeared from my pocket. I'm absolutely sure I put it there." Will's face was as hard as the cement step they were sitting on. "More evidence that the space inside the closet is different somehow. If an object exists in a different timeline, a timeline protected within the space of the closet, it would cease to exist outside of that space. The letter disappeared when I stepped into the hall, but my memory of it remained because I was inside the closet when I read it. It's the only explanation."

It was Hal's turn to confess. "There's something else. I found this on the rug in Mom's room the other day. She must have dropped it. That's when I knew Will was right— something weird is definitely going on." Hal opened her hand to reveal a tiny plastic bracelet, like the kind you get during a hospital stay. It was pink, and on the front was a label that said "Horace, Baby Girl."

"It's my baby bracelet, from the hospital," Hal explained. "Mom has been complaining about it for years, because she wanted to save it but Dad threw it away. Mom brings it up every time they argue. Then all of a sudden, there it was. I think Mom went to the past to get it."

Hal could almost see the questions bubbling in Esther's head, but just then Mrs. Yim called the girls inside.

"See you later," Esther said. "Don't do anything without me."

Will frowned and Hal knew he'd make no such promise.

"We need to investigate," Will said as they walked through the back door into their kitchen. "We need to figure out how to activate the TTD so that we can go back in time."

"What if that makes things worse?" Hal asked. As much as she wanted to know what Mom was doing, her stomach fluttered at the thought of traveling through time herself.

"Worse than what?" Will answered. "Worse than a mother who hates you so much she'd rather you were still a baby?"

How could Will think that? "Mom doesn't hate you," she

said. "She just—I don't know, gets overwhelmed sometimes. She wants the best for both of us, that's all."

"And she gets to decide what's best, right? Every day, all the time."

There was no use arguing when Will got in one of his surly moods. Besides, he was right. They needed to get to the bottom of this.

O—O—O

It was three full days before Will and Hall could examine the TTD again.

"How are we going to activate a device we can't get our hands on?" Hal asked. For the second day in a row Mom hadn't let them out of her sight. "I never realized before how she sticks to us like glue."

"I've been trying to tell you that family togetherness is highly overrated," Will said. "Now you see what I mean. Be patient. Eventually she'll have to leave us home alone."

"Remember, we do this together," Hal stated firmly, and Will nodded in agreement. His mild-mannered sister could be stubborn at times, and this was one of those times. Esther had begged to be included in the action, too, but Will had held her off by agreeing to fill them in on their findings every night after dinner. So far there'd been nothing to report. Finally, on the third day, an opportunity presented itself in an unexpected way.

Like most Saturday mornings, Will sought sanctuary in his room, hoping to avoid Dad as he stomped through the house, hair sticking out like electrified wires, searching for abandoned items to throw away. Will read quietly under a blanket, hoping his parents would forget his existence until Dad exhausted himself and collapsed in front of the Sports Channel, usually around lunchtime. In the Horace house, cleaning and yelling went together like thunder and lightning, so Will was used to hearing his parents' raised voices reverberate through the house. But this particular Saturday morning was different. What started out as Dad's standard "Let's get rid of some junk," followed by Mom's wary "Let me go through it first," quickly escalated when Dad carried Will's old booster seat to the curb without asking Mom's permission. Mom retrieved the seat, obviously peeved, and Dad didn't try to hold back his anger.

"No one has used that seat in years! What's wrong with you?" he shouted.

"I said I wasn't ready to get rid of it yet. We agreed!" Mom shouted back.

"When will you be ready, when the kids go off to college? We need the space!"

"For what?"

"For future storage."

"It has sentimental value."

"What's sentimental about an old falling-apart car seat? It isn't even up to safety code. No one can use it!"

"Why can't I have a say in this? Why do you have to be such a control freak?"

"Maybe if you had more control I could have less. This place is a mess! Admit it, you're becoming a hoarder! And you're living in the past!"

"And you have no attachment to anything but your TV. You'd toss us out with the trash if you could!"

Etc....

Etc....

Etc....

... until Dad stormed out of the house, slamming the door behind him. Will peeked out of his room and found Hal standing in the hallway, close to tears. "We have to do something," she said.

Mom sniffed at the bottom of the stairs and took a deep breath. "Kids, I'm going out for a bit," she called in a fake cheery voice. "Will you two be okay?"

"Sure," Will answered. When Hal opened her mouth to speak, he covered it with his hand. "Take your time, Mom. We'll be fine," he added. He heard Mom grab her keys and walk out the door.

"What'd you do that for?" Hal asked, shoving Will's hand away.

"This is our chance." Will rushed to the closet and grabbed the TTD from its home among the old pictures. They sat on the floor outside of the closet, Will turning the device over and over in his hands. He pushed every button in every combination he could think of, then handed it over to Hal and she did the same. Nothing happened.

Will placed the TTD on the floor between them, trying to compel it to life with a piercing stare.

"We'd better put it back," Hal said finally. "Mom could be back anytime."

Will's shoulders sank. "There must be some way to activate this stupid thing." He wondered if they should risk another try at Mr. Salazar's, but just then he heard a noise on the stairs. Chester was pacing toward them as usual, but purring louder than Will had ever heard. When the plump gray tabby passed the TTD, he gave it a swipe and the inanimate box sprang to life, chiming a repeating melody of five notes that sounded familiar, although Will couldn't place it. A round blue light blinked on in the upper right corner.

"It's on!" Will shouted, grabbing the TTD. "Come on!" They raced to the closet and stood just inside with the door slightly open. Will held the TTD with both hands, methodically pushing the buttons on the front of the device.

"What are you doing?" Hal whispered.

"I'm punching in yesterday's date. I figured we should start small." When Will completed the number sequence he took Hal's hand. "Just in case we have to be touching," he explained. "We want to go back together." They waited expectantly for five, ten, twenty, then thirty seconds. Although the light remained on, nothing happened.

"Try again," Hal said. "Set it for noon yesterday. We were in the kitchen, remember?"

Will punched in yesterday's date again, followed by 12:00. When still nothing happened he tried again and again, using every variation of symbols representing date and time he could think of. Although the TTD flashed and sang, they remained, firmly planted, in the hall closet.

Will heard a scratching sound behind him and saw Chester's paw reach in and pull the closet door open.

"Go away Chester," he said. "There's no room for you in here."

Chester ignored Will and brushed past him to a rolled-up carpet remnant below the bottom shelf in the corner. He clawed at the underside of the remnant, purring.

44

"That's not your scratching post. Out!" Will said.

Chester continued to scratch, now purring loudly. Will bent to pick him up, intent on tossing the cat out into the hall, but Hal stopped him.

"Wait," she said. "What if he's trying to tell us something? Remember in the video Mom reaches down for something? What if that's it? What if it's that rolled up piece of carpet?"

Will unrolled the carpet and laid it in front of them. "Okay, now."

They stepped onto the carpet and were immediately encased in a clear glistening tube. On the screen of the TTD a picture appeared of Will and Hal at the kitchen table with Rebekah and Esther. Will touched it, and in an instant, they were sucked into a swirling whirlpool to yesterday. Only Chester remained in the closet, still and silent as a sphinx.

Chapter 5

REWIND

"Score!" Esther shouted. A paper football hurtled over the goal post Will formed with his fingers. Will blinked several times, waiting for his head to stop spinning. Hal, across the table, was holding a nail polish brush midair with a look of astonishment on her face.

"What's wrong?" Rebekah asked.

The brush dropped and bright pink splattered across Hal's white polo shirt. "We did it," she gasped. "We came back."

"Came back where?" Rebekah asked, but Esther jumped up hard, tipping her chair over behind her.

"She's saying they came back in time!" she exclaimed.

"Shh," Will cautioned. "Mom will hear."

Right on cue, Mom entered the room. "Everything okay?" she asked. "Did someone go boom—er, sorry, I mean did someone fall?"

"Just my chair." Esther smiled apologetically. "You know what a klutz I am."

"We were just about to go outside," Will said hastily. He was up and through the door in a few quick movements. Esther bounded after him and Hal followed, dragging Rebekah along.

Once they were out of Mom's hearing, Hal and Will launched into an explanation, interrupting each other every few seconds.

"For us it's Saturday morning," Will said.

"Mom and Dad were having a fight," Hal added. Will frowned. Did she have to tell everyone everything?

"Anyway, we grabbed the TTD and we finally got it to work," Will said.

"And here we are," said Hal.

"So now what happens?" Rebekah asked. "Do you go back, or do you just live out the day as usual? And if you do, will everything happen in the same way?"

Will reviewed the events of his life since yesterday afternoon. Gluten free, vegan pizza for dinner and a boring Friday night watching TV. Nothing worth reliving there, and he certainly had no desire to witness his parents' Saturday morning argument again, even from the refuge of his room. "We go back," he said.

"Wait," Hal argued. "If we stay, maybe we can fix things."

"Fix what?" Esther asked, but her words faded as Will felt himself caught in a vortex of light and wind. He closed his eyes, trying to keep from barfing. When the current around him settled, he found himself standing in the closet with his sister, holding the darkened TTD. Chester turned and strode away.

"We're back," Will said. "But I don't know how or why." He looked down at his watch. "Do you remember what time it was when we came in here?"

"A little after ten, I think. What time is it now?"

"A little after ten," Will answered. "Come on, let's check my computer." He slipped the TTD back into the shoebox and turned to go.

"Don't forget this," Hal said. She rolled up the carpet and returned it to the corner.

"Let's see what happened," Will said, clicking on the webcam icon. They watched the video of themselves in the closet, messing with the TTD until Chester came along. After a tiny blip they saw themselves returning the TTD and the carpet and leaving the closet.

"Just like the video of Mom," Will said. "We returned only a second after we left."

"But we were there for ten minutes at least," Hal said.

"I don't think it matters how long you stay in the past," said Will. "You still return right after you left."

"Did you push any buttons to get us back here?"

"No. I didn't have the TTD. It must have stayed back here."

"What about Esther and Rebekah? What will they remember?" asked Hal.

"Good question. Let's find out," Will said. "Call Rebek."

As Hal went to find her phone, Will heard the back door open.

"Everybody okay?" Mom called.

"Fine," Will answered flatly. He'd known Mom wouldn't stay away for long.

Mom jogged up the stairs and glanced at Will as she passed his room. Without any of her usual reminders she walked around the corner, entered and exited the closet, and disappeared into her bedroom just as Hal returned.

"Was that Mom?" Hal asked.

"Yep. She's been in and out of the closet already."

Hal's shoulders slumped. "Wow. She must be upset. I wish I could tell her we know. Maybe we should."

"Not yet," Will insisted. "If she knew we've discovered her secret she'd probably hide the TTD and the carpet and we'd never find out what's going on."

"We know what's going on. Our mother is visiting the past because she's sad. Maybe if we talk to her about it we can help her."

"There's a lot we still don't know. Aren't you curious about how all this started? Where did she get the technology from? She didn't invent it herself. What did Rebek say?"

"They're both sick. She remembered being in the kitchen yesterday and then rushing outside to talk, but she seemed fuzzy about why. Then she and Esther got sick to their stomachs and went home. Their mother is making them stay in today."

"I felt a little spinny when we traveled," Will said. "Did you?"

"Now that you mention it, yeah, I did, just for a second. Do you think that's related? It could be a coincidence that Rebek and Esther got sick right after we left."

"Maybe. But what if time travel creates a disturbance in the atmosphere? Not for the people that are doing it so much, but for the people around them. Like how when Dad drives he never gets carsick but everyone else in the car wants to vomit."

Hal began to pace. She kicked a dirty pair of gym shorts out of the way to create a clear path. "If that were true, we would have gotten sick every time Mom traveled back in time. Unless she's going back to before we were born. And knowing Mom, I doubt that very much."

"Good point," Will said. "I hardly ever got sick when I was a kid. I used to fake a stomachache to stay home from school, but Mom never fell for it."

"Me neither. I got perfect attendance awards most years. If Mom is travelling back to our past, being around her didn't make us sick."

"Okay," Will said. "But I still think this sudden illness is suspicious. We need to do more research."

"By that you mean we need to go back again, right?" Hal asked.

"Right. And not back to yesterday. Back to when it all began for Mom. And that means waiting for another crack at the closet and the TTD."

"It could be days before that happens."

"Or we could chance it in the middle of the night. In the meantime, we need to approach this scientifically. We need a list of questions," Will said. "What are the rules of time travel? How far back can you go? How did we get back to the present? That kind of stuff."

"Everything okay, you two?" Mom opened Will's door and poked her head in. "What are you talking about?"

Uh-oh. If Mom overheard them with her big nosey ears all could be lost.

"Just messing around," Hal answered. "Just playing a game."

"Okay. I'm going to bake some cookies. I'm sure your father will enjoy them when he watches the game later. Want to help, Halia?" Mom looked peaceful and dreamy, like someone who had just woken from a long nap in the sun and not like someone who'd had a massive fight with her husband only an hour ago.

"Sure, I'll be right down," Hal said. When Mom left, Hal turned to her brother, "Meet in my room at midnight tonight. With a list of questions," she whispered resolutely.

Will nodded and Hal ran downstairs into the alternate reality of mixers, dough, and chocolate chip cookies.

○─○─○

Hal heard a knock on the door just before her alarm sounded. She dove across the room to hit the off button before letting Will in.

"You'll wake Mom and Dad!" Will hissed.

Hal sat down at her desk and rubbed her eyes. "How did you get up without an alarm?" she asked.

"Easy. I didn't go to sleep. We need to be quiet. Dad is still downstairs."

"Okay," Hal said, opening her laptop. "Here's my list of questions. Where's yours?"

"In my head," Will said. He lay on top of his sister's bedspread and stared up at the ceiling.

Hal frowned. "I thought we were supposed to write them down."

"I wrote mine in my head," Will said. "I won't forget

them."

"You don't even follow your own rules," Hal complained. "All right, here goes." She put her glasses on and began to read. "One, why is Mom travelling back in time? But I guess we already know the answer to that. Two, how far back does Mom go? Three, what does she do when she goes back in time? Four, when did all this start? Five, how can we help Mom?" She looked up expectantly. "That's it."

Will sighed.

"What's wrong?" Hal asked. "You said to write down questions."

"I find your lack of imagination disturbing," Will said. "I should have known your questions would be all about Mom."

"Isn't that the point? Aren't we trying to figure out what Mom is doing so we can fix it, fix our family?"

Will didn't answer, but he didn't have to. Hal knew that fixing Mom was way, way at the bottom of his to-do list.

"Whatever," Will said finally. 'Okay, first let's go over what we already know. We know that time travel is possible through a device we're calling the TTD and a small piece of carpet."

"What should we call that?" Hal interrupted. "How about the Magic Carpet?"

"This isn't Aladdin," Will said. "We also know we were able to set the TTD to an exact point in time. But we didn't set anything to return to the present. I suspect some sort of failsafe preset was involved."

"Preset?" Hal asked.

"Yeah, like the TTD was preset to return us after just a few minutes. That way we couldn't stay in the past for too long and, you know, mess things up, maybe. Next time we'll try to tell it how long we want to stay."

"All right. What else do we already know?"

"We know that the TTD took us to ourselves in the past."

"Who else would it take us to?"

"What I mean is, we landed at the kitchen table, exactly where we were at the date and time we set. We weren't there *with* our past selves; we *were* our past selves."

"I get it. We didn't go back and watch ourselves in the past."

"Right. I think that means only one version of yourself can exist within a particular moment in time."

"Okay," Hal said, squinting. "We were our past selves. But we knew we'd traveled back."

"I was getting to that. We know that time travelers retain their present knowledge of people, places, and events. We remembered everything from the present."

"So, we were in our past bodies with our present brains." Hal said. She took off her glasses and wiped them on her pajamas. "How far back would that work, do you think?"

"What do you mean?"

"Well, what if we went back to when we were babies. Would we be in our baby bodies with our present brains? That would be really weird."

Will sat up and looked at his sister with an admiring smile. "I take back what I said before about your lack of imagination. You're brilliant!"

"Don't say anything you'll regret later."

"I mean it. You're a genius. Think about what you just said. We could go back to when we were babies..."

"If you were a baby I'd be a little kid, like three or four years old."

"Whatever. Anyway, people would assume we don't know what's going on around us, like little blobs. But we'd be totally aware, taking it all in."

"Like I said, that would be really weird."

"Yeah, but don't you get it?" Will jumped up in excitement. "No one would bother to hide anything from us because they'd assume we wouldn't understand anything. We'd see and hear everything."

"Like little baby spies," Hal mused. "Weird and a little icky."

"Icky?"

"Do you want to go back to wearing diapers? And drooling all over yourself?"

"I see what you mean," Will said. "But it's temporary."

Hal took a deep breath. "Fine, I guess. Let's get to your list."

"Right. My list. Here are my questions." Will paced as he spoke. "One, who gave Mom the time travel technology? And why? Two, what are the rules of time travel? How far back can you go? Since we jumped into our past selves I'm guessing you can only travel within your own lifetime. We need to find out for sure. And how long can you stay? Can you alter the timeline?"

"That's all under one question?" Hal asked.

"Yeah. Three, does time travel affect you physically? Does it affect the people around you? I still say Esther and Rebek's sudden sickness was suspicious. And four, my biggest, most important question—and this has to do with the rules, too—is time travel limited to the past, or can you travel to the future? If you jump into your own body, does that mean your body has to be present in the place you're travelling to? Because if that's so, travel to the future would be impossible. Our bodies aren't there yet."

"That's your most important question?" Hal asked. "Why?"

When Will took a minute to answer, Hal knew she wouldn't like what was coming.

"Going to the past is cool, but what if we could travel to the future? Think of what we could see, what we could do," he said. "And if time travel is real, maybe space travel is real, too. What if all that stuff, all the make-believe sci-fi stuff I've been thinking about my whole life is real? I need to know. You get that, right?" Will flopped down on the bed again, as if he'd exhausted himself with so many words.

Hal gaped at her brother. "You don't care about helping Mom at all, do you?" she asked.

"Of course, I care. I was the one who noticed something was wrong, remember? I'm just saying this is bigger than Mom or us or our boring little family. We have the whole universe at our doorstep!"

Hal stood and walked toward the door. "I happen to like this boring old world and our boring little family, even if you don't. I don't care about the future. I want things to be the way they were before all this started. You can go now." She opened the door. "I'm going to sleep."

"What about going back?" Will asked. "I thought we were going to try again tonight."

"No, thanks," Hal said. "Good night."

Will rose and walked into the hallway, where he stood motionless for a moment. Then he shrugged and started toward the closet.

"Wait," Hal hissed.

"What? Change your mind?"

"No. But remember your promise. Don't go without me."

Will stared at her impassively.

"Will," Hal said louder, "You promised."

"Ok," Will agreed finally. "This time." He walked off to his room and shut the door behind him.

Hal knew her brother. He'd keep his promise for now, but she'd better not press her luck.

O—O—O

"Why all this interest in potty training?" Mom asked on Monday morning. She was bent over her tomato plants, searching for hornworms.

"Just curious," Will answered. He and Hal sat at the patio table, ducking their heads under the umbrella to avoid the sweltering sun.

"Well, let's see. Your sister potty trained earlier, but that's typical for girls. She was around two and a half, I think, and you were closer to three. When I go in, I can check your baby books. I'm sure I kept track."

Figures, Will thought. Mom probably kept a detailed record of every time they pooped or spit up. Even passing gas might get a mention in some notebook somewhere, knowing Mom.

"That's okay, I just wanted a general idea." Will and Hal exchanged looks but Mom didn't notice.

"It's not like you to be interested in babies," Mom said, giving the tomatoes a final once-over. Will was spared the effort of continuing the conversation when Mom's phone blared from inside her pocket.

"Oh, hi, Ted. Today? I don't know. You know I don't like to work when the kids are home. Uh huh. Uh huh." Mom sighed. "I see. Okay, I can spare a few hours, I guess. See you soon." She hung up and smiled apologetically. "Sorry guys, looks like I have to go to the farm. Someone called in sick and apparently there's several large camp groups coming today. Will you be okay for a while? Or do you want to come with me?"

The idea of standing around the Queens County Farm Museum watching a hoard of camp kids feed the goats was unthinkable to Will. He'd rather be a goat. "No thanks," he said quickly.

"Halia, how about you? You can get some volunteer hours in with the younger groups."

"Oh," Hal said, "yeah, that would be good." When she noticed Will's dagger eyes, she rescinded. "But I'd better stay home and get some reading done. Summer is zooming by."

"It's still June, Halia, but okay. You do some reading too, William, you hear? No screens while I'm gone. And stay inside with the doors locked. And don't open the door for anyone..."

"We know, Mom," Hal interrupted. When they heard Mom drive away, they sprinted up the stairs.

"What was all that about potty training?" Hal asked.

"Just trying to avoid pooping in my pants if possible."

"You almost made Mom suspicious."

"I doubt that. She'd never suspect we figured out what she's doing. She doesn't think we're that smart."

"Are you kidding?" Hal objected. "She's always telling us how smart we are."

"Yeah," Will answered. "Book smart. School smart. But not smart enough to include us in anything important."

"Don't be so hard on Mom. She's doing the best she can."

"Is she?" Will opened the closet door and reached for the TTD.

Hal unrolled the carpet remnant and placed it on the closet floor. "I've been thinking about this next trip, trying to decide how far back we should go," she said. "The goal is to find out how this all started, right? When did you first notice Mom acting weird?"

"I've always thought Mom was weird," Will replied.

"I'm not kidding."

"Neither am I. But I first noticed the closet thing—I don't know, months ago. It took me a while to realize something was up."

"So, should we go back a few months?" Hal asked.

Will brushed the hair out of his eyes. "I don't think that's far enough. If we want Mom to stop being careful about her secret, we need to go back further—back to a time she thinks we won't be aware of what's happening. I say we go back to when we were really little. Take a look around, see if we notice anything. Then we can work forward from there."

"Won't that take a lot of time?"

Will stared at his sister. "We have a time machine. If we always come back a second after we left, we have all the time in the world."

Hal's eyes brightened. "Wow. We can stay in the past as long as we want."

Will chose to ignore the warning bell clanging in his ear. "We're agreed then," he said. "I'll set it back to when I was two and you were four." He examined the silent, dark TTD. "One problem. We still don't know how to turn it on."

They stood on the carpet square in the closet, staring at the small device that had the ability to send them back through time. Will ran his fingers over its smooth, dark surface. "How did we do it last time?" He closed his eyes, trying to remember. "It just sort of turned on by itself."

"Maybe the battery is dead," Hal said.

"Hal, this is a time travel device. I don't think it runs on double A batteries."

"All right, don't get snarky." They slumped to the floor, staring at the rug as if the answers they needed were hidden in the nylon fibers. Hal suddenly jumped to her feet.

"It didn't turn on by itself!" she exclaimed. "It was Chester! Chester walked by and the thing turned on, remember?

"How could this have anything to do with Chester? He's just a cat."

"Didn't you say last night that anything is possible? I'm telling you, it was Chester!" Hal insisted. She crawled down the hall on all fours, calling, "Chester! Where are you?" When she passed Will's room, she saw a paw reach under the door.

"There you are," Hal said. She opened the door, scooped up the purring cat, and ran back to Will. As soon as they got close, the device clicked and played the same five-note chime it had the last time. Will saw the blue light in the corner flash on.

"We're in!" he exclaimed.

"What a good cat!" Hal crooned, but the good cat swiped

at her and she dropped him to the floor. With an indignant meow he twitched his tail and walked off.

"Okay, setting date and time," Will said. "Eleven years ago from today."

The screen lit up with a picture of Mom and Hal sitting at the kitchen table. Hal looked to be about four years old.

"Oh my gosh," she gasped. "It worked."

"This time before I touch the screen, I'll try to tell it how long we want to stay." He punched in 1:00, which he hoped would mean one hour.

"Ready?" he asked, excitement bubbling just below the surface.

"Ready," Hal answered.

When the chimes and the spinning stopped, Will looked around in awe. He knew he was in his own house, but everything looked so different. He was seated on the living room floor in front of a pile of Duplo bricks, within sight of Mom and Hal at the kitchen table. From his vantage point he could see into the dining room, too. Most of the furniture was older and worn, although some of the big pieces, like the china hutch and the dining room table, were the same. Everything was enormous. Even the Duplos in front of him seemed twice their normal size. The sofa was as big as a house and the room itself stretched the length of a football field.

Although the furniture was mostly in the same places, all of the bottom shelves were filled with picture books and there was a gate blocking the staircase. The old beige canvas toy bin sat off to the side, filled to overflowing. It looked different than Will remembered, not quite complete. Then Will realized that this was before he'd watched Toy Story for the first time and made Mom stencil the words "To Infinity and Beyond!" across the front. Will looked around for Chester, wondering if the cat would seem like a tiger to him now, but he remembered that Chester hadn't been born yet. He stood and took a few steps, hoping for a better look, but he lost his balance and landed on his swooshy diaper that, thankfully, was empty. He looked down at his pudgy legs and laughed.

"What's so funny in there, buddy?" Mom called. "Did you go boom?"

Will wanted to answer, "Yeah, Mom. I went boom," but he knew they'd have to be careful to play the part of little kids or Mom would get suspicious. He stood again, this time concentrating on keeping his balance. His head felt heavy, like it was pulling him toward the floor. He put out his arms and leaned back to stop himself from toppling over. Then, slowly, he put one stubby foot in front of the other and stomped into the kitchen, Frankenstein style. Hal was finger-painting under Mom's close supervision.

"What a pretty picture you're making!" Mom exclaimed.

Hal looked down at the glob of colors in front of her and frowned. Will stifled a laugh.

"Here's your baby brother!" Mom sang out. "Would you like to sit up here and paint with us?" Her tone was higher pitched and even cheerier than Will was used to. Before he could respond he felt himself being lifted into the air and strapped into a booster seat at the table. Mom placed a large sheet of paper in front of him and spooned a mountain of green paint in the middle. Will placed his hands in his lap.

Hal continued to swirl the slimy paint around with her fingers, but when Mom wasn't looking, she scrawled OMG along the side. Will reached over and smudged the letters out just before Mom saw them.

"Oops, use your own paper, buddy," Mom said. "That's your sister's painting."

"I'm finished," Hal said. "I'm going to get down now."

"Okay," Mom answered. "Go wash your hands before you touch anything."

"I know, Mom," Hal answered in a voice dripping with teenaged impatience. Will shot Hal a warning look but it was too late.

"Excuse me," Mom said. "Watch your tone please, young lady."

"Oh—sorry Mommy," Hal said quickly and disappeared into the bathroom.

"Four going on fourteen," Mom mumbled. She turned to Will and asked, "How are you doing, bud? Don't you want to paint?" She grabbed Will's hand and smooshed it into the goopy mess.

"I wanna get down, too," Will answered, hoping he sounded like his two-year-old self. Apparently, he'd missed the mark.

"My, aren't we all so grown up today!" Mom said. "Good talking, buddy! I knew you had it in you!" She unbuckled Will and carried him to the bathroom, where Hal was standing on a stool by the sink, still rubbing paint off her soapy hands.

"No playing in the sink," Mom said. "Finish up and then help your brother. Will, don't touch anything until I come back." Mom turned to the mess in the kitchen.

"Wow, is she bossy," Hal whispered.

"You're supposed to be a little kid, remember?" Will said.

"You'd be used to being bossed around. Let me wash this gook off my hands."

Hal scooted over and Will stepped up to the stool, but lost his balance and toppled backwards again. "You're going to have to give me a hand," he said. "The stool is too high."

Hal giggled and pulled her brother up next to her. "It's so funny, being in these little bodies! Did you notice how huge everything looks? Look at this sink. It's the size of the Grand Canyon!"

Will had to admit the sink looked pretty big, even if the Grand Canyon was a slight exaggeration. "I know," he said. "and Mom looks like the BFG."

Hal reached to shut the water off but Will stopped her. "She'll hear us talking," he hissed.

"Oh, right," Hal said. "You're better at this spy stuff than I am. What do we do next?"

"We take a look around, but don't be obvious."

"What exactly are we looking for?"

"Anything out of the ordinary. And be careful how you sound. I don't think I talked much at this age, so I'm gonna stay quiet."

"That'll be a huge difference," Hal said.

"Watch the sarcasm," Will reminded her. "You're four, remember?"

"Right."

"Let's go, guys." Mom entered the bathroom, turned the water off, and handed them a towel. Hal jumped off the stool and Will toddled down with help from Mom. "Play in the living room while I start dinner," Mom instructed.

"Bossy," Hal mouthed, but Will only shook his head

in response. He pointed to the stereo system on the entertainment center.

"Mommy, can we put music on?" Hal asked innocently.

"Sure, honey." Mom bustled into the room and picked up the stereo remote. "There you go," she said, and was gone again in a flash. Disneymania filled the room.

"She's so different. Not just bigger, but like she's in a hurry," Hal commented.

"Whatever. I don't notice anything suspicious. Do you?"

"No. Different, but not suspicious. But I'm still not sure what we're looking for. Did you think she'd leave the TTD laying around the house?"

"No, of course not," Will said.

Hal walked over to the toy chest and rummaged around. "Wow! I remember this stuff!" she exclaimed. "I loved this thing!" She pulled a plastic cash register out and set it on the floor.

"Before you try to force me to play store, remember our mission," Will whispered. "We're looking for evidence that Mom is time travelling."

"Well I don't see any. If anything, she seems more focused, without that sad, dreamy look. She's more—I don't know—more with-it, I guess."

"That makes sense. She has no need to time travel back to when we were little because we are little. Maybe we came back too far."

"Maybe. But if she got the TTD when we're older she'd be more careful about hiding it from us. So how would going back do us any good?"

Will shook his head and shrugged. Hal was right. His plan

had a fatal flaw. The younger they were, the less the likelihood that Mom was time traveling, but the older they were, the more careful Mom would be around them. He needed a better idea.

"How long do you think we've been here?" he asked.

"Half an hour, maybe. We still have some time left. Come on, let's play!" Hal dug into the canvas chest, greeting toys as if they were old friends. "Ooh, here's Mr. Potato Head! And my Etch A Sketch!"

Will picked up a yellow Matchbox Corvette and halfheartedly rolled it back and forth across the floor. "I need to get back home," he muttered.

"Don't be a party pooper," Hal said. "This is fun!" Will watched his sister pull toy after toy out of the bin, cooing over each one. At the very bottom she found a blue pony with a long pink mane and held it close. "Here she is!" she said, whirling with joy. "I think I still have her packed away somewhere."

Will rolled his eyes and looked at the digital time display on the stereo. Only a few minutes left. He didn't know how much longer he could stand to watch his sister do the happy dance. He felt relieved when he heard a knock at the front door.

"Be right there," Mom yelled, rushing to turn off the music. She opened the door and ushered in Gram, holding a cake plate, with Gramps right behind her, wearing the dark blue windbreaker Will remembered so well.

Will and Hal stared, transfixed, as if time were standing still. Gramps, with his spikey gray hair and his stubbly chin and his worn-out baggy jeans. Gramps, with his crooked teeth and his easy, constant smile. Gramps, the coolest guy in the world, in spite of his corny jokes. His face was a little less wrinkled, but there he was—Gramps. Hal dropped her little pony and started to cry.

"What's wrong, honey?" Gram asked. "Did you hurt yourself?"

Hal's cry became a wail.

"I don't understand it," Mom said. "She was fine just a minute ago." She rushed over to Hal and picked her up.

"Maybe she thinks we're here to babysit. Don't worry, honey," Gram said, "Mommy and Daddy aren't going anywhere. We're just here for dinner."

Hal refused to be comforted. She buried her head in Mom's shoulder and sobbed as Mom carried her into the kitchen. Gram followed, clucking in dismay.

Gramps unzipped his jacket and sank into the sofa. "What'd ya got there, Will? Can you show me your car?"

Will looked down at his hands and realized he was still holding the yellow Corvette. He let it fall to the ground and crawled to Gramps on all fours. When he reached Gramps' leg he held on tight, choking back the tears.

"Hey, bud, I'm happy to see you, too," Gramps said, patting Will's head. "Come on, let's play." Will didn't move. He smashed his face into Gramps' leg, feeling his throat close and his stomach turn upside down. Gramps let an awkward minute pass, then tried to pry Will loose, but Will only hung on tighter. "What's wrong, buddy?" Gramps asked with concern. "Hey Alex, come in here a minute," he called.

"She's still busy with Halia," Gram answered. Will could hear his sister crying her heart out in the next room.

"Goodness, you, too, Will?" Gram asked, walking toward him. "What's going on today?"

"I don't know. Hal acts like she's just lost her best friend and this one is hanging on for dear life," Gramps said. Will squeezed with all the strength is his chubby two-year-old arms. "I'm losing circulation in my leg," Gramps joked. "Gimme a hand here, will ya?"

Together he and Gram gently pulled and Will felt himself being wrenched away and lifted into the air. His stomach flipped again and he shut his eyes to stop from throwing up. For a few seconds he felt himself spiraling in a whirlpool of time and tears, but then he was in the closet, back in the present with Hal. He dropped the TTD and ran to the bathroom, where he did throw up for real.

Chapter 6

DEBRIEF

Without saying a word to each other, Will and Hal retreated to the refuge of their rooms until Mom returned a few hours later. Will pretended to be reading, hoping Mom would leave him alone, but no such luck. She shooed them outside, insisting it was a beautiful day and they needed fresh air in one breath and cautioning them not to go far in the next. They sat silently at the picnic table in the yard, listening to the cars go by, not meeting each other's eyes.

"I guess I wasn't ready for that," Hal said finally.

"Yeah. Me neither." Will wandered over to the hedges and plucked off a handful of leaves.

"Don't let Mom see you do that. She's still pretty bossy," Hal said.

Will nodded and ripped the leaves into tiny bits.

"I don't know any other kids our age who are forced to go outside, for example," Hal continued.

"Yeah."

"Just to sit here in the yard and do what? Soak up the vitamin D, I guess."

"Yeah."

"I want to go in."

"Yeah."

"I was having so much fun, and then he was there. He was just so real," Hal said.

Will looked up from his pile of decimated leaves. "Hal, he was real."

"You know what I mean. I just never expected to see him again." Hal wiped a tear away. Her sadness rolled toward Will like an ocean wave.

Will carefully placed the bits of leaves in the palm of his hand and blew them into his sister's face.

"Hey! Cut it out!" Hal protested. "My contacts!" She jumped up just as the text alert on her phone sounded. "It's Rebek. I'm telling her we did it and to come over. We need to debrief."

That was more like it. The spell was broken. "Okay. But Hal, one thing."

"What?"

"Let's not tell them about Gramps, okay? Let's keep that just between us."

Hal nodded. "Okay." She took a deep breath. "This time travel thing is risky, isn't it? It can hurt."

"Yeah, I'd say so. But I think it will be worth the risk. Do you?"

"I don't know. Maybe. If it helps Mom."

Will looked his sister directly in the eye. He needed her to understand. "Because Hal, I'm doing this. No matter what." He didn't say, with or without you, but the unspoken words hung in the humid air.

To Will's surprise, Hal smiled. "Okay. Got it. Willful William, at your service." Hal used the name Mom had given her brother years before, whenever he refused to go along with her plans (which was about every day). "Meet Willful William, Thomas the Tank Engine's new friend," Mom would say. "He has so many lessons to learn!" She'd tickle Will and he'd finally obey, mostly to get her to stop, but Mom didn't seem to get that.

"Whatever," Will said. The gate swung opened and Esther bounded into the yard, followed by a more subdued Rebekah.

"What was it like?" Esther asked. She bounced up and down on her toes in bursts of kinetic energy, dispelling the last remnants of sadness that had followed them from the past.

"Pretty unbelievable," Will answered with a satisfied grin.

Hal jumped in. "We were there with Mom, in our little kid bodies. Everything was the same, but different. Bigger."

"Everything seemed bigger because you were smaller," Rebekah said. "It's a matter of perspective."

"Right," Hal agreed. "And the weirdest thing was that we remembered everything, and we could think and talk the same as now. We had to be careful not to give ourselves away."

"Wow," Esther said wistfully.

"What do you guys remember about Friday?" Will asked.

"Friday?" Rebekah wrinkled her brow in concentration.

"That was the day we got sick, right?"

"Yeah," Esther answered. "We must have eaten something bad. One minute we were sitting around talking, and the next we were throwing our guts up."

"I don't think I've ever been that sick before," Rebekah said.

"But you do remember talking with us on the front steps, right?" Will asked. "Do you remember what we were talking about?"

Esther and Rebekah shook their heads. "Couldn't have been anything important," Esther said.

"Actually, it was," said Hal. "That was our first time travel trip. On Saturday morning we went back to Friday—the day you got sick, but you weren't sick when we got there. You were fine. We told you that we were time travelling."

Esther looked doubtful. "I think I would have remembered that, Hal," she said.

"But you didn't remember. That's just it," Will said. "We were only in the past for a few minutes, but still, you should remember that we talked about it."

"Even if that's true, I don't see what it has to do with anything," Rebekah said.

Esther stopped bouncing and stared at Will. "You're trying to figure out the rules, aren't you?"

Will nodded. "I think, maybe, that you aren't allowed to tell people you're visiting from the future. Some kind of atmospheric disturbance happens if you do, to stop the people from remembering it. Like a failsafe to keep time travel a secret."

"Will we remember this conversation?" Esther asked. "I

71

really don't want to throw up again."

Will rubbed his eyes. "You should be fine, because we're all from the same time signature right now."

"I think I get it," Esther said. "We can talk about time travel, but we can't know if you're time travelling right then, or else we'll get sick."

"And we won't remember the conversation," Rebekah added.

"I think so," Will said.

"Okay," Esther said. "What else? Did you learn anything?"

"Yeah, kind of," Will answered. He'd talked enough for a while, so he looked to Hal to fill in the details, as usual. But Hal had put her head down and closed her eyes and Will knew she was thinking about Gramps again.

"We didn't find any answers," Will said, "but we did realize a flaw in the plan." He waited again.

Hal opened her eyes and stared at the freckles on her arm.

"And?" Esther said. "Are you going to tell us about this flaw or do we have to travel to the past to find out for ourselves?" Will kept looking at Hal, but now her eyes were fixed on the butterfly that had landed on the table.

"Or maybe we can travel to the future to skip the lulls in the conversation," Esther said.

"Okay, okay," Will said. "Here's the problem. If we go back to when we were little, like we did this morning, it's less likely Mom is using time travel. But if we don't go back far enough, it's more likely she's being careful to hide stuff from us. See what I mean?"

"Hmm," mused Rebekah. "You might have to figure out some other way to get information."

"Like what?" Will asked.

"Well, your mother got this technology from somewhere. Maybe she's communicating with whoever gave it to her now, in the present."

"Good point," said Will. "I've been thinking about who that might be."

"Me too," Esther said. "There are a few possibilities. First, the government. Maybe your mom is part of some kind of secret government project."

"Like a test subject," Rebekah offered.

"Why would the government choose our Mom, of all people, to test out time travel?" Will asked.

"Another good point," Esther agreed. "Of course, there's always the possibility of aliens."

"And you don't actually know for sure if someone gave this technology to your mom. She could have found it," said Rebekah.

"So, aliens left time travel tech laying around somewhere, like maybe the grocery store, and Mom picked it up?" Will said, frowning. "Not likely. Anyone who's smart enough to create time travel is smart enough to keep track of their stuff."

"Lucky we've ruled out the government, then," Esther said.

"What if there was some kind of spaceship crash and your mom found the crash site?" Rebekah asked.

"Where, at the Queens County Farm? I think we might have heard about that. Again, not likely."

"Maybe she stole it," Esther said.

Will scowled. "Let's keep this within the realm of possibility."

"We're talking about time travel," Esther countered. "None of this is within the realm of possibility."

"The existence of aliens is far more possible than our mom stealing something," Hal said, sitting up. "I doubt we'll find out anything here, in the present. I think we should go back again, even further this time."

"Why?" Esther asked.

"I don't know. It's just a feeling I have," Hal said, and Will thought he saw a glimpse of longing cross her face. "We should go back again, and we should stay there longer and have a closer look around."

"Are you sure you aren't more interested in playing with your old toys again?" Will asked.

Hal looked stung. Will didn't want to hurt his sister, but he meant what he said. Hal was a little too happy back there and it made him nervous.

"Maybe I'm doing this with or without you," Hal said irately. "Come on, Rebek. Let's go inside." She left in a huff and Rebekah followed.

"That went well," Esther said. "What's up with her?"

"Whatever," Will shrugged. "I guess I'll go in too. See ya."

"Hold on a minute," said Esther. "I want to ask you something."

"Yeah?" Will figured Esther wanted to compare the rules of time travel in *12 Monkeys* the movie with *12 Monkeys* the TV show or some such thing, and he wasn't in the mood. He'd talked enough for one day.

"I want to come," Esther said.

That, Will hadn't expected. He stared past Esther, at a loss for words.

"We could figure out a way," Esther continued, as if she were anticipating his objections. "We could go back to a day we know we were together, like a birthday party or something. Your mom would be totally distracted and we could snoop around together."

Will hesitated again. He liked Esther and all, but he was barely getting the hang of this time travel stuff himself. He wasn't ready to share it with anyone except Hal and he didn't know if he ever would be. He frowned and said nothing.

"Well?" Esther asked.

Will shook his head and looked down at his hands. Esther's expression went from hopeful, to disappointed, to angry.

"Okay, I get it," she said. "I'm the Asian sidekick in the story, right? I stand by, give you advice, do a few math calculations maybe, but never get in on the action. Well no thanks!" Esther turned on her heel and stomped off.

Will wasn't sure how he'd managed to make everyone mad at him in the span of a few minutes, but there he was, by himself, feeling guilty but not really knowing why. He was about to retreat to his room when he heard a cough over the fence. Mr. Salazar was stooped over his cucumbers, inspecting the vines carefully.

"Hey," Will said, walking toward him.

"Hola, Will," Mr. Salazar answered, not looking up. He placed a stake close to a vine and pounded it into the ground with a mallet.

"Do you need any help?" Will asked. Gardening was not his favorite thing, but he felt like being near Mr. Salazar right then even if that meant getting his hands dirty.

"Sure, come on over," Mr. Salazar replied. Will walked around the fence to the yard next door with Chester at his side.

"Where did you come from?" Will asked Chester. "I didn't know you were out here."

Mr. Salazar handed Will the mallet. "I need stakes to tie up all of these vines," he said.

Will wondered if Mr. Salazar had heard their conversation, but he didn't ask. It felt good just to bang one stake after another into the soft earth. But when he thumped the last stake, it resisted. He tried again, but the stake refused to enter the ground. Will kept at it as if his struggle with the pointy stick was personal, until finally Mr. Salazar stopped him.

"Let's see what's in the way," he said, digging into the spot with a trowel. When the metal edge clinked against something hard, Mr. Salazar dug up a small, flat rock.

"Try now," he said. Will tapped the stake into the dirt easily.

"Force is not always the best course of action," said Mr. Salazar. He sat on the wooden garden bed frame. "Sometimes one needs to be flexible."

"I guess you heard what we were talking about," Will said. "We should be more careful."

"Perhaps," answered Mr. Salazar, "although I suspect most people would not take your conversation seriously."

"But you do, right? You believe us? About the time travel stuff, I mean."

"I have no reason to doubt you or your friends."

"Good. What do you think we should do?" Will asked.

Mr. Salazar said, "I think you know what to do, but if

you forget, maybe this will remind you." He handed the troublesome rock to Will. "I must go in now." He walked toward his backdoor with Chester following.

"Chester, come," Will called, knowing his cat didn't obey voice commands. "I think he likes your house better than ours," he complained.

"He probably still remembers," Mr. Salazar replied.

"Remembers?"

"Yes, remembers when he was a kitten, before I presented him to your mother as a gift. Go home now, Chester, that's right." Mr. Salazar reached down to scratch Chester behind the ear and Will thought he whispered something to the cat. Chester promptly turned, ready to follow Will.

"You gave us Chester?" Will asked, but Mr. Salazar was already out of hearing.

○─○─○

Chester allowed the boy to carry him into the house and didn't refuse the treat he offered, paltry as it was. He followed the boy up the stairs to his room and stationed himself in the doorway, front legs extended and claws at the ready. When he felt certain that all was quiet, he closed his eyes and pondered, again, how the destiny of so many could depend on the actions of these unpredictable and fragile creatures.

Chapter 7

WITH OR WITHOUT YOU

Hal had been fuming when she came in earlier, but, as usual, her anger soon faded. Why was it so hard to stay mad at her brother? She'd had no problem throwing some jerk's backpack into the pool, but Will was different. Will needed her in ways he didn't understand. They didn't argue often, maybe because there was no winning an argument with Will. She always came away with the same sinking feeling in her stomach, so even when she won, she lost. It was no wonder she was always the one to make things up.

This time Hal was determined to hold out a little longer. During dinner she hadn't made eye contact with Will, and since Mom and Dad were bickering again it seemed safer to stay in her own world. Now she sat on her bed, engulfed in a feeling of defeat. When she heard a knock at her door, she didn't get up.

"What?" she said in her most annoyed voice.

"It's me," Will answered. "We need to talk."

Hal stared up at the ceiling and pushed down the urge to forgive and forget. "It's been a long day. We'll talk tomorrow."

Hal heard a faint "whatever" before Will moved on. How like him to give up so easily. If the roles were reversed, if she'd been the one standing outside Will's door, she would have tried harder, that was for sure. She wouldn't have left until he agreed to talk and she made things right. But the roles were not reversed. Will was gone and here she was, alone. The memories of the day crashed in on her like a tidal wave, and Hal felt exhausted under their weight. She wanted to sleep but she couldn't turn off her buzzing brain. Over and over she relived the high of being a little kid again and the low of seeing Gramps. She took comfort in the memory of combing her little pony's long, silky hair and let her mind drift to all the times she'd played with the silly thing without a care in the world. Suddenly, Hal knew what she wanted to do.

"With or without you" she whispered, ignoring her rising guilt. If Will could push his feelings away, so could she. She got out of bed, turned off her light, and slowly tiptoed down the hall to the closet, stopping dead in her tracks when she realized she needed Chester. If he was in Will's room, she'd have to give up her plan. But there was Chester, waiting patiently. When she opened the closet door, the cat followed her in. Hal set the carpet square out and retrieved the TTD from its hiding place. Now, for the date. She wanted to be as young as possible; what date should she choose? A birthday would be perfect! But what if Gramps turned up again? She didn't see how she could avoid him. Hal steeled herself. She'd be ready this time.

Hal could only remember back to her fifth birthday, but she wanted to be younger than that. She'd seen pictures of her third birthday, and everyone seemed to be having a great time. She quickly set the date on the TTD and waited for the chimes to take her to a time before her family was falling apart.

Hal didn't remember the car seat feeling so tight—come to think of it, she didn't remember the car seat at all. Once she stopped spinning she pushed her body forward as hard as she could to loosen the straps, but it was no use, the harness snapped her right back in place. She might as well relax. Will sat next to her in a rear facing baby seat.

"Everything okay back there?" Mom asked. Hal smiled at how familiar that question sounded. Mom had been asking that for a very long time.

Will started to fuss and within thirty seconds his whimpers erupted into a full-blown cry. "Okay honey, we'll be home soon," Mom said, but when Hal looked around she saw they were stuck behind a truck that was trying, unsuccessfully, to make a left turn at a busy intersection. The streets were unfamiliar to Hal. She remembered that they'd lived in a different neighborhood until she was four. Will's shrieks got louder and mingled with horns blaring from all directions.

"Any day now, moron!" someone shouted from a nearby car.

"I'll never get used to the rudeness here," Mom sighed. "Halia, please try to quiet your brother."

Hal tickled Will's chubby leg and made a silly face. Will quieted, staring at her with the pensive look she knew so well.

Then his face squinched up and turned red and Hal caught a whiff of dirty diaper. I can't wait to tell him about that, she thought.

When the traffic finally cleared, Mom wove around jaywalking pedestrians and double-parked cars until she came to a four-story red brick apartment building. "Now to find a parking spot," she said. They circled the block four times until finally a black Toyota signaled it was leaving. Mom waited patiently in front of the car, her turn signal flashing, but the second the spot was empty a red Porsche approached from behind.

"Oh no, he doesn't," Mom said, gritting her teeth. Hal watched in amazement as well-mannered Alexis Horace from Pleasant Valley, Idaho, the embodiment of midwestern courtesy, jumped out and blocked the intruding car. She waved her arms and shouted, but Hal couldn't make out what she was saying because the windows were closed.

The Porsche door opened and a long, thin man wearing a sleek leather jacket unfolded himself and towered over Mom. His platinum hair was tied back into a ponytail that fell to the middle of his back. He remained silent, but his stare was sharp as a knife. Mom did not back down. Although she spoke quietly, Hal could tell by her gestures that this guy would park his car here over Mom's cold, dead body.

Mom finished her lecture on parking etiquette, folded her arms, and waited. The man still hadn't said a word. He turned his head and peered into the car, looking Hal straight in the eye with the slightest curl of his lip. Mom took a few steps to her right to block the man's view and without knowing why, Hal gripped her baby brother's hand. A second later the man tucked back into his car and drove away. Mom parked in a series of lurches and jolts that left Hal feeling like a pinball.

By this time Will had started crying again. "Okay, okay, another minute," Mom said, the tension in her voice rising. Somehow, she managed to get Hal, Will, the diaper bag, the cake, and two plastic shopping bags through the large glass doors of the apartment building, into the lobby, up the elevator, and into an apartment that Hal did not remember.

"Your father's not home yet," Mom said, shouting above Will's screeching. "Glad he could find time to work out while I do everything else," she said, but she didn't sound glad at all. Where was the bright, sunny Mom that Hal knew? Somehow this version of Mom, this cross, frazzled mess, had replaced her. While Hal wished for old Mom, new Mom rushed the cake into the kitchen and ran back for the grocery bags that were still hooked to the sides of the stroller. Meanwhile, Will's squawks intensified.

"I know, I know," Mom shouted from the kitchen. "I just need to get this stuff in the fridge." Hal wished she could help, but she didn't think her three-year-old body would be much good at putting groceries away. She tried to distract Will again, but the smell of poop overwhelmed her.

"He's got a dirty diaper," Hal yelled to Mom.

"I know," Mom said as she entered the room and scooped up the screaming baby. "Will, Will, I've had my fill, gotta chill, so take a pill" she chanted under her breath. Hal was stunned. She'd never imagined her patient, loving Mom simmering with sarcasm toward her own child.

Hal followed Mom into a large bedroom and looked around. There was a queen-sized bed, a toddler bed that she guessed was hers, and a crib all crammed into the one room. Hal hadn't known they'd ever lived in such tight quarters. Mom stood at a changing table with Will. "Great," she mumbled. "Where is the new package of diapers?" Hal thought Mom was about to step away from the table when she suddenly stopped, swayed, and held on to the edge.

"Not this time," Mom said in a softer, calmer voice. "No one is going to fall today. Mommy's right here." She looked around for Hal. "Honey, can you get a clean diaper from the bag?" Mom asked sweetly. "We don't want our little bundle to fall on his head. No emergency room for him!"

She's doing it, Hal thought. She's time traveling. Mom's bad-tempered frazzle had vanished and here stood the Mom that Hal knew, the kind, serene Mom who never raised her voice. Mom finished the job and picked Will up, hugging him close. "There's my sweet boy," she cooed, covering Will with kisses. She paced back and forth, holding Will tight and humming a familiar melody. Where had Hal heard it before? Oh! Mom was humming the same hypnotic chime the TTD made when it activated. Will's cries turned to whimpers and he fell asleep on Mom's shoulder.

"Time for a nap," Mom said, laying Will gently down in his crib and leading Hal to the small bed in the corner of the room. Mom tucked Hal under the soft pink coverlet and handed her a velvety brown teddy bear. Buttercup! She loved Buttercup so much! What ever happened to him?

"Sweet dreams," Mom said. "When you wake up, it will be time for your party." Mom kissed Hal and left, leaving the door ajar.

Hal rubbed Buttercup's smooth fur against her face with

the most delicious feeling of contentment. She snuggled into her pillow and smiled dreamily, about to drift off when she heard Mom's voice coming from the living room. Hal hadn't heard the apartment door open. Was Mom talking on the phone? She shook herself awake. Time was almost up. She crept out of bed and sneaked down the hall, thankful that she didn't weigh enough to make much noise on the carpeted floor.

"It worked, Fost. Thank you," Mom said. "I've always regretted this day so much, but now it's all fixed." Hal could see Mom standing in the middle of the room, holding a composition notebook. She was definitely not talking on the phone, but Hal couldn't see who was in the room with her. When she crept closer to get a fuller view, what she saw hurled her backwards in shock. There, a few feet away from her mother was a tall, thin, glowing creature in a shimmering robe that seemed to be made of light. The creature had long, curly, silver hair and features that Hal decided were distinctly female. If Hal had tried to picture what an alien looked like, this being would have been it.

Hal gasped and turned away. As she ran back to the bedroom the spin of time travel overtook her and she found herself back in the closet, grasping the TTD.

Chapter 8

THE JOURNAL

Will shot his sister a look of disgust.

"I said I was sorry," Hal said for the third time as they walked along the crowded sidewalk in the drizzle. "Can't we move on?" she begged.

This time, Will didn't give his sister the courtesy of a dirty look. Now she wants to move on, he thought, when it suits her.

"Come on," Esther said, bumping Will with her shoulder. "Where's that 'whatever' when you need it? How about a little shrug? For me?"

"No one thinks you're funny," said Rebekah.

"We need to focus on what I saw," Hal said. "I thought you'd be ecstatic. I saw an alien, for goodness sakes!"

"Yeah, but I didn't," Will answered, still not making eye contact. "If you had included me, we both would have seen an alien."

They stopped in front of Lucy's Pizzeria. As Esther opened the door, the aroma of melting cheese and tomato sauce on rising dough pulled them into the narrow shop.

"How many slices?" Hal asked her brother. "I'm treating."

Will shook his head. "I can't believe you think you can buy my forgiveness with a stinkin' slice of pizza."

"Pizza and a comic," Esther said. "Remember, she promised we'd go to the comic store, too."

Will and Esther slid into an orange booth while Hal and Rebekah ordered.

"She's right," Esther said. "You need to move on. This is huge."

Will nodded reluctantly.

"Besides," Esther continued, "you need her. She's the mobile one, remember? What can you do alone if you're stuck in a baby seat or a crib?"

Will had been too furious at Hal's confession to think through the logistics of a trip that far to the past. Esther was right—he couldn't do much behind the bars of a crib. By the time Hal came back with the pizza, Will was ready to talk.

"Describe it again. The alien, I mean," Will said. He slurped up a mouthful of ice from his soda and chewed.

"I told you. Tall, shimmering, silver hair. Just what you'd think an alien would look like. Like what you'd see in the movies. And I think it was a she."

Will frowned but Esther choked and spit cola on her pizza.

"What?" Hal asked.

"It seems odd that a real alien would look like it came out of an earth movie. What are the chances?" Will asked.

"And I suppose this alien was Caucasian, right?" Esther added. "Are you sure you didn't dream the whole thing up? You said you were about to fall asleep when you heard their voices."

"I know what I saw, and I can prove it. I think Mom was keeping a journal of her trips into the past. We need to go back and find that notebook," Hal said.

"Agreed," said Will. "If Mom really is chronicling her time travel, that notebook should contain a boatload of vital information. It's too bad you didn't see where she keeps it."

"What if you went back to the exact same day and time, but set the TTD to stay longer?" Rebekah suggested. "That way you could get a better look at the alien and the journal."

"Makes sense," Will said.

"Plus, we can snoop around while Mom is distracted by the party," Hal said.

"And it doesn't hurt that you'll get to celebrate your third birthday again, right?" Esther asked with a smirk.

Hal grinned. "Yeah, there is that."

"Remember the mission," Will said sternly. "We'll try tonight when Mom and Dad are asleep." He shoved the last of the pizza into his mouth and stood. "Let's go."

They walked to the comic book store, brushing past one annoying shopper after another. Esther pushed her way forward and squeezed next to Will.

"Listen," she said, "I know you haven't noticed the sad look in my eyes so I'm going to say this again straight out. I want to go with you."

Will's gaze stayed fixed on the uneven sidewalk. Absently, he put his hand in his pocket and felt the rock Mr. Salazar had dug up in his garden. "I get it," he said. "I just don't see what good it would do."

"Does it have to do any good? Can't you just do this because we're friends?"

Will didn't answer.

"We are friends, right?" Esther asked. She stopped and grabbed Will's arm. "And if you say 'whatever' I'm going to kick your butt." She searched Will's face until he finally made eye contact. Then she smiled. Will's face remained impassive.

"I know you're smiling on the inside," Esther said.

"Okay," Will answered. "We'll figure out a way. But first, I go back with Hal, to see if this so-called alien is real."

O—O—O

That night at dinner, if Mom thought Hal's sudden interest in the good old days was strange, she didn't show it.

"What was our old apartment like?"

"How old was Will when he started walking?"

"Did we always take a nap at the same time?"

"How long did we sleep?"

The more Mom reminisced, the more dreamily distracted she became, until Dad finally had enough and declared, "No more questions." After a heated exchange about who got to control the conversation, Mom left the table in a huff. Hal thought she heard the closet door open and close upstairs. Will answered her look of concern with a shrug. They helped Dad clean up in silence.

Later, Hal fiddled with her hair at her dresser mirror while Will leafed through a stack of comics. It was taking forever for Mom and Dad to go to sleep.

"One thing I don't get," Hal said. "How come I didn't get sick, back there in the past, when I realized Mom was time traveling?"

"I wondered that, too," Will answered. "I think it's because you were time traveling, too. Somehow that made you immune."

"I guess that makes sense." Hal wove her hair into a braid and then loosened it again with her fingers. "Do you think she went back before, when she got mad at dinner and left in a huff?" she asked.

"Yeah, probably. I guess all that talk about the past was too much for her," Will answered.

"She's like an addict," Hal said sadly. "Still, she did save you from falling on your head. That should count for something."

"Except that she was the one who dropped me on my head in the first place. She's fixing her own mistakes."

"I bet lots of people wished they could do that," Hal said.

"Maybe. Except she's making a whole new bunch of problems in the process," Will said. "That's why it's not worth going back. Going to the future would be so much better."

"But you said we can't go to the future because there'd be no bodies to jump into, right?"

"Maybe," Will said again, and Hal heard the disappointment in his voice. She tried to empathize, but her parents' latest skirmish was still on her mind and figuring out how to help Mom had to be her priority. Hal moved to her desk and tried to distract herself with cat videos until, finally, she heard Mom go to bed while Dad snored on the couch downstairs. Will grabbed Chester from his usual spot in the hall and in no time, they were in an unfamiliar room at a strange apartment in miniature bodies on Hal's third birthday.

"We're getting good at this," Hal said when she stopped spinning. She was pleased to see that she'd gotten the timing right; they'd landed during naptime, but (at Will's insistence) after the incident at the diaper table.

"Help me get out of here," Will hissed.

Hal slipped out of bed and tiptoed to the crib. She heard voices coming from the living room. Mom was doing most of the talking, but now and then a delicate, laughing voice chimed in that Hal knew belonged to the alien. "That's her," she whispered excitedly. "She sounds angelic."

Will stood in the crib, holding onto the slats. "I have to see it," he said. He grabbed the crib railing and tried with all his might to lift his lower body over the side, but his fat little legs seemed glued to the mattress. He tried a second time, but it was no use. "Give me a boost," he said desperately.

Hal reached through the slats and gripped Will's ankle with both hands. "On three," she said. "One, two, three!" She gritted her teeth and pushed up as hard as she could. Will hit the bar with his belly and hovered in midair.

"Pull me over," he gasped.

"I can't reach you," Hal said, stretching up on her tiptoes. She looked around the room frantically for something to climb on, but there was nothing.

"I can't breathe," Will said. Hal jumped as high as she could and hit Will's shoulders, pushing him backwards. The crib squeaked as he hit the mattress with a thud.

"What's going on in there?" Mom called from the

hallway. Will managed to lie down and close his eyes just as Mom entered, frowning and clutching the journal in one arm. "Halia, why are you out of bed? Are you trying to wake up your brother?" She glanced at Will, who was faking sleep with deep, even breaths. Mom smiled dreamily and knelt at Hal's side. "Back to sleep, or you'll be cranky for your party." She kissed Hal gently on the cheek.

Hal realized that this was still future Mom, the Mom who missed her little kids so much she'd figured out a way to go back in time. Counting on the hope that this Mom wouldn't be able to refuse her, Hal made a quick decision.

"Can you read your book to me?" she asked in the sweetest little kid voice she could manage.

"Well, I guess we have time for just one book. How about *The Cat in the Hat*?"

"No, I mean your book," Hal said, pointing to the journal that Mom was still holding.

"This book?" Mom asked, surprised. "This is Mommy's book. It doesn't have any pictures."

"That's okay. I just want to see your writing. When I grow up, I want to write just like you." Hal batted her eyelashes at Mom adoringly. "Because you're the best mommy in the whole world," she added for good measure. She heard a soft, gagging sound come from Will, but he managed to compose himself when Mom looked in his direction.

"He must be dreaming," Mom said quietly. "Okay, we can look at my book for a few minutes, but then you have to promise to go to sleep. Deal?"

"Deal," Hal answered, and they snuggled up on Hal's little bed. Mom made up a story about a girl and a unicorn as she flipped through the pages of the journal. Hal took in as much of Mom's writing as she could, sometimes asking Mom to stop and tell that part again so she could have more time on a page.

When they got to the end, Mom closed the notebook and tucked Hal under the covers. She waited a few minutes while Hal faked sleeping before she left the room.

"Did you get a good look?" Will whispered.

"Pretty good, but maybe we can find it and sneak a peek during the party."

"We aren't going to the party," Will said, and Hal felt herself whirling back to the present.

"What happened?" Hal asked once they were back in her room. "I thought we were staying longer this time."

"We stayed long enough to accomplish our goal. We couldn't risk staying longer than that. We still don't know the ramifications of time travel."

"But I wanted to stay for the party," Hal slumped onto her bed. "I wanted to see everyone and play with my toys and blow out the candles on my cake."

Will shook his head. "There was no need."

Hal jumped up in anger. "How come you get to decide that? Next time I'm setting the TTD!"

"Calm down, you'll wake them," Will replied. "What did you find out from the journal?"

But it was too late. Dad was stumbling down the hallway. "Go to bed, both of you," he ordered, half asleep. "It's late."

"We'll talk tomorrow," Will said as he slipped out of the room. Hal heard his bedroom door close. There was nothing left to do but go to sleep.

"Maybe we'll talk tomorrow, if I feel like it," she mumbled from under the covers. "Or maybe I'll just keep it all to myself." But already her anger was fading and she knew she'd tell Will everything she'd learned from Mom's journal. She drifted off, dreaming of dancing in a field of yellow daisies with little brown bear named Buttercup.

Chapter 9

ESTHER'S PLAN

"Because we can't all fit," Will said. He tossed a pebble and heard it clank off the side of the metal swing set. The girls loved to swing at the park, and although he'd never admit it, Will didn't mind the feeling of soaring through the air with only bits of plastic and metal separating him from the sky.

"And Rebekah doesn't even want to go," Esther added.

Hal looked to her best friend, swinging next to her. "Is that true, Rebek? You don't want to give it a try? We could go back to the eighth-grade dance."

The wind blew through Rebekah's hair. She always swung the highest and the longest, moving in perfect unison with the motion of the swing. "No, thanks. I'm satisfied right here in the present."

"Well, I want to go. Come on, we won't stay long," Esther pleaded.

Will sighed. "It doesn't matter how long we stay, remember? As far as anyone will know, we'll only be gone for a second."

"What if you run into the aliens?" Hal asked.

"We're going back to last week. There were no aliens around," Will said.

"Fost and Tuley, Mom called them in the journal," Hal said. "Fost was the one I saw. She looked exactly how Mom described her—tall, silver, shimmering."

"What about the other one?" Esther asked.

"From what I could tell, Tuley looked different every time Mom saw him. She wrote something about an eagle. He was sort of part man, part eagle. I wish Mom had drawn pictures."

"Maybe the aliens have the ability to change their appearance," Will said.

"At least now we know the how, or part of the how," Rebekah said. "Did the journal say anything about the why? Why did your mom start going back in time? And why did these aliens give her the technology in the first place?"

"She went back to fix stuff," Hal answered. "That much we know. I saw her stop Will from falling on his head. And she wrote about other times when she went back." She glanced at her brother uncertainly, but he wasn't looking in her direction. "It seemed like she was worried about Will."

"We know *Mom's* why," Will said, "but we don't know the rest of the why. Why would aliens choose our Mom? What's so special about her?" Will launched off the swing in midair and landed in a squat. He straightened up and began to pace in front of the swings, just out of kicking reach. The question haunted him. Why would aliens contact his mom?

95

Why wouldn't they contact him? He was the one who longed to meet them, to fly away with them, to explore the strange vastness of space. Will was tired of his comics and movies and video games. He wanted more.

"Let's go," Hal said, jumping off the swing and leading the way home. While the girls bickered about a plan, Will trailed behind, lost in thought. He didn't mind doing this favor for Esther, but let them figure out the logistics.

Esther turned and walked backward. "Earth to Will," she said. "Are you listening? It's agreed. Hal and Rebek will distract your mom while we use the TTD. Okay?"

Will almost said "whatever," but when he saw the excitement on Esther's face he nodded instead.

"But distract her how?" Hal asked. "She's not going to leave you two home alone, that's for sure."

"You just have to keep her outside in the yard," Esther said. "Sit down on the patio for a talk. You know, ask for advice. Your mom loves that."

"True," Hal answered, looking to Rebekah. "School work or boy trouble?"

"Either, I guess," Rebekah said.

"Stick to boy trouble," Esther butted in. "You want this to be believable. It's summer, and even you wouldn't be worried about school work yet."

As Esther had predicted, Mom could not pass up the opportunity to hand out advice, and due to the delicate nature of the topic, luring her to the privacy of the patio was easy. Will and Esther sat at the kitchen table, feigning deep involvement in a game of Risk. After a few minutes they made their move. Chester, who had been asleep on the sofa, followed them upstairs as if he knew he'd be needed. Will opened the door to the closet and stepped in. He placed the carpet square on the floor and turned to Esther.

"Are you sure you want to do this?" he asked.

Esther's face lit up in eager anticipation. "Are you kidding? Let's go!"

She stepped in and Will closed the door. "Okay," he said, looking down at the TTD. "I'll set it for last Wednesday at 2 pm. We were all hanging out at the pool that day. Get ready to feel a little spinny."

"What's wrong with the cat?" Esther asked. Chester was pacing around their legs with his ears turned back and his tail wagging like crazy.

"I don't know," Will said. "He's usually calm. His purr activates the TTD." Will reached down and scratched Chester behind the ear, but the cat was having none of it. He swiped at Will's hand and left a red stripe with his sharp claws.

"Hey!" Will said. "What's wrong with you?"

"Maybe he's not in the mood."

"If he doesn't cooperate we're not going anywhere," Will said. "Here, hold this." He handed Esther the TTD and picked Chester up. "What's wrong?" he whispered, scratching under Chester's soft, furry chin.

Chester was usually a sucker for a chin scratch, but not today. He lurched out of Will's arms, knocking the TTD out of Esther's hand on his way down. The device hit the wall hard and landed at Will's feet, back panel off and intricate parts exposed. But Chester was not done. He pounced at the TTD, holding it down with one paw while he clawed away at it with the other.

"Chester, what are you doing!" Will exclaimed. "Stop!" He tried to brush Chester away with his foot, but the cat kept clawing, now meowing loudly. In a few quick movements Will opened the closet door, tossed Chester out, and closed the door again.

"That was really weird," he said.

"When did lazy old Chester become an attack cat?" Esther asked, her voice shaking.

"He's never acted like that before. I don't understand it."

Esther gathered up the pieces of the TTD and handed them to Will. "Is it broken?" she asked. Will frowned. Without the TTD there would be no more time travel, for them or for Mom. What would she do when she found out they knew her secret? More than that, what would Will do if his plans to meet real aliens ended here today? The idea of finishing out the long, boring summer and then going back to another long, boring school year as if none of this had happened was unimaginable. He was on the brink of something big, something life-changing, and he wasn't about to see it end now. Will pieced the TTD back together as best he could. Miraculously, the device activated. He punched in the date and time and set the duration of the trip for ten minutes, but his hands were shaking and he may have hit a few numbers more than once. A blurry picture of whirling motion appeared on the screen. Will tried to clear it, but it was too late. A sparkling column encased them and they were on their way.

Will prepared himself to land in last Wednesday, but something very different happened. They remained in the portal, spiraling on and on but not feeling the least bit dizzy. Bright circles of light flashed around them like fluorescent orange hula hoops, spinning in time with an effervescent tune that started with the familiar chimes of the TTD, but then enveloped them in a full, magnificent melody. The music filled Will with a sense of wonder he'd never felt before.

"You didn't say it was anything like this!" Esther said, and Will was surprised he could hear her above the music. Her voice was crystal clear, as if it were coming from inside his head and not from someone standing next to him.

"Because it wasn't like this!" Will exclaimed. He relaxed and let the music fill him. So this is what it feels like to be happy, he thought.

Then, as quickly as it had begun, it was over. Will and Esther stood in a brightly lit white hallway with a rounded ceiling and no doors or windows. The music was replaced by complete and utter silence.

"Do you think we died?" Esther whispered.

"Only if there are cats in heaven," Will replied, pointing to Chester, who was rubbing around his ankles.

"Now he wants to be friends," Esther said.

"How did he get here? He wasn't in the portal with us." Everything about this trip was different. Will forced himself to stay calm. "Maybe we went back too far, to before we were born," he suggested. "We could wait here for the ten minutes to be up. The TTD should take us back automatically."

Chester meowed and sauntered down the hall, pausing every few feet and turning to look back at them.

"I think he wants us to follow him," Will said.

Esther hesitated. "Should we?"

Chester walked on and disappeared around a corner.

"Maybe we should wait here," Will said. "No telling where

this will take us." What if this hallway led to something dangerous? Will didn't want to be responsible for Esther's safety. He searched Esther's face, expecting to see worry and fear. Will wasn't very good in the comforting department. He usually left that to Hal. Esther met his eyes and smirked.

"Yeah, right. Let's go back and forget the whole thing. I'd much rather be sitting around eating your mom's almond butter sandwiches." She took a few steps and then turned to Will. "What are you waiting for? Come on."

They proceeded cautiously, excitement growing in Will by the second. Although his heart was racing, he forced himself to take slow, steady steps. They turned the corner and entered another long corridor. Will could just make out a figure at the end.

"Do you think that's God?" Esther asked.

Will strained to see more clearly. The figure definitely looked like a man, and a familiar looking man, at that.

"I don't think so," Will said. They continued slowly, and the closer they got, the more familiar the man looked. Chester sat at the man's feet. Finally, Will broke into a grin.

"It's Mr. Salazar!" he said, sprinting the remaining distance with Esther following close behind.

"What are you doing here?" Will asked. "How far into the past did we come?"

Mr. Salazar smiled. "Hola, Will. Hola, Esther. Welcome to the future."

PART II – FUTURE

Chapter 10

ALTERNATE

The metal cuffs rubbed against Will's wrists. Arms pinned behind his back, he squirmed. His shoulder muscles were starting to stiffen up and he knew from experience that pain was imminent.

"Get in," Detective Santiago said. He held Will's head and guided him into the back seat of the patrol car, then slid into the front seat next to Officer Chun. They drove through side streets and out to the main road, quieter now than usual because of the time of night.

"Here we are again, Horace," Chun said. "Some people don't know how to quit while they're ahead."

Will remained silent.

"Nothing to say for yourself?" Chun asked. "You were plenty chatty an hour ago when you thought you were making a sale."

Will let the words pass through him as if he were a hologram.

Santiago shook his head sadly. "We gave you a break last time, Will, out of respect for your mother. I don't particularly enjoy arresting my neighbor's son. But this is the third time. No more breaks."

Will stared at a jagged rip in the upholstery.

"Here's your mother now," Santiago said when they'd parked in front of the precinct.

Will imagined falling into the void of the upholstery tear.

Out on the sidewalk, Mom rushed over, her face a painful mix of anger and distress. She wasn't wearing a coat, although the autumn night air was raw. Hal followed a few steps behind, clutching her hoodie closed and crying.

"I'm sorry, Alexis," Santiago said. "This time we'll have to book him."

"I understand," Mom said, her voice cracking just a little. Will looked away.

Two familiar-looking Asian girls and their parents walked by briskly. The younger one turned back for a second and said, "That's the kid from school—the bad one that gets in trouble a lot."

"Esther, Rebekah, let's go," their father called from a few steps ahead. "It's late."

Will allowed himself to be led up the concrete steps to the front door of the precinct, but when he reached the top step, his foot seemed to pass through the cement into nothingness. He braced himself for a fall, but to his surprise he remained suspended with nothing solid beneath him. The sights and sounds around him blurred until the precinct faded away and Detective Santiago's face melted and reshaped into the comforting image of Mr. Salazar.

"It's okay, Will," said Mr. Salazar. "You're back now."

Chapter 11

THE FUTURE IS GREEN

Mr. Salazar and Chester led the way out of the stark white tunnel into the warm sunlight of a grassy field. Esther was the last one out. The instant she cleared the exit it sealed and disappeared into a foothill of a low mountain range.

"Where'd it go?" she asked. She considered that she might be dreaming, or more likely stuck in Will's nightmare. He was sweating and shaking all over.

"This place is shielded from view. Only a few trusted friends know of it," Mr. Salazar replied.

Parked nearby was a small vehicle that emitted a slight, green glimmer. It reminded Esther of a golf cart, except it had no wheels. On the inside of the cart were four seats, but no controls of any kind. Mr. Salazar reached in and pressed his palm against the smooth interior surface. From nowhere, a compartment popped open, revealing a shiny metal container.

Mr. Salazar twisted open the lid and poured a thick, green liquid into it. "Drink this," he told Will.

As Esther waited with the patience of an active volcano, Will gulped the liquid down, wiping his mouth with his sleeve when he was done.

"Okay now?" Mr. Salazar asked.

Will nodded and Esther erupted. "What the heck happened back there?"

"Come," said Mr. Salazar. "I'll explain while we ride." Then, to Esther's astonishment, he slid into the front passenger's seat while Chester took the driver's seat.

"Now I know I'm dreaming," said Esther. "Don't tell me that cat can drive."

"It's purr-activated," said Mr. Salazar. "Much like the technology that got you here."

If Esther hadn't been shell-shocked at the events of the last few minutes she would have laughed. Instead, she felt annoyed that Mr. Salazar would joke at a time like this. Then Chester purred the cart into movement and they lifted a few feet off the ground, through the field to a narrow strip of shiny green plastic-like material, where the cart seemed to pick up speed on its own. They were the only vehicle on the road. Chester put his head between his paws and went to sleep.

"Activation drains him of energy. He's exhausted now," Mr. Salazar explained. "We'll travel the rest of the way on chloro-solar power."

Esther gave a disbelieving snort.

"I know you have many questions," said Mr. Salazar. "I will attempt to answer as many as I can. First of all, as I said before, you have traveled to the future."

Esther looked around as the wind whipped through the open cart. All she saw were green grass, tall trees, and blue skies. This didn't look like the future to her. Where were the ultra-modern buildings with sharp angles and sleek surfaces? And most importantly, where were the flying cars?

"How far?" Will asked. It was the first time he spoke since they'd arrived. His voice was weak and the wind swept up his words so that they were barely audible.

"We don't have far to go," Mr. Salazar answered. "I want you to meet some friends of mine."

Will shook his head and slumped further into his seat.

"He means how far in the future are we?" Esther shouted over the wind. Mr. Salazar pressed his palm against the interior of the cart again and a thin plastic barrier encased them, creating instant calm. The only sound that remained was Chester's quiet snore.

"That's better," said Mr. Salazar. "By your units of measure, we are many hundreds of years in the future. You arrived here because of Chester's manipulation of what you call the TTD."

"You're saying that a cat brought us here?" Esther asked, still incredulous.

"Yes. I could attempt to explain, but I'm not sure you'd understand. Perhaps you have more pressing questions. I think Will would like to know what he experienced in the Altvume."

"The what?" Will whispered.

"The Altvume allows us to explore alternate timelines. What we saw was a possible reality—something that might have come to pass if events in Will's life had transpired differently."

"I did more than see it," Will said. "I was there, in it." Esther had never seen Will cry, but she thought he was close now. She wanted to touch his hand, but she knew better. She reached into her pocket, dug out her last piece of Bubble Yum, and tossed it onto Will's lap.

"Yes," said Mr. Salazar. "I programmed the Altvume with you as the subject. I felt you needed to experience that possible reality to understand your mother's use of time travel."

"You couldn't just tell him?" Esther asked. "How about we put you in the Altvume and see what would happen if the cat drove the car into a ditch?"

Will put the gum in his mouth and tossed the crinkled wrapper at Esther. It bounced off her nose and fell to the floor, where it disappeared with a sucking sound.

"What was that?" Esther asked.

"We've learned to recycle everything with the use of nanotechnology," Mr. Salazar answered.

"Of course you have," Esther replied.

"Where are we going?" Will asked.

"To the Historical Society, where I work," Mr. Salazar answered. "It is just beyond those hills." They sped along, hovering above the slick, green strip, still surrounded by lush, grassy fields. The minutes stretched on with no other vehicles in sight.

"Why are we the only car on the road?" Will asked, taking the last sip of the liquid Mr. Salazar had provided. "Where are all the people?"

"Most people choose a quicker method of transportation," Mr. Salazar explained. "I chose this method in order to give Will time to recover. Since he seems to be feeling better, would you like to speed up our trip?"

"Definitely," Will and Esther said together.

"Okay, then. Here we go." Mr. Salazar waved his hand and they rose into the air, suddenly surrounded by a host of vehicles scooting in all directions.

"Flying cars! I knew it!" Esther said.

"Why couldn't we see them before?" Will asked. He held on to the seat in front of him, watching vehicles speed over, under, and around. Some looked like small planes, while others resembled cars or SUVs, but all had the same green glow as their flying golf cart.

They were shielded from our view. We've discovered that the human mind does better with fewer distractions. Most people choose a serene sky background when travelling." A cross between an SUV and a compact jet made a sharp left in front of them.

"How do they stop from crashing?" Will asked.

"When I programmed our destination, the road flyer registered a flight plan automatically and sent it to the other vehicles. Sit back and relax—we'll be there in a few minutes." Mr. Salazar reached over and absently scratched Chester behind the ear. "Almost time to wake up, my friend," he said softly.

Soon Esther could make out dozens of clusters of low, green spheres glistening in the sun. "We're in the future," she whispered to Will. "In a flying car. Being driven by a cat."

Will stared through the clear barrier that separated them

from the sky and nodded. For all the excitement he showed he could have been watching a SpongeBob rerun, but Esther knew better. Esther knew that behind his passive expression he was bursting with joy and anticipation. She kicked his foot and said, "It's okay to look happy. Your face won't crack and fall off."

Will kicked her back. "Like yours already did?"

"When I looked at you."

"Whatever," Will said, and Esther was glad for that little bit of normal. A moment later the road flyer slowed and descended.

"We're landing now," Mr. Salazar said. "When we arrive, I'll introduce you to my friends. They will help answer your questions."

They parked the road flyer at the edge of the city and jumped on a long, rectangular transport that would take them the rest of the way. Chester pranced off in the opposite direction without so much as a goodbye meow.

"This will take a bit longer, but the levitrans is safer," Mr. Salazar said. Esther wasn't sure what he meant. Safer how? There were other people around, but she got the distinct impression that Mr. Salazar didn't want to be overheard, so she kept quiet and ran her hand over the smooth, invisible shield that held her in her seat as they glided a few feet off the ground. One thing was sure—the levitrans beat the bumps, rattles, and jolts of the Q65 bus any day.

"Why are all the buildings round?" Esther asked.

"This shape is easiest to replicate quickly. Look there and you'll see what I mean." Mr. Salazar pointed at a globe that seemed to be adding smaller globes to itself. "We've learned that buildings serve us best when temporary and easily altered. And so, the landscapes of our communities are always changing, depending on the need."

As they got closer, Esther heard the muted sound of chimes playing a simple, elegant tune. The air was full of the faint, sweet melody, and although she couldn't figure out where it was coming from, the music made her feel light and happy and filled with possibility. She watched the round clusters transform as, one after another, circles formed and disappeared under a fine green shine.

"Like blowing bubbles on a wand," she commented softly.

"Yes," said Mr. Salazar, "these 'bubbles,' as you call them, are clustered together to form communities spread throughout the planet. We've learned that crowding too many people into small spaces is not healthy for mind or body."

"But how do you fit all the people in these little clusters?" Esther asked. "During our time there were over seven billion people. There must be even more now."

"Yes, considerably more, but space was never the problem, even in your time. It was uneven distribution that once caused overcrowding in some areas, while others remained underpopulated. Our technology allows us to use the entire planet efficiently, even those places that were previously uninhabitable."

Questions popped up in Esther's head like fireworks on Fourth of July. Did that mean people live at the bottom of the ocean? Or at the top of Mount Everest? What about Antarctica? Could she buy a house, or a bubble, on the moon? How much would it cost? Did they even still use money? But before she could ask anything, the levitrans stopped and

Esther's focus shifted to the large sphere in front of them that was emitting the same green shimmer she'd noticed everywhere.

"What's with all the green?" she asked as they approached the structure. "And how do we get in?" She couldn't see an opening of any kind. The exterior of the sphere felt soft and squishy but she couldn't push in more than an inch.

"You use chlorophyll for energy somehow, don't you?" Will asked. "That's what powers the vehicles and the buildings, and that's why everything is green."

"You're on the right track," Mr. Salazar said, "but it's a bit too complicated to explain right now." He placed his hand on the glistening green exterior of the sphere. Immediately a round entrance appeared and they stepped through it.

"Welcome to the Historical Society." Mr. Salazar led them quickly through an empty corridor with rippling green, cushy walls. They walked through an archway into a hall filled with people clustered around tables and work stations. The curved walls were covered in screens where images blinked and changed at the wave of the person viewing. Small and large holographic figures appeared and disappeared throughout the hall like ghosts in a graveyard.

A group of kids about Esther's age approached them cautiously, glancing around as if they thought they were being watched. They brushed past Esther and Will and motioned for them to follow.

"Hasten," said a brown-skinned female in a bright pink headdress that blossomed around her like a rose. She led the way to the end of the hall, past open archways, until they came to a dead end.

A boy who looked Asian came forward and pressed his hand to the wall. A tiny bubble appeared, grew, and extended out until a round sphere had been added to the building.

"Thank you, Jikon," Mr. Salazar said.

Jikon stepped through and motioned for the others to follow. Esther wondered if he might be Korean, but she had never heard that name before.

Once they'd entered, the archway sealed and Esther could no longer hear the sounds of the people she'd passed. She was able to take a good look at the six teens who surrounded them: three males and three females, all of different height, shape, hair color, and complexion. They wore brightly colored, loose fitting clothes made of a light, silky material, and now their cautious expressions were replaced with huge grins as if they were greeting long lost friends. Next to Esther, Will slouched and put his hands in his pockets. He loved meeting new people—not.

Esther expected the usual nods and grunts of awkward introductions, but instead, the group encircled them, holding hands and chanting in a language she had never heard—and coming from Queens, that was saying a lot. Some of the words sounded like English, but they were put together in a way that Esther could not understand. They chanted and danced in a series of intricate steps, left, right, forward and back, raising their arms and lowering them in rhythm to the chant, which got louder and softer with the tempo of the dance. Esther squirmed and Will looked like he wanted to crawl into the nearest hole, except there weren't any holes in this pristine world. Finally, the circle broke and the dancers formed a straight line facing Will and Esther. They chanted the same phrase over and over—something about a waterbed? Of course, that made no sense, and Esther wanted to laugh out loud. Apparently, no matter how advanced the civilization, the theater-nerd gene lived on. Will looked to Mr. Salazar for help.

"Stop, please, my friends," he said. "Our customs are not familiar to our new arrivals. You have studied their time period. Please adapt accordingly."

"Regretful, Time Leader," said the girl with the pink headdress. "Modify all."

"Thank you, Okoko," Mr. Salazar replied. The future kids stared straight ahead, blinking rapidly but otherwise motionless.

"This will take a moment," Mr. Salazar said.

"What did they call you?" Will asked. "Time Leader? What does that mean?"

"Exactly as it sounds. To you, I have appeared as Mr. Salazar, your retired neighbor. Here, I am the Leader of the Time Team, a branch of the Historical Society. Our role is to study history. These are my coworkers."

Coworkers? Esther thought. These kids were no older than she was. Did he mean students? Interns, maybe?

"What are they doing?" Will asked.

"They are engaging their language updaters. Language and communication styles change over time. Their present mode of communication may not be understandable to you."

"Are they robots?" Esther asked.

"I assure you, they are as human as you and I, with a few modifications. Long ago we learned to supplement our knowledge by uploading information directly into our brains.

They should be ready any second now."

"But where are they uploading the information from? And how?" Will asked. Before Mr. Salazar could answer, the group trance ended.

A small, pale, blond girl approached Esther with her fist extended. "Yo, I'm Astra. Dap me up," she said.

Esther shifted her weight and looked to Will. Helpful as ever, he shrugged.

"Er, okay," she said, bumping the girl's fist weakly.

"You seem uncomfortable," Astra said. "Did I get it wrong?"

"I think you confused 'dap' with 'dab,'" said a tall, thin, boy with brown skin and black hair.

"I think my use of early twenty-first century vernacular was correct, Gyasi," Astra said. "To 'dap' is to bump fists, while to 'dab' is to move like so..." She threw her arms out in the dance move that Esther hoped she'd never see again in this or any century. "I'm sure Esther will hit me up," Astra said, extending her fist again.

"I think you mean 'back me up,' but sure," said Esther, with an even weaker fist bump.

"Perhaps let's stay away from slang for now," said Mr. Salazar. "Adjust vocabulary, please." Again, they stood transfixed for a few seconds and then relaxed.

A girl who hadn't spoken yet approached Will with a warm smile and stuck out her hand. "I'm very pleased to meet you, Will," she said. "I am Samaya." Her thick, dark brown hair rested on her shoulders in intricate braids. Esther thought she looked Asian, but definitely not Korean.

Will kept his hands in his pockets.

"Is this not the formal greeting?" Samaya asked, confused.

"It is," said Mr. Salazar, "but I think you may be overwhelming our guests. Let's sit down." At the wave of his hand, a circle of soft chairs rose from the floor. When Esther sat, the chair molded perfectly around her body.

"This is comfy," she said, sinking in. "I think I could get used to it here."

The smiles around her faded just enough for Esther to notice. Mr. Salazar gave a long, sad sigh. "What?" Esther asked. "What did I say?"

"They're not going to let us stay long," Will said. "That's it, isn't it?"

"As usual, Will, you've understood the situation." Mr. Salazar rubbed his stubble beard absently. "It would be impossible for you to stay for more than a brief period of time."

"Why?" Esther asked. She turned to Will. "Like you're always saying, we have a time travel device. We can return to our time a few seconds after we left, no matter how long we stay here, right?"

"That's true," said a tall boy with short, wavy brown hair, a square jaw, and broad shoulders. He reminded Esther of the guy who played Superman, whatever his name was, and she took an instant dislike to him. He kept talking. "But people might notice changes in your appearance if you stay away too long. I'm Robbie, by the way."

"Huh?"

"Robbie. That's my name."

Will snorted.

"I heard you, *Robbie*," Esther said. She turned to Will.

"What does he mean, change in our appearance?"

"Esther, think. When Hal and I traveled to the past, we jumped into our own bodies as they existed during that time. We have no bodies in the future. Haven't you wondered how we're here?"

"Well, excuse me for being a little too overwhelmed with alternate realities and cats flying cars to ponder the rules of time travel. Please enlighten me, Your Brilliance."

Gyasi's open expression turned to confusion. "I thought they were good friends," he whispered to the others.

"Let me explain," said Mr. Salazar. "Travel to the past and travel to the future are two very different operations, with different 'rules,' as you call them. Will is partly correct—in the future there is no body to enter. However, all living things leave an energy signature, even after they are gone. When you travel to your future, that energy draws you and causes your body to materialize here. Although you may return to the moment that you left, your body will have aged as normal while you were away. If you stay for any length of time, people are bound to notice differences when you return." He glanced over his shoulder where the opening to the room had been. The others were quiet, listening.

"I'm guessing we're not supposed to be here," Will said.

"Correct, and we don't have much time," said Samaya. With both hands she shaped a bubble the size of a beach ball out of thin air.

"Our team studies important points and people in history," said Gyasi, waving over the bubble. Esther expected to see it fill with an image of the President or the Pope, maybe, but no, there was Will's mom, digging in the dirt in her small garden.

"My mom?" Will's voice rose. "You're saying my mom is important in history? What, does she run for office or something?"

"Nothing like that," said Mr. Salazar. "Alexis remained relatively unknown throughout her lifetime. She never became famous, yet her work to create a greener environment inspired others, who then inspired others." Mr. Salazar pointed to the green walls that enclosed them. "The green movement eventually led to the technology that sustains us today. Only those of us who study time closely realize the vital influence she had." The images in the bubble flickered and transformed as he spoke—Will's mom picking tomatoes in her yard, planting in a field, marching at a rally, speaking to a small group in someone's living room, and then to a large group in a school auditorium.

"Think of it like a web, with every life a strand affecting every other life," said Astra.

"And every time a bell rings an angel get his rings," Esther muttered.

"That's wings," Robbie said.

"You know that movie?" Esther asked.

"All beginning students of Time History study the principles of *It's a Wonderful Life*," said Astra, flicking her hand until a frazzled George Bailey tore around in the bubble. "The film is the basis of our proverb, 'Every life is a watershed.'" Suddenly Esther realized what the team had been chanting at the end of their opening number.

"We're getting off track," Okoko interjected. She waved and the bubble flickered again. There stood Will, but not this

Will. It was the Will they'd seen in the Altvume, a little older and a lot scruffier, hands shackled behind his back, being shoved into a police car on a dark, deserted street. "Something happened to change your mother's influence, Will," Okoko said, "something involving you. Changes to the timeline resulted in the events you experienced in the Altvume. Those changes so negatively affected your mother that she did not fulfill her destiny."

Now the Time Team raised their arms and the bubble grew and engulfed them. The walls fell away and Esther found herself in the road flyer, traveling over lush green fields under a bright blue sky. Then, as if she were being fast forwarded inside a movie, large, jagged buildings appeared, deteriorated, and were replaced by even larger, spikey towers that stood against an ever-darkening sky. A force of water rushed from the horizon, crushing every edifice under its powerful current. Esther felt herself submerged in the pounding ocean, yet she remained dry.

"Okay, we get the point!" she shouted, not sure anyone heard her muffled voice. She looked to Will, who smirked and offered her a fist bump. Of course, he'd be enjoying this. Finally, the waves subsided and the simulation faded.

Jikon spoke. "Your mother was given the ability to travel back in time to correct those aberrations."

"That doesn't make sense," Will said, shaking his head. "If someone changed the past to affect your present, how would you even know about it?"

"It's hard to describe," Samaya said. She flicked her hand and again, an ocean wave arose around the edge of the room and rushed toward them, breaking over their heads. As Esther ducked and covered, Samaya continued calmly. "Time travels in waves. Events don't affect the timeline instantaneously."

"Enough with the water," Esther complained. "Do you people have to be so dramatic? Haven't you ever heard of a marker board? PowerPoint, maybe?"

"Keep in mind that there are many types of time waves," said Jikon. As he spoke, the smaller bubble reappeared before them and within it a calm sea stirred peacefully against the shore. "Some skim the surface of time, like shallow ocean waves. This is the type of wave that altered your development, Will. Fortunately, we were able to detect it and intervene before it was too late. Since we don't know who altered the timeline, we don't know who we can trust. That's why we brought you here in secret."

"If you gave Mom the TTD," Will asked, "who are the aliens?"

The Time Team exchanged confused glances.

"We know of no aliens involved in your history," Gyasi said. "In fact, we've only recently developed the technology for intergalactic space travel."

"There were aliens," Will insisted. "My sister saw one in our past, talking to our mom."

Mr. Salazar waved his hand and a sparkling jet stream sprang up from the bubble and was enveloped in a waterfall. "This may be the result of a sneaker wave—a time wave that rises up without warning and overtakes all other waves. They are unpredictable and quite dangerous."

"If a sneaker wave is at work," said Okoko, frowning, "you may have experienced the results of actions before they are initiated—like the effect happening before the cause." At the flick of her hand the waterfall reversed and disappeared into the bubble.

"I think I'm getting sea sick," Esther said. "Do you have any idea what they're talking about?" she asked Will.

"Sort of, but not a hundred percent. This kind of stuff takes time."

"And time is what we've run out of," said Mr. Salazar. The curved wall across from Esther began to ripple. "We've been discovered."

"No!" Will shouted. "Not yet! We just got here!"

"I'm sorry," Mr. Salazar answered. "Will, you now know how important you are. Remember, every life is a watershed." Mr. Salazar stood and Esther closed her eyes to stop the spinning that had suddenly overtaken her. Seconds later she was in Will's kitchen, the voices of her sister and Hal streaming in through the open window.

"No!" Will screamed again. He ran up the stairs to his room and slammed the door. Esther followed, sitting in Chester's usual spot in the hall. She knew she'd be waiting for a while.

Chapter 12

MESSES

Hal scooped a mess of slimy pulp from the pumpkin and dumped it on the newspaper that covered the kitchen table. "Are we roasting the seeds?" she asked.

"Of course," Mom answered. "And we'll carve out a big smiley face. Maybe that will cheer your brother up. He loves Halloween."

Poor Mom. If she thought a crooked-toothed jack-o'-lantern and a couple of Twizzlers would shake Will out of the funk he was in, she was as clueless as Will said.

Mom took a handful of seeds to the sink and ran the water over them. "He's been so sad since Mr. Salazar went back home. And then Chester going missing at the same time— we're all sad about that."

Dad, who'd been sitting at the counter with his laptop, didn't look sad at all. "Will needs something, that's for sure," he said, "and this trip is just the thing. He loved it last time."

"Right, every kid needs a trip to a nuclear reactor laboratory when he's feeling down," Mom said.

Hal scooped out the last of the guts and carried the pumpkin over to the sink, where Mom rinsed and patted it dry.

"Can I carve the face?" Hal asked.

"Sure, but be careful with the knife." Mom turned her attention back to Dad. "Are you sure you aren't taking him there to spite me?"

"This may come as a surprise, Alexis, but not everything is about you. Your antiquated 'no-nukes' policy has nothing to do with our trip to MIT. It's a great school and Will needs to start thinking about the future."

No one noticed Hal catch her breath—Will had been thinking about nothing but the future, but not in the way Dad meant. Mom exuded cold silence and after a few minutes Dad shut his laptop and stalked off. Mom closed her eyes and took a deep, cleansing breath. She turned to Hal.

"Let's see the face, honey," she said brightly.

Slowly, Hal turned the pumpkin toward Mom.

"Halia, I said a happy face!" Mom exclaimed. Hal's pumpkin had sorrowful eyes and a turned down mouth. She'd even carved tiny teardrops dripping down the pumpkin's cheeks.

"What's the problem with this family?" Mom asked in frustration. "No matter what I do, we just can't seem to be happy." She wiped her hands on a towel and headed for the stairs, leaving Hal alone with her sad new friend.

"Funny question, coming from her," she said to the

pumpkin, "since she's the problem." Hal looked over her shoulder, glad that her words had only been heard by a squash. "I guess that's not quite fair," she said. "We're all the problem, in one way or another."

The pumpkin stared up at her silently. On the floor above, Hal heard the closet door open and close, Mom's soft footsteps, and Dad's loud voice as he banged on Will's bedroom door.

"Let's go," Dad barked. "We've got a good four hours on the road ahead of us. I pulled a lot of strings to get us on the reactor tour. We don't want to miss it."

Will didn't answer, which was no surprise to Hal. Ever since summer he'd been as uncommunicative as the pumpkin, and as sad. Sadder. And angry. Her brother had never been Mr. Happy, but now he was so much worse. His brief visit to the future had left Will devastated. He'd tried to get back time after time, sometimes with Hal, sometimes with Esther, and sometimes alone. It was no use—without Chester's help the TTD was useless. There'd be no more time travel to the past or the future unless the cat returned.

Now Will barely left his room except for school, which he tried to get out of as often as he could. He told Hal that he planned to quit the day he turned seventeen, and no amount of arguing could sway him. Hal was glad that was still several years away. She worried about her brother every day, and today was no exception. Will had not actually agreed to take this road trip with Dad, but Dad, of course, had plowed on with his plans anyway. Hal sat at the bottom step and waited. More and more she found herself here—not on the step, but waiting in-between the moments of some impending crisis, steeling herself for the inevitable explosion. But this time the explosion did not come. Instead, Will emerged from his room wearing his gray hoodie. He slung his backpack over his arm and followed Dad down the stairs. Hal shifted out of the way to let them pass. They left without saying goodbye.

Suspicion crept up on Hal as she went back to the kitchen to clean up the pumpkin mess. Why had her brother gone so willingly? What was he planning? Something was off. She threw her scruples about privacy in the trash with the dirty newspaper and ran up the stairs into Will's room. She opened his top dresser drawer and sure enough, the stash of money he kept in a Star Wars tin was gone. Hal wasn't sure how much Will had saved up, but since he rarely shopped, she thought it was a considerable sum. Will intended to run away.

Hal went to her room and threw herself on her bed, staring up at the pink and white stripes on her ceiling. What should she do? Should she text Dad? And say what? She had no proof that Will was planning anything and besides, telling on her brother felt like an act of betrayal. After all they'd been through together, she felt she owed him more than that. Once again, she waited in-between the moments of an approaching storm.

Through her open bedroom door Hal heard voices coming from Mom's room. Maybe Mom had someone on speaker phone. Hal pictured her mom standing in the mountain pose while complaining to her friend, Charlotte, or Aunt Judy, like she often did after a fight with Dad. She tiptoed down the hallway and pressed her ear to Mom's door. No doubt about it, Hal heard at least two voices other than Mom's, and they weren't Charlotte's or Aunt Judy's. They spoke in hollow, rhythmic chimes that were different from anything Hal had ever heard, but at the same time oddly familiar. Although she didn't want to be discovered, she took a chance and opened the door just a crack. There, surrounded by dazzling light, stood Fost and Tuley, the aliens Mom had written about. Fost looked exactly as Hal remembered, tall and thin, in a silver, shimmering robe. She'd never seen Tuley before, but she remembered Mom's description. His broad body had human shape, but was covered with soft brown feathers. His facial features were human, too, but his head was crowned with the long white feathers of an eagle. Although the aliens faced the door where Hal peeped in, if they saw her they didn't let on, and Mom was too mesmerized by their tall, glowing presence to pay attention to anything else. Hal opened the door a little more and listened.

"I'm afraid your device will no longer work," Fost was saying. "The past must remain closed to you now."

"But why?" Mom said, clearly distressed. "I've been able to fix so many things."

Hal heard Tuley speak for the first time. "Too much interference is dangerous," he said in deeper tones, and again, as he spoke Hal sensed something familiar. "Others are interfering, too. There's nothing more you can do."

"But we still have so many problems," Mom said sadly. "I wasn't finished yet."

Under the tuft of soft white feathers, Hal thought she saw Tuley roll his eyes. Fost, though, responded more sympathetically. "You've done the best you can. Your children have to find their own paths, and you must fulfill your destiny. You need to be fully present for that to happen."

Mom nodded her head slowly and sighed. "I think I understand. But..." she hesitated, "I, I don't know if I can stop. Please don't take it from me." Mom sat on the edge of her bed, hid her face in her hands, and cried. It was all Hal could do to stop herself from rushing in.

Fost and Tuley exchanged glances. Tuley approached Mom, speaking more gently now. "We can help with that," he said. "Your addiction is partly our doing." He reached out his hand and placed it on Mom's head. "We can soften the time travel experience in your memory so its force is less powerful."

Fost placed her hand on Tuley's. "Remember, not too much," she said to him. "Memory wiping is forbidden. Don't steal her past from her."

With his other hand Tuley pointed toward the door and Hal felt a wave of calm come over her. She awoke an hour later on her bed, not sure of how she'd gotten there.

○─○─○

Will slumped next to Dad in the car, backpack at his feet. He'd tried sit in the back, but Dad had insisted, "I'm not your chauffeur," so Will was stuck in the front seat. For the past hour he'd done his best to nod and grunt just enough so as not to be accused of ignoring Dad. When Dad finally got tired of talking, Will closed his eyes and tried to sleep, but it was no use. His memory took him back to the day he'd soared through the air in a road flyer and the desperation that had become his closest companion welled up again. He pushed his palms into the cushioned seat until he felt nothing.

"Passing a rest stop soon," Dad said. "Bathroom break?"

Will shook his head.

"Cat got your tongue?"

Will's look of disdain was the only answer Dad deserved.

"Okay, I shouldn't have mentioned the cat. I am sorry he's gone missing."

"No, you're not. You hated Chester."

"Not true," Dad insisted. "I didn't hate him. The stupid thing just got in the way sometimes."

Will almost laughed. He almost told Dad how not stupid Chester was, but, why bother? Anyway, a rest stop now wasn't in Will's plan. Not yet. "I don't need to stop," he said.

"Okay then," Dad answered. Seemingly satisfied that Will had spoken a full sentence, Dad let Will be and spent the next several minutes yelling along with Bruce Springsteen about being born in the U.S.A., as if anyone cared. Signs for Bridgeport approached.

"I'm hungry," Will announced.

"Now?" Dad asked. "We're not even close yet."

"I didn't eat breakfast. And I have to go to the bathroom."

"You said you didn't have to go."

"I have to go now. And I'm hungry."

"Okay, okay," Dad said, exasperated. "We'll find some place to eat in Bridgeport."

"The Colonial Diner," Will said. "I checked it out online. Good burgers." Will wasn't exactly lying—he had checked the diner out, but not for the quality of its burgers.

Dad smiled. "Alrighty then. I could go for a burger and some nice, greasy, nonorganic fries. Plug it in." Will found the diner on the navigational app while Dad crossed three lanes of traffic to reach the exit, cutting off a minivan and a motorcycle in the process. Through raindrops blurring the windshield, Will counted the blocks of broken sidewalks and worn curbs. Almost there. His heart was pounding when, a few minutes later, they turned into a small parking lot.

"Order me a burger and a Coke," Will said, heading toward the bathroom. He hoped Dad wouldn't notice his backpack and ask questions, but Dad seemed taken with the diner's ambiance.

"These seedy little places have the best food," Dad exclaimed as if he hadn't eaten in years. He followed the waiter in the opposite direction without looking back.

Will figured he had five minutes, ten tops, to make his move. As soon as he was out of Dad's sight he slipped back outside and hurried down the street in the direction of the bus station. He pulled his hood up and rushed along dirty sidewalks, past rusty chain link fences, storefronts, service stations, and factories, ducking under awnings wherever he could to stay out of the rain. Finally, he reached an underpass and waited, hoping the torrent would let up and listening to the cars and trucks roaring over his head. He'd have to get going again—time was running out.

A silver Subaru Forester pulled up in front of Will as he was standing there, trying to be invisible. The window rolled down and a kid who looked about sixteen ducked his head in Will's direction. "Need a ride?"

In that instant Will heard every stranger-danger warning Mom had pumped into him since he was four buzzing in his head. To shut them up he opened the door and jumped in. The car smelled like weed.

"Thanks. I'm just going to the bus station."

"Sure," said the kid. He didn't offer his name and Will didn't ask. "But if you're running away, the bus station is the first place they'll look. Trust me, I know." The kid smiled. "Are you sure you don't want to go somewhere else?"

"No thanks," Will said.

"You also know that they won't sell you a ticket without a parent's signature, right?"

"Yup," Will said.

The kid shook his head. "Whatever." He hung a U-turn and within five minutes Will spotted the transportation terminal enclosed behind a long row of glass panels. He hopped out with a grunt and the Subaru sped off. That could be me a few years from now, Will thought. It wasn't the future he had in mind.

The terminal was busy enough on a Saturday afternoon that no one noticed a kid in a gray hoodie sitting alone on a bench. Will zipped open his backpack and retrieved the folded scrap of paper that he'd found in his locker last week. He studied the words scratched in unfamiliar writing: Bridgeport Bus Terminal 10-26 1:15 pm. He checked his watch—five more minutes to wait and hope that Dad didn't get there with the cops first. Five more minutes until, maybe, something good, something important would happen. Will put the note in his pocket and waited. He didn't know what he was waiting for, but he clung to a tiny molecule of hope with all his might.

People scurried around from every direction, dragging suitcases, duffle bags, and backpacks with them. Will tried to focus on their faces. Most people looked tired and dull, glued to phones or tablets. No one looked familiar. Across from Will, a mom tried to keep three little kids occupied while the dad stood on the ticket line. Out of the corner of his eye Will saw a man with a squeegee and spray bottle getting ready to wash the glass panel door. He was wearing a familiar brown work shirt. Could it be? Will turned his head quickly, but no— while the man had a similar build, he was not Mr. Salazar. Is that who Will expected to turn up here today? Or was it one of the kids he'd met? Samaya, or Jikon, maybe? Would he know them if he saw them, dressed in regular clothes? All through last summer Will had tried to keep his memories of the future kids fresh—the Time Team, they'd called themselves. He'd tried to remember their faces, and he'd even tried to draw them, but really, his artwork sucked. Esther was a little better, but Rebek was the only real artist among them, so, no help there. By the time school started Will's memories of the Time Team were fading, and now he wasn't sure if he'd be able to pick any of them out of a crowd. He kept looking anyway.

Unfortunately, when Will did see a familiar face approaching, it wasn't from the future. It was his very own present Dad, running toward him like an angry bull yelling into a cell phone. Following him was a concerned looking police officer.

"He's here! I'll call you back," Dad shouted. He grabbed Will by the arm and yanked him to his feet.

"What were you thinking?" he cried. "You scared the life out of me!"

Will looked at his watch. 1:14 pm.

"What, am I keeping you from an appointment?" Dad shouted. He tightened his grip on Will's arm.

The police officer stepped forward. "Everything okay now?" she asked.

"Fine," Dad said. His shoulders relaxed a little as he turned toward the officer. "This is my son. We'll head home now. Thanks for your help, Officer Sierra."

"Sure. I just need some information for my report. Do you have identification on you?" she asked Will.

Will handed the cop his school ID. He checked his watch again—1:15 pm exactly. He looked around desperately, and although the spectacle of angry Dad had garnered some attention, not one of the faces turning toward them was from the future.

"Son, I'm going to ask you something, and I want you to tell me the truth," Officer Sierra said. "You're not in any trouble. Were you meeting someone here?"

"Meeting someone?" Dad asked. "We were on our way to MIT. Who would he be meeting?"

"Sir, this happens all the time. A kid meets a predator online posing as a teen. They make plans to meet up. You and your son are lucky. It doesn't always end this well."

Dad's expression changed from anger to worry. "Is that true, Will? Did you make plans to meet someone here?"

Will remained unruffled. "I'm not an idiot," he said, but the note in his pocket got a little heavier. Technically, he was hoping to meet someone here, but not in the way Dad and this cop thought. There was no point trying to explain, so Will kept his mouth shut. It didn't matter anymore, anyway. Nothing was happening and soon he'd be stuck in the car, on his way to being stuck in his life.

Officer Sierra handed back Will's ID. "I'll leave you to sort this out," she said. "But son, whatever is happening, running away is not the answer." She looked Will straight in the eye and smiled sympathetically. "Really, you should count your lucky stars today."

Will snorted. Yeah, lucky. If getting the best thing in the world and losing it on the same day was lucky, he was lucky. If sitting in your stupid room playing stupid video games and reading stupid comics about people traveling through time instead of doing it yourself was lucky, he was the luckiest kid alive. Will had no interest in counting his lucky stars. He wanted to fly among them.

Dad led the way to the car and Will followed dutifully. He looked at his watch—1:20 pm. Will knew he'd get an earful all the way home, but he was too disappointed to care. The rain had stopped but the sky was still dark. A peal of thunder crashed so loudly that Will almost missed another smaller sound coming from under the car.

A cat purring.

Chapter 13
GETTING BACK

"So, you weren't running away?" Esther asked.

"Of course not," Will answered through the din of voices bouncing off the cafeteria walls. "Everybody knows kids aren't allowed to buy bus tickets without parents' approval."

"I didn't know," Hal muttered.

"I was meeting Chester, except I didn't know it was Chester," Will said.

Esther shoved a fish stick into her mouth. "You're saying Chester left a note in your locker?" she asked.

"Don't talk with your mouth full," Rebekah said.

How many times did Will need to explain? "Someone left the note. I don't know who. I let my dad think he was taking me to MIT so I could get close to the bus station in Bridgeport. I didn't know what to expect, but there was Chester."

"You could have told me," Hal said. "I was so worried."

"Too risky. Besides, you'd have wanted to come with me and you'd have missed seeing the aliens."

"They were amazing," Hal said with a dreamy look that was so much like Mom's it made Will squirm.

"Will meets up with the cat from the future and Hal gets up close with the aliens," Esther said. "Pretty impressive weekend. All we did was visit my uncle's church in New Jersey."

Will took a swig of milk and tossed the empty carton over Esther's head into the big green trash can, prompting a dirty look from Lena the Lunch Lady, who was escorting a queasy-looking seventh grader out of the cafeteria.

"How did you explain it to your parents?" Esther asked. "Finding Chester all the way up there, I mean. Your mom must have gotten suspicious."

"My mom has no way of knowing there's anything strange about Chester. Remember, she didn't need him to use the TTD. They just think it's some kind of Homeward Bound miracle."

"They even stopped fighting for five seconds," Hal said.

"Are they mad at you?" Rebekah asked Will.

"They'll get over it."

"They think you tried to run away!" Esther exclaimed. "Your mom is probably lining up a therapist as we speak."

Will shrugged. "Whatever. Now, we need to plan our next move." He turned to Hal. "Can you arrange a sleepover Friday night?"

"I guess," Hal said.

"It's Halloween," said Esther. "I'm not sure my parents will let us out of the house."

"Stop exaggerating," Rebekah said. "It will be fine."

"Ok, good," said Will. "In the meantime, we need to look for the TTD. It's not in the box in the closet. Do you think the aliens took it?"

"I told you, I didn't see. It's all so fuzzy. I don't even remember how I got back to my room."

"We need to find it. Now that we have Chester, we have a chance to get back there. But we still need the TTD."

"Why all of us?" Rebekah asked.

"Yeah, not that I'm not grateful, but what's with all the sudden togetherness?" Esther asked.

Will figured he deserved that. He hadn't exactly been Mr. Team Player in the past. But now, after months of sitting alone in his room, he'd had enough. He had another chance at the future and he wanted to share the experience.

"Whatever," he said. "Don't come."

"Okay then," Esther said. "We're coming."

"Ladies and gentlemen, line up please!" Mrs. Bumbly called from the back of the cafeteria. "Take your trash and don't forget to recycle!"

"The future depends on it!" Esther said with a grin.

Hal and Rebekah walked off in the opposite direction while Will and Esther meandered through a maze of students to their next class.

Science was usually taught by Ms. Penning, a great believer in orderly rule. "Science is guided by law!" she would proclaim. "Nature loves symmetry!" But word had spread there was a sub that day, so students ignored the symmetrical and orderly seating chart and sat wherever they pleased. Esther made a beeline for the coveted back of the room and slipped quickly into a seat. She tossed her backpack on the desk next to her.

"Sorry, taken," she said to the five other students eyeing the spot. Will let the crowd disperse and sat down.

"You're welcome," Esther whispered.

A tall, thin, black man with gray hair wrote his name on the marker board. "Good afternoon, class," he said in a voice and accent that sounded mildly familiar. "I am Mr. Getachew, and I will be your substitute teacher today."

"I know that guy," Will whispered to Esther.

"Me, too. He subbed for some math classes last week," Esther whispered back.

"Not my classes."

"Maybe you saw him in the hall."

"I don't think so."

"Even you can't remember everything. Maybe he's in your subconscious."

"Whatever."

"You brought it up. Whatever to you."

Mr. Getachew directed his attention toward them. "Is there a question, there in the back?"

"No, sorry," Esther said. Will slumped and continued to scrutinize the sub.

"Since your teacher did not leave a lesson plan for today, I thought we'd talk about one of my research interests at MIT—nuclear energy."

Will sprang up in his seat, eyebrows raised. "What are the chances?" he said a little too loudly. Esther opened her mouth but closed it again when she saw Mr. Getachew look their way.

"Now, that's a big subject for this brief class period,"

Mr. Getachew continued, "so this lesson will provide a basic primer on the functions, benefits, and challenges of nuclear energy. Please form groups of four and complete the packet I will distribute."

For the next five minutes people shuffled their desks around, arguing about who would be in what group, until finally Mr. Getachew assigned the groups himself. Will and Esther spent the rest of the class filling in the blanks about nuclear fission, core reactors, and spent fuel. Every once in a while, Will shook his head and mumbled, "What are the chances?"

O—O—O

The idea of a sleepover on Halloween night sent Mom into a baking frenzy. She put the finishing touches of orange icing on the pumpkin cupcakes while Hal arranged the Frankenstein cookies on a platter. Even though hardly anyone trick-or-treated in their neighborhood anymore, Mom had set the jack-o'-lantern in the window. A flameless candle shone through its sad eyes.

"The living room is all yours tonight," Mom said. "Dad has a meeting and I'll stay upstairs. Aren't you going to decorate?"

"Mom, we're not little kids and this isn't a Halloween party," Hal said. "It's just Rebek and Esther, and they'll be here any minute."

"You know your mother," Dad said from the table where he and Will were playing a video game on their laptops. "Any excuse for a party."

"And you know your father," Mom replied. "Any excuse to

be out of the house."

"I meant it as a compliment."

Mom smiled sweetly. "I'm sure you did."

Chester, who had been under the table, jumped up to the chair at the counter. With a quick move he swatted one of the cupcakes to the floor, where it landed icing down.

"Chester, no!" Mom exclaimed. "Get down!"

Chester ignored her, still eyeing the cupcakes.

"Yeah, we sure did miss that cat," Dad said.

"He doesn't like it when you fight," said Hal. She picked Chester up and hugged him close, burying her face in his fur.

"Game over," Will said, and left the room. Chester jumped out of Hal's arms and followed.

"Now look what you did," Mom said. "He was finally coming around." She threw the fallen cupcake in the trash and stomped up the stairs.

Dad sighed. "Just another day in the Horace house."

"More like the Horrors House," Hal said. "You could be nicer to Mom. She's going through a lot."

Dad frowned. "Like what?"

Hal thought of how hard it must be for Mom to give up her travels to the past. All in all, for a recovering addict, Mom was doing pretty well. Hal wished she could make Dad understand, but she'd made a pact with Will to keep Mom's secret and besides, Dad would think she was crazy. She turned away and said nothing and Dad didn't pursue it.

"I gotta get to my meeting." Dad grabbed his keys and rushed out the door. The two laptops remained on the table like friends waiting for a ride to a party.

Hal heard a soft knock at the back door. "What's wrong?"

Rebekah asked as she followed Hal into the kitchen.

"Same as usual. Great way to start the night, refereeing my parents." She walked to the stairs and called, "Mom, they're here."

"Okay, have fun and let me know if you need anything." Hal heard the TV go on in Mom's room as Will descended the stairs.

"Let's get to it," he said.

"Hello to you, too," said Esther.

Hal pushed the computers to the side to make room for the sweets and they sat around the table, chewing and frowning in concentration.

"We have Chester, but no TTD," Will said. "We have to figure out another way to activate the portal."

"Even if we could get to the future," Rebekah said, "are we sure it's a good idea?"

Will and Esther looked at Rebekah as if she'd suggested the earth was flat or global warming was a hoax.

"Fine," said Esther, "don't go."

"Wait," Hal said. "If Rebek doesn't go, I don't go."

"Why don't you both go—upstairs and polish your nails? Or stare into your phones at all the cute boys who don't know you exist?" Esther said.

"You don't have to be insulting," Rebekah replied. "I'm just saying we should consider what we're doing here. Is knowing the future a good thing?"

"If you'd been there you wouldn't ask such a dumb question," Esther said.

Hal felt as if her head would explode. "I can't do this," she said. "I've had enough arguing for one night."

"Blame Miss Voice of Reason," said Esther.

"Actually, Rebek makes a good point," said Will, and the calm in his voice eased the pounding in Hal's head a little. "It's not a good idea to know too much about your own future. You could create a paradox. Like, say you knew you were going to fail a test. You might give up and not study and that's what makes you fail the test."

"Or, say Mom knew she'd be fighting with Dad all the time," Hal said. "She might decide not to marry him and we wouldn't be here."

Esther stared at Will in total shock. "Are you saying you're changing your mind?"

"Of course not. I'm just saying that knowing too much about your own future is risky. In our case, though, it's not a problem, since we're going so far into the future we won't be affecting our own lives. We'll all be long dead by then."

"That's comforting," Esther said.

"None of this matters if we can't figure out how to get there," Will added. "Any ideas?"

Seconds ticked by.

Esther bit into the Frankenstein monster's head.

Rebekah peeled the paper off an orange cupcake.

Hal leaned her head on her arm, randomly pushing buttons on her phone.

Will stared at the blank computer screen in front of him.

"Looks like it's gonna be a short planning session," Esther said.

"What about the carpet in the closet? Would that help?" Hal asked.

"I don't see how," said Will. "I tried standing on it when

we first came back, and nothing happened. It needs the TTD. We need the TTD. Without it, we're stuck here."

"It doesn't hurt to try," Hal said. "I'll be right back." She tiptoed up the stairs and through the hall to the closet. To her surprise, there was Chester, fully alert and waiting.

"I'm on the right track, aren't I?" Hal asked. Chester nudged her hand.

Hal retrieved the carpet square and crept down the stairs with Chester following. Although Mom's door was open a crack, the hilarity of celebrity game show night created a perfect sound barrier, and Hal made it back to the kitchen with Mom none the wiser. She placed the carpet on the floor and stood in the middle.

"Everybody squeeze in," Hal said. Rebekah and Esther complied, but Will looked skeptical.

"What good will that do?"

"Just try," Hal said. "You never know."

Will sighed impatiently, but stood at the edge of the carpet. "Now what?"

Esther giggled and lost her balance. "After this can we play Twister?" she asked, straightening up.

"This is pointless if we don't have the TTD," Will said.

"But we do have Chester," Hal responded. "Look."

Chester had jumped up to the table and stretched his body across both computers. He clicked the keys of one with his paws and swiped his tail over the touchpad of the other, all the while purring steadily. The carpet began to vibrate. Chester reached for Hal's phone and clawed its back open. He scraped at its insides with one paw while still hitting computer keys with the other. His purring got louder as he worked.

"He's doing it!" Hal exclaimed.

"It feels different," Will said. The vibrations from the carpet grew stronger and rose up, creating a distortion field around them. Esther slipped again, but the invisible field held her up. The shimmering air thickened until they were surrounded by a dense fog. Chester's purring grew faint, drowned out by an ear crushing, grinding din.

"Here we go!" Will said.

"I hope that cat knows where he's taking us!" Esther shouted through the clamor.

From the corner of her eye Hal saw a blurred figure enter the kitchen just before they faded away.

"What's going on here?" Mom cried, but they were gone.

Chapter 14

THE FUTURE IS GREENISH

When the clamor stopped and the fog lifted, Will saw the familiar smile of Mr. Salazar. Although he tried to appear nonchalant, Will felt his grin spreading. Esther jumped up and down, shouting "We're back!" while Hal and Rebekah gaped at their surroundings in stunned silence.

"Welcome, Halia and Rebekah," said Mr. Salazar. While he made introductions, Will breathed in the air of the future, letting it fill every cell of his body. They stood inside a sphere with green, rippling walls, just like the one they'd been wrenched from with no warning last time.

The Time Team gathered before them, but something was different. In place of their brightly colored, airy clothing were dull gray coveralls. On each of their right sleeves was a circular badge with the words, "TIME GUARD" stamped above a picture of a creepy looking guy with long, white hair and a smooth, clean shaven face. Under the picture, in smaller print, were the words "Agent of Servant Leader Snorok."

"What's with the uniforms?" Esther asked. She pointed to the face on the badge. "And who's he?"

Okoko stepped forward. Her bright pink headdress was gone and her dark curly hair was cropped short. "Are you saying there's a difference from your first trip here?" she asked.

"Yes," said Will. "You all look different. Your hair, your clothes—they're not the same." Will didn't know what these changes meant, but it couldn't be good. "And before, you were the 'Time Team,' not the 'Time Guard,' like it says on your badges," he added.

Jikon waved his hand over a display screen on a shiny green table at the center of the room.

"It is as we feared," he said, studying the symbols that sprang into the air. "We must find the interference."

"Okay, let's get the ball rolling," said Gyasi. Will sighed and Esther smirked—more feeble attempts at slang. But to their surprise the entire room began to roll.

"What the heck!" Esther exclaimed.

"Interesting," said Rebekah. She looked down at her feet, which were planted firmly on the floor. "There must be some kind of stabilizers at work to keep us upright."

"Yeah," Will agreed, "like an inertia damper." He felt like a hamster inside a ball.

"Actually," said Robbie, "the ball emits its own

145

gravitational field, which keeps us from feeling the effects of its movement."

"Whatever," Will said.

"Yeah, we're really on a roll," said Esther.

Rebekah frowned at her sister disapprovingly.

"Thanks for rolling out the green carpet," Esther said.

"Enough," said Rebekah.

"Just trying to roll with the punches!"

Will laughed, not because he thought Esther's puns were funny, but because he was overtaken by the joy of their accomplishment. They'd made it! They were in the future! His excitement shone so brightly it almost cast a shadow.

Within a few seconds they stopped rolling and lifted off the ground.

"We're flying!" Will said.

"And fully cloaked," said Astra. "Would you like a better view?" She touched the wall and the green faded into transparency. Encased in a clear ball, they rose over fields and trees, speeding through the clouds into the blue sky. In the distance, Will saw the ocean and the V-shaped wings of a bald eagle in flight. He pressed his hands against the transparent wall, half expecting to feel a breeze or smell the ocean air.

"Wow," said Rebekah.

"Amazing," said Hal.

"I'm going to vomit," said Esther.

The future kids were riveted to the images on the display.

"You see, here and here," Jikon said, grabbing and moving the pictures and symbols. "If you look closely and isolate the images you can see a slight aberration."

"And here is the cover-up," said Samaya, pointing. "Will,

do you notice any other differences?"

"Just your clothes," Will answered. "And those patches. And your name."

"Esther, anything to add?"

"I wasn't joking. I'm going to vomit." Esther turned away from the group. "I hope your cleaning nanites are working today."

Immediately, Astra touched the wall and the sky was replaced with opaque, rippling green walls. "Some people find open air travel uncomfortable." As she waved, cylindrical stools grew from the floor. "Please, be seated. You should feel better soon."

Esther looked relieved. "There is something else," she said, "maybe it's because we're in this ball, but the music is gone. The chimes, I mean. They were there, in the background last time. They made me feel, I don't know—happy or something. In fact, it might sound crazy, but you all seemed happier before."

Will focused on the faces around him. He wouldn't have noticed on his own, but Esther was right. Gone were the bright smiles and nerdy comments. This group was as serious as a calculus exam.

The mood grew even more somber. "We have no such music," Jikon said.

"And you say you've never seen the image of Servant Leader Snorok before?" Mr. Salazar asked.

"You mean the guy on the patch? Nope," Esther answered.

"He does look a little familiar, but maybe I'm thinking of someone on TV. Who is he?" Hal asked. "Why is this important?"

147

"I've suspected for some time that Snorok has been manipulating the timeline to place himself in power," Mr. Salazar answered. "That's why we've brought you back to our time. We needed confirmation."

"That's why you brought us back?" Will demanded. "So we could answer your questions?" His voice rose. "And then what? When you're done with us, you send us home again? I don't think so." He looked around like someone desperate to escape a moving train.

"Good to know people are still jerks in the future," said Esther.

"We're sorry we sent you back so abruptly," Mr. Salazar said. "We feared discovery last time. Remember, travel to the future is strictly forbidden. As soon as we found a way around that, we sent Chester to retrieve you."

"Who put the note in Will's locker?" Hal asked.

"Note?" Robbie responded. "There was no note. Chester was sent directly to your home—to your yard, to be specific." He gazed into Hal's eyes and smiled as if he had said something charming. Hal looked away shyly.

"Yuck," Esther said under her breath, but Rebekah nudged her into silence.

"We didn't find Chester at home," Will said. "There was a note telling me to go to the Bridgeport bus station on a certain day. That's where I found Chester."

"Another aberration," Jikon said. "Or possibly a sneaker wave. Our memory of events differs from yours. We need a plan."

Astra pressed the wall lightly and a navigational panel appeared. "We're almost there."

"Almost where?" Hal asked.

"We're taking you to the Science Institute," Astra replied. "Our friends there have found a way to disguise your identity."

The ball plunged into a quick descent that made Will's stomach flip. Esther put her hand over her mouth.

"We apologize for the discomfort," Samaya said. "The gravitational field doesn't work at full capacity when we're cloaked."

"It won't be long," said Robbie.

As the descent ended, Astra's fingers flew over the navigational panel and the ball took up its roll again.

"Where are we?" Will asked as they came to a stop. He knew they weren't far from the shoreline, but he had no idea what coast they were on or even what continent.

"Although you've traveled far in time, you have not gone a very long distance," Astra answered, not looking up from her work. "You are in the province of Kees, but you would know it as Massachusetts. The Science Institute is on the site of an ancient university that, in your time, was known as an institute of technology."

Will shared a shocked expression with Esther. "What are the chances?" he said.

There was no time for discussion because the ball stopped and attached itself to a large cluster of spheres. A pinhole formed in the wall opposite Will and expanded into a circular doorway. A teenage girl wearing the same style coverall as the others stepped in. Her dark hair stuck out from under a cap and her badge identified her as a Science Sentinel. She, too, was branded an "Agent of Servant Leader Snorok."

"Tassiana, thank you for coming," Mr. Salazar said.

"We must hurry. Are these the subjects?" She pulled four small vials out of her pocket.

"Subjects?" said Esther, jumping to her feet.

"What's going on?" Hal asked.

"Since travel to the future is forbidden, we had to find a way to disguise your identity," Okoko explained. "Our friends from the Science Institute adapted our DNA altering techniques so that you will not be discovered."

Will looked mildly curious. "Do we drink it or do you have to inject it?" he asked.

"Drink it," Tassiana said. "We must hurry." She held out the vials and Will took one.

"Whoa, slow down!" Esther said. "A little more info, please!"

"Are there side effects?" Rebekah asked.

"No side effects except that your appearance may change a little," Tassiana said. "Your thoughts, emotions, and memories will remain the same. The effect will last several hours and will stop anyone from recognizing you as a visitor from the past."

"I don't understand," Hal said.

"Your DNA carries a distinct time signature," Jikon said. "This will make it appear as if you are from this time."

"We may be discovered at any moment." Tassiana offered the remaining vials to Esther, Hal, and Rebekah. They did not move.

"The alternative is for us to send you home now," said Mr. Salazar kindly. "You must decide."

Before anyone could protest, Will opened the vial and drank the liquid.

Rebekah took Esther by the arm and turned to Mr. Salazar. "We'll go home," she said.

"Speak for yourself!" said Esther. She pulled away from her sister, swooped a vial from Tassiana's hand, and drank.

"I'll stay if you will, Rebek," said Hal. "At least for a little while."

Rebekah groaned. "One dose," she said, glaring at Esther. "Then we go home." They took the vials and drank.

Tassiana gave a sigh of relief. "Safe now," she said, but her serious expression remained.

Will studied his face in the table's reflective surface, looking for physical changes. He wondered if his hair would change color or his nose grow. It wasn't like he looked in the mirror much anyway, but as far as he could see, nothing.

"I don't see any changes," he said.

"You may not. We formulated a low dose—just enough to fool the trackers," said Tassiana.

Esther, Hal, and Rebekah crowded around the table to take a look.

"I look even prettier than usual," said Esther, flipping her hair and crossing her eyes at her reflection.

"As I said, the change will be small. It may be something not noticeable, like a change in earwax," Tassiana.

"Earwax is affected by DNA?" Hal asked.

"Oh yes, DNA determines wet or dry earwax..."

"Stop!" shouted Esther, "I was just starting to feel better!"

"It's time to go," said Mr. Salazar. "We've prepared temporary quarters for you. Robbie will accompany you and brief you on your cover story. Remember, no one outside of this group must know that you have traveled from the past."

Robbie smiled at Hal as if they were the only two people there. He led them through a maze of hallways to another small room, where four sets of coveralls and boots were waiting. "Wear these," he said. "We'll introduce you as new guard members from another province at dinner tonight. You'll receive a work assignment then. Make sure you say 'Time Guard' as your area of interest so you can be with us."

They slid the coveralls over their clothes and slipped into the boots, which somehow fit they perfectly. Robbie led them through more tunnel hallways to the lobby, then out into the bright sunlight. The Science Institute stood at the top of a low hill, overlooking miles of large and small thoroughfares. Nowhere to be seen were double yellow lines, stop signs, or traffic lights, and no concrete, either; instead, the roadways were made of a slick material the color of pine needles. Here and there a road flyer landed or took off, quickly disappearing under a cloak. Larger transports like the one Will and Esther had used on their last visit traveled along the wider lanes. All the structures were spheres—big, small, and medium sized shimmering green balls. Some stood alone, but most had smaller spheres attached at the sides or top.

"They look like bubbles," Rebekah commented.

"Exactly," Esther said. "Watch."

As far as they could see, globes of all sizes appeared and disappeared in shimmering clusters throughout the city.

"People add rooms as they're needed," Will explained, "and delete them when they're done."

"It's an efficient use of space," Robbie said.

"But how?" asked Rebekah.

"We've learned to tap into the essential energy of

Green World Gray

photosynthesis. The Science Sentinels can describe the process if you're interested, and if you're here long enough."

Will frowned but said nothing. They walked through narrow garden pathways under hanging, leafy vines until they came to a cluster of small interconnected spheres.

"Here's our residence," Robbie said with a smile. "Rest for awhile. I'll come for you at dinnertime." He winked at Hal and left.

Esther flopped down on a low bed. "That guy is creepy," she said.

"I think he's cute," Hal answered, sounding wistful.

Will gave Hal a sideways look. It didn't take much to turn her head. A wink from some jacked superhero type and she'd go weak-kneed and quivery. Will was about to warn his sister not to get distracted from their mission, but he realized with a start that they no longer had a mission, at least not one they would agree on. Will's only mission now was to stay here, in this time period, and he was pretty sure Hal would want no part of it. In fact, most likely she'd try to stop him. He stretched out on the bed and put his hands behind his head, staring up at the green, glistening ceiling. He'd have to think this through. He'd have to figure out how to shift Hal's focus away from him, and maybe this guy Robbie was the key.

Hal had never seen a cafeteria like this one. She gazed up into a dome the size of a cathedral. In place of the usual long tables filled with rowdy students and patrolled by dour lunch aides, small groups of young people floated above her in shimmering bubbles they'd conjured with a wave of the hand. Servers streamed into the area with platters full of leafy greens and vegetables Hal couldn't identify, even after cooking with Mom all those years. They released the platters into the air where the globes received them through slots that opened and closed seamlessly.

Hal studied the occupants of the globes as she walked through the room. They varied in age—the youngest looked around ten and the oldest would have been high school seniors, maybe, if they'd been back home. Although all were wearing the same gray coveralls, Hal spotted many different badge designations, all adorned with the stern face of Servant Leader Snorok. Along with the Science Sentinels, the Growers Garrison, Wildlife Wardens, Production Patrol, and Document Defenders hovered above and around her like bulbs on a Christmas tree.

"Notice the names?" Esther said.

"Yes," answered Rebekah. "I was just thinking that. They're all about guarding or defending, like they're in the military."

"It wasn't like that the first time," Esther said.

Robbie led them to the Time Guard and they gathered around Mr. Salazar, who placed his arms above them. A glimmering bubble formed from his hands and encased them. As Hal felt herself rise into the air, a table and chairs grew from the floor and a platter of food floated in and landed on the table.

"This is nothing like our school cafeteria," commented Esther.

"That's the understatement of the century," said Rebekah.

"Which century?" Hal muttered.

"We've studied your schools," said Gyasi. A head taller than everyone else in the group, he bowed in respect as he spoke. "We're sorry you were subjected to that."

"It wasn't that bad," said Hal. "I mean, the food wasn't great, but..."

"I wasn't referring to the food," Gyasi said. The atmosphere at the table became melancholy.

"He meant, we're sorry that you had to go to school," Okoko explained.

Hal, Rebekah, and Esther looked puzzled. "We don't understand," Hal said. "Everyone goes to school in our time. It's how we learn."

"Not everyone learns there," Will said quietly.

"How could they?" asked Samaya. "Large, cold, steel and cement buildings where children were forced into groups not of their choosing to study subjects for which they had little to no interest. Children forced to sit quietly and perform dull, repetitive tasks while the adult in charge monitored them and assigned evaluative scores." Samaya grimaced as if in physical pain.

"Speaking of which, where are all the adults?" asked Esther.

"Many have been called away on a special project," said Robbie, "related to the new science initiatives in space travel. Others have returned to their original clusters for The Nesting."

A feeling of uneasiness stirred in Hal. This was starting to sound like some weird horror movie thing.

"What's 'The Nesting'?" Esther asked. "It sounds like some weird horror movie thing."

Mr. Salazar laughed. "Not at all. It just means that they're preparing for the birth of a new child. It's that time of year."

Rebekah raised an eyebrow and even Esther had nothing to say to that.

"What about the old people?" Will asked. "I don't see any around. Except for you."

Mr. Salazar laughed again. "By our standards I am not old at all. Lifespans here are longer, and people are able to have children much later in life than in your time. Those of truly advanced years serve on a variety of councils or in our mentoring programs. They are here in the city, but not at this gathering. The long-standing institutes are run by the young."

Hal observed groups of tweens and teens milling around in total freedom. She heard Mom's voice in her head. Who's in charge here? What if there's an emergency? Who tells the younger kids when to go to bed? No one seemed worried about the lack of adult supervision, so she kept her questions to herself. She glanced in Robbie's direction and he caught her eye and smiled.

"He's here," said Astra, nodding toward the entranceway.

The man whose face was on the badges walked into the room. He was a tall, imposing figure with straight, unrelenting posture and thick, white hair that fell across his shoulders like a mane. He raised his arms and all at once the bubbles descended and fizzled away. Conversations died as if only silence could survive in the vacuum of his presence. Again, Hal thought she had seen him before, but she couldn't figure out where. Her mind searched through possible associations, and for some reason an image of a red sportscar appeared.

Maybe she'd seen an actor who looked like this guy in a car commercial, although if that were the case, Hal thought, it's no wonder the auto industry was in trouble.

Hal stood with the others and waited.

"I will introduce you as new recruits and Snorok will ask what group you will serve with. Simply say 'Time Guard,'" Mr. Salazar whispered. "Tomorrow you will receive language update implants, but for now you must do your best not to draw attention to yourselves. Remember, language evolves over time. He will speak English, but you may not understand."

"Like Shakespeare," said Rebekah.

"Exactly. Try to get the gist of it and keep your answers brief."

Snorok moved from group to group, acknowledging greetings with no more than a nod. Hal noticed the nervous expressions as he approached and the relief when he moved away. Finally, he arrived at their group. His voice was deep, but quiet. "Attending are these?"

"Recent limbs offer," said Mr. Salazar.

Hal tried to keep her face passive. She knew even a slightly confused manner could give them away. She also knew that Esther might burst out laughing at any moment, which would be just as bad. She glanced down and saw Rebekah squeezing her sister's hand. Robbie brushed Hal's hand lightly, too.

Snorok looked directly at Hal. "Choosing will?" he asked.

Hal caught her breath, startled that Snorok had used her brother's name, but then she realized her mistake. "Time Guard," she replied.

Snorok nodded. "Say?" he asked Rebekah.

"Time Guard," she said.

Again, Snorok nodded. "History keepers salient indeed," he said, contorting his mouth into an almost smile. He nodded toward Will.

"Science Sentinel," Will said loudly and with more confidence in his voice than Hal had ever heard. The others stirred faintly. Snorok raised an eyebrow.

"Changer," he said, staring into Will's green eyes. Will stared back, his face deadpan. Hal remembered all the times her brother had hidden behind that stare at school. Practice makes perfect, she thought when Snorok moved his gaze to Esther.

"Science Sentinel," Esther said without hesitation. Her face mirrored Will's impassivity, but while Will could stare down the Mona Lisa, Esther had once lost a staring contest with her pet goldfish. Hal held her breath.

Snorok looked from Esther to Will and back again. "Approval," he said, and moved on to the next table.

Hal turned to Will and Esther. "What was that? You were supposed to say 'Time Guard.'"

"Not interested in the past," Will answered. "We're in the future. Don't you want to know how things work?"

Even through her worry, Hal couldn't resist the excitement in Will's eyes. "Okay, I get it," she said. "But at the end of the day tomorrow we tell each other everything we've learned. Deal?"

"Deal," Will said.

Rebekah glared at her sister. "What's your excuse? We should stay together."

"Don't you want to know how things work?" Esther repeated.

"We're not staying long enough to find out," Rebekah answered firmly. "We said one dose, remember?"

"You said one dose," Esther replied, her voice getting louder. "You can go back without me."

"Shh," cautioned Samaya. "You must not attract attention."

"Sorry," Esther said. "You can go back without me," she repeated more quietly.

"How would I explain where you are?" Rebekah asked. "I think Omma and Appa would notice."

"Once more, with feeling," said Will. "We're travelling in time. No matter when we leave here, we can arrive back home at the same instant."

"Is that right?" Hal asked Mr. Salazar, who nodded in response. "So, I could go home right now, and Will could go home ten years from now, and we'd both arrive at the same time?"

"Exactly," said Will. "There's nothing to worry about."

"But remember," said Gyasi, "in that scenario Will would have aged normally and his appearance would have changed noticeably."

"Which is why you may stay for short periods only," added Okoko.

"You said that," Will replied, and Hal knew her brother well enough to hear the unspoken *but I don't care* at the end of the sentence.

"I believe it's safe to leave now," said Mr. Salazar. "Robbie will take you back to your quarters. Time travel takes a physical toll. You must be tired."

Esther yawned. "Now that you mention it, I'm exhausted.

I'll be asleep as soon as my head hits the pillow."

"I believe you will find the bedding adequate," Gyasi said. "What purpose will be served by hitting your pillow?"

"Perhaps it is part of a bedtime ritual, a way to release the tensions of the day," said Astra.

"Whatever," said Hal, Will, Rebekah, and Esther in unison.

○─○─○

Esther flopped over on her bed for the fourth time in ten seconds. "Adequate bedding my butt. You'd think they could have invented a softer mattress," she complained. "This is hard as a rock. Nothing like those cushy green chairs they had the first time we were here."

"What do you expect? They're soldiers now," Will replied.

Hal shifted her weight and tried to get comfortable. She didn't mind the hard bedding; normally she could sleep anywhere. But this night was anything but normal, and the more she tried to relax, the jumpier she felt. She wished they'd be staying together tomorrow, under the protection of Mr. Salazar. She could never be sure what Will would do, even when she was there to balance his risky impulses. Tomorrow he'd only have Esther with him, who was just as bad.

The light in their compartment that had been simulating dusk now faded completely to deep night. A soft hum emanated from her bed.

"Is that supposed to put us to sleep?" Esther asked through her yawn.

"Let's hope so," said Will. He turned to face the wall, his breathing slow and regular. That was Will, all right—even falling asleep was an act of resolve for him.

160

Within five minutes the steady breathing in the room told Hal only she was still awake, so she slipped out of bed and threw on her coveralls and boots. She moved her hands slowly along the curved wall of their compartment, searching for the small patch that Robbie had shown them in case one of them wanted to leave during the night. She found it, and with a little pressure a slim opening appeared and she was able to slide out onto the path. There, standing off to the side a few yards away, was Robbie.

"Oh," said Hal, "I'm surprised to see you here. I thought everyone would be asleep by now."

Robbie smiled but offered no explanation for his presence. "Are you having trouble sleeping?" he asked.

"Yeah, I guess. I thought maybe a few minutes in the night air would help." But the air had not changed at all with the setting of the sun. It was still pleasantly mild. The leafy green shrubs surrounding them smelled like her favorite bubble bath and seemed to reach toward them, inviting them for a stroll. In companionable silence, Hal and Robbie ambled side by side down the path.

"I guess you've learned to control the weather," Hal said finally.

"In a way. It is what you would call spring, and our clusters benefit from the ambient effects of our power synthesizers, which are not far from here. We find it convenient to keep the temperature steady so that we can focus fully on our work. Are you uncomfortable?"

"No. Actually, it's almost too comfortable for nighttime. Sometimes a little cool air feels good, you know?"

"Ah, yes, I think I understand. Would you allow me to take

you somewhere colder?"

"You mean in one of those flying car things?" Hal asked. Adventure beckoned, but it was late and the others might worry if they woke to find her gone. "I don't know—shouldn't I be getting back soon?"

"Frivolous time travel is usually not allowed, but I think I can take some liberties. I have what you might call 'connections.'" Robbie smiled and Hal attempted to look suitably impressed. "Do I have your permission? I promise to return you to this very moment. You'll be able to get a full night's sleep."

Suddenly, sleep was the last thing on Hal's mind. "Sure," she said, trying to keep her voice casual, as if evening rendezvous with cute boys were part of her usual repertoire.

"Stay close," said Robbie. He circled his arms around Hal and even though they were barely touching, Hal felt her heart flutter. A translucent green sphere encased them for a split second and then dissolved. Standing atop a high slope, Hal breathed in the cold, fresh air of winter. She squinted at the reflection of bright sunlight on the soft, white drifts of snow all around.

"This is a little colder than I meant," Hal laughed.

"Should we go back?"

"No, it's great," Hal said, letting her eyes adjust. "Where are we?"

"We've traveled to last winter, a few miles outside the city cluster."

Hal scooped up some snow and packed it together. "I don't really feel the cold," she said. "Except for my hands."

"Your coveralls are designed to accommodate all

weather," Robbie explained. "Would you like to go for a ride?"

Hal looked around, half expecting to see some sort of futuristic sled driven by a snow leopard waiting for them. "In what?" she asked.

Robbie reached down to his feet and arched his hands upward, forming a hollow half sphere that sat on the snow like a green teacup on a white saucer. He took Hal's hand and they climbed in, Hal in front leaning on Robbie, who put one arm around her.

"What is this thing we're in?" Hal asked.

"We call it a snow globe. I can close it around us or keep it open. Which would you prefer?"

"Open, for sure!"

"All right. Ready?"

"Don't we need a push?"

"Like this?" Robbie stuck out his free hand and generated a pulse that sent them on a heart-racing, stomach-leaping trip down the hill. Hal screeched with delight as they picked up speed. They hurtled down and down, faster and faster, the feel of the frosty air in their faces and the sound of the snow crunching beneath them. Just when Hal thought they might take flight, they reached a flat open space and spun to a halt.

"Awesome!" Hal exclaimed after she'd caught her breath. She surveyed the long, steep hill that now rose above them. "I'd say let's do it again, but I don't think I want to walk back up."

"No need," Robbie said. He reached out his hand and the snow globe backtracked up the hill, seemingly on its own.

"This feels like cheating but I'm okay with it," Hal said, blinking in the bright sunlight. "I bet this would be even more fun at night."

She hardly felt Robbie move, but an instant later snowflakes touched her eyelids as they fell lightly through the dusk.

"Better?" Robbie asked.

"Perfect," Hal said, and leaned back just a little. Now that the sun wasn't blinding her, off in the distance she could make out two people engaged an epic snowball battle. They ran toward and away from each other, pelting and ducking in what looked like a long-practiced dance.

"Is that...?" From this distance she couldn't be sure, but the harder Hal stared, the more the figures resembled Will and Esther. She waved at them furiously.

"Best not to attract attention," Robbie said. "Remember, frivolous time travel is forbidden. You mustn't tell anyone we were here."

Hal let her hands fall back into her lap. "But how could that be Will and Esther? Did they follow us?"

"Time travel can be complex," Robbie answered. "Whenever they are from, I assure you it's not the night we left. Future events may vary, and they may never experience this night at all. I caution you not to ask too many questions, for your own protection."

Protection from what? Hal wondered. She had the feeling Robbie was keeping something from her, but unwilling to spoil the magic of the moment with questions and distrust, she let it go.

"I must take you back now," Robbie said.

"Thanks for tonight. I loved it," Hal said when they appeared outside her quarters. She smiled up at Robbie, but suddenly he seemed troubled. Without returning her smile, he formed an entrance in the wall and waited for her to step through. Hal lay motionlessly on her bed, letting the hum lull her into a fitful sleep.

Will looked longingly at the parked road flyers as he and Esther sped along on the levitrans. Since they were only going a short distance, he'd have to be content riding close to the ground. Not that he was complaining. I'm in the future, he reminded himself every now and then. Finally, the wonders he'd only imagined were a reality. Will could have enabled a thin transparent shield to protect him from the wind, but the warm gusts hitting his face served as a kind of pinch to be sure he wasn't dreaming. Esther's hair whipped around her head like a hundred flags blowing every which way. Under the chaos of the windstorm, she was smiling.

A Science Sentinel that reminded Will of a sixth grader he'd seen on one of his many visits to Mrs. Bumbly's office had shown up at their quarters that morning. Will didn't know the sixth grader's name, but this kid's name was Damaso. He was shorter than Will, with buzzed hair, dark eyes and brown skin, and to Will's relief, he wasn't much of a talker. After a quick stop at the lab, they boarded the levitrans that sped them past the clusters to the dreamy, slow-moving river.

"Now what?" Esther said. "Do we hop on a boat?"

Damaso looked confused. "Boat?" His eyes glazed for a few seconds and then came back into focus. "A small vessel used only in water will not be necessary," he said. Without slowing down, the levitrans slid into a short, narrow conduit that spat them out just above the clear, blue water. There was no splash and no rippling sound, just the quacking and honking of ducks paddling at the river's edge. Overhead, a blue-gray heron flapped and glided through the sky.

They crossed the river at a narrow point and were soon speeding past more bubble clusters until they stopped in a large, open field. "My unit is there," Damaso said. He jumped off the levitrans and trotted toward a group of coverall-wearing kids a few hundred feet away. Will and Esther followed. They found Tassiana and three other female Science Sentinels pacing and waving at the ground like zombies with metal detectors.

"What are they doing?" Esther asked.

"Scanning the radiation waves," replied Damaso.

"Where are the scanners?"

"They must be imbedded," said Will. "Like the language updaters we got this morning." As much as Will had wanted the updater, he wasn't crazy about needles. He'd been bracing himself for a subdural injection with a long, razor sharp needle, but instead some guy had tapped the back of his neck with a little plastic tube. Instantly he found he could understand the butt-backwards talk of the future.

"Okay," said Esther. "What are they looking for?"

Damaso replied, "Centuries ago, a nuclear accident at this site resulted in the release of radiation. We are studying the remnant waves."

"Remember that sub we had for science last week?" Will asked Esther. "What was his name? It started with a C."

"Getachew."

"Right."

"That starts with a G, not a C."

"Whatever. Anyway, according to him, some uranium isotopes can last millions of years." He turned to Damaso. "Is that what you're studying?"

"Yes, but there is no need to worry. We've learned to harness the energy of plant flavonoids to negate the damaging effects of nuclear radiation. What remains is harmless, but useful for study."

The other Science Sentinels approached.

"Ready," said a tall girl with short red hair.

Damaso took a devise the size and shape of a tennis ball out of his pocket and tossed it a few feet away, where it hit the ground and burst into a sphere large enough to surround them. Will half listened to Damaso introduce the other Science Sentinels, preoccupied by the questions that had germinated in his head overnight. This was his chance for some answers. The redheaded girl waved a work station into existence and held her palm over its flat surface. A holographic screen emerged, flooded with words and symbols that Will couldn't understand. With a nod, he signaled for Esther to step away from the group with him.

"Find out what you can about this radiation stuff," he said. "I'm going to see what I can get out of her." He nodded toward the redhead.

"She has a name."

"Okay. What is it?"

"Amy Pond."

"Come on."

"Buffy Summers."

"Come on," Will repeated, scowling.

"You should have listened. It's Frona. She didn't give her last name but you can call her 'Frona Whatever' since that's the next word you'll say."

Will stopped the word from escaping just to prove Esther wrong. "Oh, Frona," he said in the most courteous voice he could fake, "can I ask you some questions?"

"Of course," Frona answered, "we've been instructed to give you full access." Will relaxed a little, relieved that he wouldn't have to trick her into giving him secret information. "Wave your hand over the screen and the language updaters will adjust the text for you," Frona instructed. As Will obeyed, the symbols formed words he could read, but he still couldn't understand the content.

"Currently, we are studying the communicative properties of alpha radiation." Frona moved her fingers over the display and an image of purple waves appeared. "We've found that messages can be embedded in the waves, which is exciting because of the uranium's long half life. Would you like to hear more?" Frona smiled. She spoke slowly and with the patience of a kindergarten teacher instructing a not-so-bright five-year-old.

"No, thanks," Will answered. "Can you tell me more about that DNA changing stuff? How far does it go?"

"What do you mean?"

"Like, what if I wanted to change my appearance completely, so that no one would recognize me? Could I do that?"

"Yes, of course," Frona said.

"What if I wanted to become something completely different, like a bird, say?"

Frona squinted thoughtfully. Her green eyes almost matched the color of the rippling walls. "It is theoretically possible, but the formula would need to be developed further. We are still quite young in this field."

"Okay, cool."

"So far, we've only developed the ability to change DNA slightly and for brief periods. In fact, we will need to get back to the Science Institute soon if you plan to stay much longer. It is almost time for another dose. Damaso, have you finished?"

"Wait, one more thing," Will said. "It's about time travel. Whose job is it to create the device that makes it possible? Is it you guys or the Time Team—I mean Guard?"

"The Time Guard studies history and watches over the timeline to protect it from tampering," Frona replied. "But the Science Sentinels are responsible for creating the technology that made time travel possible. My grandparents worked on the initial designs," she added proudly.

Will decided to test the limits of full access. "How can I get one?" he asked, trying not to sound desperate.

"One what?"

"The device that sends you back and forth in time. We call it the TTD. It looks like a cell phone or a TV remote."

Frona's brow furrowed. "I'm not familiar with that term."

"The little rectangular thing that you use for time travel."

A girl who hadn't spoken before stepped up to the display. She was the shortest person in the room, and she couldn't have been more than 10 or 11 years old. "I believe I know what Will means," she said. She pulled at the air above the panel and a rotating 3D image of the TTD appeared. "Here is an example of the prototype. It was called the Past Finder. The device was meant to be given to historians from the past to explore their history more deeply. The Ancient Peoples Dictates outlawed them and they were not further developed."

"The what?" Will asked.

"The Ancient Peoples Dictates. The council decided that time travel was too risky in the hands of anyone living before 19 mille."

Will had no idea what "19 mille" meant, but he didn't want to get sidetracked by asking. He couldn't let himself be sent home with no way of returning to this time period. As he was calculating his next move, Esther spoke up.

"His Mom had one—a TTD, I mean. Some aliens gave it to her. That's how all this started."

Frona nodded. "Perhaps aliens we have yet to meet are tampering with our timeline. We must inform the Time Guard."

"They know," Esther said. "They thought it might be a creeper wave."

"A sneaker wave," Will corrected. He stepped closer to the girl who was still examining the holographic TTD. She'd removed the back and was isolating and enlarging the mechanisms piece by piece to get a closer look. Will remembered the day he'd seen the swirling innards of the TTD in Mr. Salazar's garage. He'd come a long way since then and he wasn't going back. He wished he'd paid attention to the girl's name.

"Er, what's your name again?" he asked.

She didn't look away from the spinning gears and wheels. "I am Dali."

"Okay, Dali, how can I get one of those devices? A prototype, maybe?"

Dali stopped a gear in mid spin and faced Will. "Why would you need one?"

"Look," Will said, "maybe it's allowed, maybe it isn't. But technically, we're not even supposed to be here, right? So, you're already breaking the rules."

Dali looked to Frona and Frona looked to Damaso. They stepped away and conferred quietly. The other two girls stopped their work and joined in.

"Very subtle," Esther said to Will. "You probably just got us kicked out of here."

Will waited in glum silence. He'd fought so hard to get here and he'd keep fighting to stay, but he knew the truth. At the wave of a hand he could be sent home and there was nothing he could do about it. Unless he had his own TTD.

"So how about it?" he asked.

"Yeah," Esther jumped in. "How about it? You said full access, and I think it's only fair..."

"You misunderstand," Damaso interrupted. "We are wondering why you would need such a device to travel in time, when you can do so much more directly with tempderms."

"Perhaps people of your time enjoy the ritual involved in using external machinery," said Tassiana, "like people who preferred to use physical driving mechanisms decades after vehicles were equipped with auto-navigation. I have heard of such things."

"Wait a minute, the last time we were here a cat did the driving for us," said Esther.

Damaso and the others smiled. "Yes, they insist on

171

driving," Frona said, as if she were talking about someone's older brother who just got his license and thought he was a NASCAR superstar.

Will receded into the background as Esther chattered on. He needed to understand fully what had just transpired. Once he did, he felt like he'd escaped from the gravity well of a black hole. He sent Esther a look that said "go with me here." She quieted down, ready to follow his lead.

"Getting back to those tempderms things, Demetri," Will said, "how can we get some?"

"Damaso," Esther said.

"Whatev...I mean, Damaso. We'd like to receive your latest time travel technology."

"We must get back to the institute for your DNA dose," Frona said. "Once there, we can equip you with tempderms and any other modifications you'd like."

Will's years of emotion-repressing experience kicked in and he managed to make it through the exit without bursting. Esther was another story. She shot out to the open field like a solar flare and ran a ring around the group.

"Race ya," she said as she came alongside Will.

Will ignored her, concentrating on the next steps in his plan.

"Scared?" Esther asked.

"There is nothing to fear," Frona said. "As long as you take the dose within the next hour you will not be discovered."

"He's scared of losing a race," Esther said. "Again." She sideways lunged at Will, but when he ducked out of the way, she fell into Damaso.

"Klutz," Will said, and took off running. "They gave you

turtle DNA!" he yelled over his shoulder.

Esther jumped to her feet and chased after him. "Cheater!" she shouted, but her voice was swallowed up by the sound of Will's whooping.

Chapter 15
FAMILY FIRST

"You let them do what to you?" Hal asked, pacing around the circumference of their quarters. "How many devices did they implant in your body? The language updaters were a necessity, but that was supposed to be the end of it."

"Watch this," Esther said, grinning. She waved her hand at the table in the middle of the room and a three dimensional screen instantly appeared. "Anything you want to know? We now have total access. Let's start with something simple—world government." She waved again, but nothing happened. "Okay, more basic, maybe. Let's check the weather." Still no images appeared. "How about the dinner menu for tonight?" Nothing. "I don't get it," she said. "It worked before."

"You have to find the category of information and isolate your request," Will said, stretched out on his bed. "It's not magic."

"It looks like magic when they do it," Esther answered. She waved her hands some more and succeeded in bringing up a menu, but it disappeared before she could latch onto any data. "A little help here," she said, but Will didn't stir. He stared up at the ceiling, a million miles away.

Hal and Rebekah shared a worried look. "What does this mean?" Hal asked.

"What?"

"You know what. You can control your ability to travel in time. You have access to all their science. You don't plan to come home with us."

Will sat up and faced his sister. "It's not personal. And I'll be able to come home whenever I want."

"But you won't," Hal said. "You know you won't. We'll never see you again."

Will's silence was all the answer Hal needed.

"What about Mom and Dad?" she asked. "Don't you care what this will do to them?"

"I will come back, once in a while," Will said. "Maybe. Like, for your birthday."

"Very convincing," said Esther. "But aren't you forgetting something, Will? You have to go back. Remember the waterbed thingy?"

"Huh?" said Hal and Rebekah together.

"Stop trying to be funny. It's watershed," Will said. "It was something they said the first time we came, when things were different here. 'Every life is a watershed.' We never found out what it meant."

"A watershed is an area of land that carries water to other places," Rebekah said. "Without it, water can't reach lower levels."

"Thank you, Dora the Explorer," Esther said. "And we do know what it means, even if Will won't admit it. Your mom is important to the future. She's like a watershed. Change flows through her so that good things can happen later. And Will is important to your mom, so he's a watershed, too. If your mom stops her crunchy organic stuff, for whatever reason, bam, the future sucks. All this glorious green is replaced by the kingdom of darkness."

"And someone is already interfering," said Rebekah. "We learned more about that today. Jikon and the others were able to see where the changes were made, but not who made them or why."

"And that someone is pretty smart about covering up," Hal said. "Robbie told me that." She tried to keep her voice steady when she said his name, but she didn't succeed and had to put up with Esther's smirk.

"Yes, which makes me wonder," said Rebekah. She gathered her hair to one shoulder and ran her fingers through it.

"Care to tell us what you're wondering, oh wise one, or must we wait for you to complete your beauty regimen?" Esther said.

"A few things. First, if someone is smart enough to tamper with the timeline and not be found out, isn't he or she smart enough to know we're here? I'm sure that creepy guy Snorok suspected something last night. So why are they letting us slide? Second, why would the science people give two kids from the past unlimited time travel ability? Unless someone doesn't want you to go home—someone who's trying to change the timeline."

"Or someone who's trying to repair the timeline," Will said, and Esther nodded in agreement.

"What do you mean?" Hal asked.

Esther explained. "Mr. Salazar knows that sending Will home with no way to get back is a bad idea. He tried it once and Will nearly had a mental breakdown, remember?" Will looked down at his hands. "Sorry, but it's true," Esther continued. "So, he gives Will time travel. Will is happy, your mom is happy, and the future is rosy green."

"That makes no sense," Rebekah said.

"You know what I mean."

"But Will can't travel back and forth to the future without our parents noticing," said Hal. "He'll age while he's here. And my mom will know what's going on—she already saw us leave and she'll want an explanation when we get back. If she knows Will is living in the future, she'll worry day and night. And what about the hurt she'll feel if her son chooses to grow up without her? Won't that change the timeline?"

"It might," Esther said. "But that's our only option."

"Except for the option that we all go home and Will lives a normal life. He grows up like a regular person and becomes a great scientist. He gets married, has a family—he's happy. We're all happy. What about that option?" Hal knew she sounded desperate, but she didn't care. Her goal of a normal family life was slipping through her fingers like a holographic butterfly.

"There is another way," Will said. He joined Esther at the table and waved a stream of data into the air. "I took a look at their brain research. They know how to alter human

177

memory." Will scrolled through several lines of text and swiped at an icon of a dog. "I'm not sure how it works, but the data is right here." A small hologram of a Chihuahua wagging his tail and licking a man's face appeared. The dog was jumping, yipping, and slobbering all over like in one of those dog-reunites-with-his-human videos. Then a woman in gray overalls approached the dog and waved her hand at his head. The dog moved back and stood at alert. When the man approached, the dog tucked in his tail, lowered his head, and growled.

"Oh, wow," said Hal. "Poor dog."

"It makes sense that they can do this," Rebekah said. "Compared with altering DNA, altering the neurons that make memories would be easy."

"So?" Hal asked. She tried to ignore the uneasy fluttering in her stomach.

"What if I could alter Mom and Dad's memories of me? Even take them away completely? If they couldn't remember me, they wouldn't miss me and we'd all be happy, right?"

"That's cold," Hal said, "even for you."

"It's merciful," Will answered. "They couldn't miss me because they would never know I existed. Like the dog."

"They're not dogs, they're people. And I would know."

"You'd still see me. I'd visit you in secret. Mom and Dad could think I'm some kid at school. What's wrong with that?"

There was so much wrong with Will's idea that Hal didn't know where to begin. Her brother was further gone than she'd realized.

"Will has a point," Esther said. "You can't miss what you never knew."

"How would you like it?" Rebekah said to Esther. "What if someone took your memories away?"

"Of you? I don't know, but I'm willing to give it a try."

"Please don't fight," Hal begged. "It won't help."

"Okay, okay. Of course, I would miss Rebekah," Esther said. "Eventually. How many years are in a millennium?"

"Esther, please," Hal said.

"Sorry. Only trying to provide a little comic relief."

Just then Robbie's head popped through the gelatinous green wall and hung there like a whack-a-mole turned on its side.

"No need, I see," said Esther. "Hello, Robbie."

"May I enter?" Robbie asked, and stepped into the sphere without waiting for an answer. "It's almost time for dinner, and I have your next DNA doses." Will and Esther downed their doses immediately, but Hal held onto hers and turned toward Rebekah.

"Ready?" she asked.

Rebekah placed the vial on the table. "Not this time," she said. "Send me home."

Hal hadn't thought things could get any worse, but she'd been wrong. "Now? Already? Why?"

Rebekah smiled sadly. "We don't belong here. It isn't natural and it isn't healthy. All this talk about the past and the future is stopping you from living where you're supposed to— in the present. For better or worse, that's where we belong. All of us." She focused her gaze on her sister.

"I took the dose and I'm staying," Esther said. "But I'll meet you back there, Halloween night, same time, same kitchen. Okay?"

Rebekah softened. "Okay. Don't keep me waiting like you always do." She gave her sister and Hal a hug. "Bye. See you soon. Be safe."

Robbie stood above Rebekah and cupped his hands over her head, then arched them downward to form a sheer green bubble around her. She smiled one last time and was gone.

"How do we know she's okay?" Esther asked.

Robbie called up a holographic wave on the table display. "She's fine," he said. "She returned to the appropriate time and place. From her perspective, you will arrive with her."

"I still don't totally get that," Esther said, "but I'll take your word for it. I'm hungry. I hope they have lime Jell-O for dessert."

O—O—O

As much as she was enjoying the attention of this cute boy sitting next to her, Hal felt sadness beckoning. She missed Rebek already, she missed her mom, and the truth was, she wanted to go home, where it was still Halloween night.

Will and Esther sat across the room with the Science Sentinels. No floating bubbles tonight, by order of Servant Leader Snorok. Although Hal couldn't hear what they were saying, she could see her brother listening attentively to a red-headed girl, looking her straight in the eyes. That must be the Frona that Esther had mentioned. As Frona spoke, Will nodded, his eyes alive. Every now and then Will smiled, and not his usual sarcastic smirk, but a broad, animated grin, as if he had just won the lottery. Hal hated to admit it, but she had never seen her brother look so happy. In fact, she realized, she'd never seen him look happy at all.

Robbie touched her hand lightly. "You seem sad." His kind blue eyes searched Hal's and she felt her face grow warm.

"I am sad," she said. "This, all this, was supposed to fix our parents, but it doesn't look like that's going to happen." She motioned toward Will. "I don't think he's coming home."

"Can we go for a walk?" Robbie asked. "There's something I need to tell you."

Wouldn't you know it? Finally a guy was about to express his undying love for her and she was too preoccupied to enjoy it. What if Robbie asked her to stay? Could she be like Will? Could she leave everything behind?

"Sure," she answered. As they left the dining hall Hal looked back at Will, but he was far too captivated in his conversation with Frona to notice her. Only Mr. Salazar, who was sitting nearby, nodded as they passed.

They strolled through paths lined with fragrant shrubs under a canopy of hanging leafy green vines. Of course, the weather was perfect, as it had been since they'd arrived (except for her winter excursion with Robbie). Hal thought of home, where it was autumn and where a sea of hoodies waited to enter school on chilly mornings. Once Halloween was over it was only a few weeks till Thanksgiving and then a few more till Christmas, Hal's favorite time of year. Pretty soon she and Mom would start shopping, baking, and wrapping full force. Esther and Rebekah's church would be rehearsing their Christmas program and Hal would participate, like she always did, since they didn't have a church of their own. And next week was homecoming. She certainly couldn't miss that. She'd convinced the planning committee of the perfect theme: "Blast from the Past." With a little creativity the school gym would soon look like a 1950s dance hall. Maybe a stupid school dance couldn't measure up to real time travel, but for Hal, it was enough. She could never be like Will.

"May I purchase your thoughts?" Robbie asked.

"Huh? Oh, it's 'a penny for your thoughts.'"

"What is?"

"The expression you're trying to use. It's 'a penny for your thoughts.'"

"Ah. A penny for your thoughts, then."

"My mind was just wandering, I guess."

Robbie looked concerned. "Do you need medical assistance?"

Hal laughed. "No, it's another expression. I was just thinking about everything coming up back home—homecoming, the holidays, all that."

Robbie stopped and stared straight ahead for a few seconds. "I've uploaded the definition of 'holidays,' but I can't find 'homecoming' in our database. What is it?"

"It's something schools do. There's a football game and a dance. But we don't have a football team, so we only have the dance."

Robbie stopped again. "To dance is a verb, but you are using it as a noun." He tilted his head in a very android-like fashion. "I understand now. We have nothing comparable. What is it like?"

"A dance? Fun, mostly," Hal replied. "You go with your friends and, well, dance. Sometimes people hook up too, but mostly it's a lot of jumping around to the music. Except this year there'll be real dancing, because of the 50s theme. We're learning the Lindy Hop—that's a dance—in gym class. It's fun. Want to try?"

Awkwardly, Hal took Robbie's hands and led him in a few dance steps forward and around to the count of eight. Robbie swayed toward her with a confused smile, but when he didn't move his feet they ended up in a tangled mess.

"Uh, I guess this isn't working," she said. "Sorry."

"No need to apologize," Robbie said. "My culture does not value musical movement as your does."

"You did, before," Hal said. "Esther told us. The first time she and Will were here the kids danced, and she heard music all over the place."

"Perhaps. But in my timeline I have not experienced music or dance."

"Oh. I'm sorry," Hal said again.

"Do not be. One cannot miss what one never knew," Robbie said.

Where had she heard that before?

"You said there was something you wanted to tell me," Hal said.

"There is, or show you, actually. We're almost there." They strolled along in silence for a few minutes until they came to a large sphere that was covered in shiny clover. Thousands of thin, green shafts of light shot out from a million tiny leaves into the night sky, intersecting in perfectly formed geometric patterns.

"Wow," Hal said. "It's beautiful." She leaned on Robbie's arm and let the warm glow of the lights fill her until she wasn't feeling so sad anymore.

"This is one of our energy synthesizing centers. Would you like to have a look around?" Robbie asked.

"Sure."

They slipped in through an opening Robbie formed, and what Hal saw took her breath away. She'd expected some kind of futuristic factory, but instead she was surrounded by layers of soft, rolling green balls crisscrossing in a swirling maze that reached up to the very top of the sphere.

"Will would love to see this," said Hal. "How does it work?"

"The balls draw energy from plant life and send it upward to a sky station. There it's synthesized into usable form and released into the atmosphere, where it attaches to earth's gravitational force. We can access the energy anywhere we go."

"But how? You can't just pull energy out of the air, can you?"

"We have many microscopic devices imbedded in our bodies to focus energy. Will and Esther have been given a few. It's simple, really."

It didn't sound simple at all to Hal. Again, she wished that her brother could see this.

As if he'd read her mind, Robbie said, "You care a great deal about your brother, don't you?"

"Yeah, of course. Like my mom says, family first, always. Do you have a family?"

"Yes, but families here are different than they were in your time. I have siblings, and parents, of course. I don't see them often because of the work I've chosen. Except for my uncle."

"Your uncle?"

"Yes. Snorok is my uncle, although our relationship has

been held in secret. And I must warn you of what is to come."

The warm fuzzies that Hal had been enjoying evaporated in an instant. She didn't know much about Snorok, but she knew they were hiding their identity from him and that he couldn't be trusted. She took a step away from Robbie.

"Warn me of what?"

"I have made Snorok aware of your presence. He will deal with Salazar tonight. You will not be safe."

Hal turned to run but the exit had sealed up. "Let me out!" she shouted. "I have to warn them!"

"You must not," said Robbie. "But you need not face the Servant Leader. Try not to be angry with me." Hal realized, too late, that Robbie had not been outside her quarters last night by coincidence. He'd been spying on them for Snorok. Before Hal could say another word, Robbie reached over her head and activated the temporal bubble that would send her home.

"How could you?" she screamed, trying to hang on, but feeling herself spin through the irresistible force of time.

"It is as you say. Family first."

○─○─○

Will knew something was wrong the minute Snorok walked into the dining hall, surrounded by a group of thugs from the future wearing "Probity Force" badges. With the nod of his head, Snorok sent them to Mr. Salazar's table. They approached, palms raised, Snorok close behind.

Will checked his watch to be sure there was plenty of time before he was due for his next dose of DNA altering formula. He needed to stay calm. Beside him, Esther was pumping

Damaso for information about the mechanics of changing physical form.

"You're saying I could become any animal I wanted? A whale? An elephant?" she asked.

"It will take further study, but yes, eventually," Damaso replied. "But you would not need to restrict yourself to our current animal registry. With practice you could create your own forms as well."

Will interrupted. "Esther, look," he said, motioning toward the group descending on Mr. Salazar, who stood, looking grim, and spoke quietly to Snorok. They walked together to the center of the room, where a platform emerged and elevated Snorok. Will could swear Snorok grew a few inches as he rose above the crowd. Mr. Salazar remained below with a guard on each side.

"I'm sad to announce that Leader Salazar of the Time Guard has broken the Ancient Peoples Dictates," Snorok said.

"He doesn't look sad," Esther whispered, and she was right. Snorok oozed malicious satisfaction.

"He has allowed—no, enabled—ancient individuals to travel to our time."

"Who's he calling ancient?" Esther said.

"Shh," Damaso warned. Snorok nodded again and four members of the Probity Force approached Will and Esther's table, palms outstretched.

"Are they saluting us?" Esther asked.

"They have imbedded force fields to keep you from fleeing," said Tassiana. "I'm afraid you've been discovered."

The guards led Will and Esther to Snorok, where they stood with Mr. Salazar.

"Something tells me we're going home," Esther whispered.

"We'll be able to get back," said Will.

"You hope."

Snorok continued. "The Ancient Peoples Dictates are sacred and unbendable, designed to protect the integrity of the timeline."

"That is laughable, coming from you," Mr. Salazar interrupted, his gentle voice suddenly thunderous. Every eye in the room focused on him. "You, Snorok, have polluted the timeline to place yourself in power. These ancient ones have been brought from the past to prove your deceitfulness. They will give testimony to my words."

Murmurings rose, but subsided with a wave of Snorok's hand. "Testimony will be given at your tribunal." He pointed at Will and Esther. "These intruders, however, must be sent back in accordance with the Dictates. Time Guard, come forward."

Jikon and Okoko approached, looking like they carried the universe on their shoulders.

"I'm sorry," Okoko said softly. "We must send you home now."

"Whatever," Will said. He was already planning his trip back. They'd need to figure out how they were discovered in order to avoid it next time. Maybe a higher dose of the DNA altering formula would do it.

Okoko and Jikon raised their hands above Will and Esther's heads, and Will closed his eyes and braced for the spin that would send him home.

"Wait!" Snorok commanded. He pointed toward Will and Esther, who floated up until they were just below Snorok's height. The Servant Leader looked down on Will with cold steel in his eyes. Will matched his gaze with his usual blankness. Neither looked away.

"These trespassers may not be permitted to retain any memory of what they have seen here," Snorok declared. "All experiences related to time travel shall be wiped."

"Wait!" yelled Will. "You can't do that!"

"Memory wiping on humans is forbidden!" Mr. Salazar said. "You do this to protect yourself from discovery."

Snorok smiled with false patience. "I do this to uphold the Ancient Peoples Dictates and to protect the timeline from your tampering. You will have opportunity to defend and counter-accuse at tribunal." He placed his hand on Will's head as Will struggled to get away.

"No!" Will cried again. "Don't let him!" But it was too late. A few seconds later he was spiraling into his kitchen, where it was still Halloween night.

Green World Gray

PART III– PRESENT

Chapter 16

HAPPILY NEVER AFTER

Hal was still spinning as the four of them stumbled off the carpet. Chester jumped down from the table and ambled away, leaving blank computer screens behind. Hal grabbed Will by the shoulders. "Are you okay?" she asked in a panic. Mom was watching intently. Here it comes, Hal thought, finally, the big time-travel-truth-telling blowout. Mom was sure to know what they were doing, since she'd done it so many times herself. But Mom didn't say a word. Instead, she announced she was sick to her stomach and left the room in a haze. Right, Hal remembered—knowing that someone in your present had traveled in time led to a severe case of time travel influenza, complete with memory loss. Mom would not remember what she'd seen tonight.

In the meantime, Will's expression was glacial. "Relax, Hal, it's just a game," he said. "Hey Es, save me some cookies."

Esther lobbed a cookie to Will but it hit the table and broke into pieces. She and Will jumped into a game of cookie hockey, flicking a piece of Frankenstein's head back and forth until Esther missed and it flew to the floor. Hal and Rebekah watched in stunned silence.

"What, aren't you gonna tell me to stop wasting food?" Esther said to her sister. She picked up the cookie piece and tossed it into her mouth. "Or not to eat food off the floor?"

"I was so worried!" Hal said. "Robbie sent me back! He's Snorok's nephew!"

"Enough, Hal," Will said, not looking up from the cookies. "Game over for now."

Esther laughed. "What kind of name is 'Snorok,' anyway? Sounds like a rock that snores."

Before Hal could respond, Rebekah pulled her aside. "I don't think they remember," she said. "Any of it."

"How can that be?"

"Will told us that the Science Sentinels knew how to manipulate memory. Remember the dog video?"

Hal watched Will and Esther slurp down milk and devour cookies as if they hadn't eaten in days. "Any Jello-O?" Esther asked, and a glimmer of recognition crossed Will's face but swiftly vanished.

"You're right," Hal said. "Snorok must have wiped their memories before he sent them back." Will began building a house of cookies, studying his construction with the focused intensity that Hal knew so well. She'd last seen that look when her brother had scrutinized the science database before they'd gone to dinner—what, an hour ago? Or hundreds of years from now? Will had mastered the technology of the future so quickly. But now, all the knowledge he'd gained was gone and here he was, playing with cookies. Hal finally understood her brother's chronic, unhappy indifference. He'd simply been born in the wrong century.

"What should we do? We have to tell them!" she whispered.

"I don't think they'd believe us," answered Rebekah. "I wouldn't. Would you?"

"I guess not. But look at them." Esther was balancing a cupcake on the roof of the very unsteady cookie house. She lowered her head in concentration and in a deft move Will pushed her nose into the icing.

"This means war!" Esther exclaimed, and they jumped into action, chasing each other around the kitchen in all out cupcake combat. Hal couldn't bring herself to laugh. She felt her brother's loss even if he didn't.

"So, we just let them go on as if nothing happened?" she asked.

"What else can we do? Besides, they won't miss what they don't know," Rebekah replied. "Maybe it's better this way."

"Maybe," Hal agreed. Maybe things could go back to normal now. Maybe Will could stop dreaming about the future, and maybe Mom would stop living in the past. Maybe their family could be happy. Maybe, maybe, maybe. For the rest of the night Hal tried to hold on to her maybes, sinking under the weight of her brother's what-might-have-beens.

O—O—O

And so, autumn pressed on just the way Hal had described to Robbie. Homecoming came and went, and although Hal didn't have a date, she didn't care. Robbie's betrayal still stung, and she'd had enough of guys for a while. They ate an organic Thanksgiving dinner with Gram and Uncle Jason's family and with hardly any parental drama, other than the typical, "this trash won't take itself out" kind. Before Hal knew it, Dad was dragging Christmas decorations down from the attic and Mom lit up like the Rockefeller Center tree. She blinked in and out of rooms, wrapping holly around anything that wasn't moving. For the first time in a long time Mom was fully present, and even if her brightness was blinding sometimes, Mom was happy. Dad, too, seemed content, and his Saturday morning clear-outs took on a milder tone. Things were good, and Hal began to believe that Rebekah was right. They were all better off here, in the present, living the life they were meant to live.

Then there was Will—the same old restless, unattached Will she'd known for her whole life. Hal had to admit she missed the time travelling version of her brother, the one who was excited and ready to risk everything to experience life in the future, the Will whose joyfulness bubbled under the surface of his cool demeanor. Whenever Hal felt a twinge of guilt over letting that Will disappear, she reminded herself that it wasn't her fault. Besides, even if Will wasn't perfectly happy, at least he was here. At least they were a family, like they always had been. Maybe it was poetic justice that the person who'd contemplated wiping his parents' memories had suffered the very same fate. As winter came and went Hal concentrated on forgetting her own memories of time travel. She and Rebekah hardly ever spoke about their experience, and when they did it was mostly to reassure each other that things had worked out for the best.

One afternoon in early April, the Horace and Yim siblings stayed after school to set up their science fair projects. Hal and Rebekah were working together on testing the effect of microwave radiation on yeast fungus. Esther's project involved comparing amounts of chlorophyll in leaf pigments, while Will was studying the life habits of bald eagles.

Hal scoured through online research with Rebekah, when across the room something caught her eye. Instead of typing, Will was absently waving his hand at the computer screen just like he'd done to gain access to the science database in the future. Hal froze and nudged Rebekah.

"Do you see that?" she whispered. "Look what he's doing."

They watched for a few seconds until Will's hands dropped down to the keyboard. He regained focus as if nothing had happened and began to type away.

"It's like he remembered for a second," Hal said.

"I know," replied Rebekah. "Every now and then Esther does something like that, too. For example, did you notice her topic?"

"Yeah," Hal said. "Do you think she remembers all the green energy talk?"

"She might. I guess they couldn't completely clear the memory engrams."

"Do you ever feel bad for them?" Hal asked.

"I did in the beginning. But I hardly think about it now."

"We haven't talked about it for ages."

"I know," Rebekah said. "Esther seems to be doing okay, though."

"Yeah, Will, too. That's one thing I can't figure out. Why

did Snorok leave our present as it is? I mean, even though he took their memories, Will is fine. He's not getting in trouble or anything. And if Will is fine, then Mom is fine, and the future is fine, like the first future Will and Esther saw. How does Snorok gain from that? He wasn't in power that first time."

"True," said Rebekah. "It doesn't make sense. Why didn't Snorok do something to hurt Will, or stop him from returning? That would have damaged your mom and set the ball rolling for the dark side to take over."

Hal smiled in spite of herself. "Remember when we were in that rolling ball? That was pretty cool."

"Yeah, it was," Rebekah answered. "But I'm glad to be home," she added quickly. "I guess we'll never know what future will come to pass. I don't think we're meant to."

"I guess not," Hal said, and went back to her data search, resigned to letting their time in the future remain in the past.

The science fair presentations were in the evening so that the parents could attend. The projects were set out on tables, ready to be oohed and aahed over by teacher evaluators with clip boards and smiling parents making believe they were interested in other kids' work. Every year the teachers chose a winner of the science fair. Hal hated that. Why did everything have to be a big competition? She thought back to Samaya's description of school and shuddered.

After a while Mrs. Bumbly told everyone to have a seat so she could make the big announcement. She cleared her throat, waiting for the buzz to subside.

"Good evening," she said, "and welcome to Go Green Academy's tenth annual science fair. Although I will shortly announce this year's winner, it's important to remember that science is not a competition." Right, Hal thought. Sure, it isn't. "Scientific investigation is crucial to the future of the planet." Well, at least she got that right. Hal tried to make eye contact with Rebekah, who was sitting one row back with her parents, but Rebek was looking down at her hands. Mrs. Bumbly raised her voice and declared, "We must remember that here at Go Green Academy, you are all winners!" Cue applause.

"This year's winner was chosen for his attention to detail regarding the plight of the American Bald Eagle." That was Will's project! Mom sat up straight, beaming as if her son had just been elected president, but Dad looked at Will skeptically, as if some terrible mistake had been made. "This student has shown great improvement in all areas, and his science project is a fine example. In fact, this student was so involved in the project that we started to think he would turn into a bald eagle!" Diplomatic laughter ensued. "Ladies and gentlemen, please congratulate eighth grader Will Horace, this year's winner of the Go Green Academy Science Fair!" Polite applause followed from everyone except Mom, Dad, and Esther, who pounded their hands together as if they were trying to break the sound barrier. Esther was especially animated, hooting and jumping out of her seat. Hal hadn't seen her so excited since—she pushed away the memory of Esther taking in the sights of the future.

Will stood dutifully and walked to the front. He plugged in his flash drive and hit some keys until up popped a photo of a bald eagle standing majestically on the edge of a cliff. He clicked through a series of pictures as he spoke in a quiet, even voice.

"Bald eagles only live in North America," Will began, clicking to the next slide. "They're not really bald, but their heads are a different color from their bodies, so some people think they look bald. I don't think so." Click. "They have a wingspan of six to seven feet and when they fly their wings are flat. That's how you can tell them apart from vultures." Click to a video of a bald eagle in flight. "Unlike people..." here Will sent a deadpan look directly at Mom and Dad "...bald eagles mate for life." A few people laughed nervously. Click. "They have the biggest nest of any bird because the male and female build it together." Click. Will kept his eyes fixed on Mom and Dad. "They also share parenting duties like taking care of their eggs and feeding their young." Click. Dad looked away, but Mom stared straight ahead with a smile plastered on her face.

"Bald eagles molt like other birds, but scientists aren't exactly sure when or why. For my project I reviewed data from three different eagle cams. The chart I made shows some differences in molting times." Will pointed to his poster display at the back of the room. "You can read it for yourself if you want. The important thing about molting is that bald eagles never lose all their feathers at once." Will's expression became wistful. "They can always fly, no matter what." Will was silent for a few seconds, squinting as if trying to remember something. When he continued, he seemed to deflate. "People believe all kinds of myths about bald eagles. They think when eagles get old they can grow a new beak and feathers and be reborn. But that's not true. Bald eagles live about twenty years, and then they shrivel up and die just like we do." At that Will sat down, and Hal felt as if her heart would break.

"Well, that was an uplifting ending," Dad said, but Mom nudged him to be quiet and began her turbo clapping. The rest of the audience followed suit.

Hal turned around and saw that Esther was sobbing into a tissue.

"What's wrong?" she heard Rebekah whisper.

"No idea," Esther replied.

But Hal knew what was wrong, and so did Rebekah, even if she didn't want to admit it. Better to cope with the pain of loss than the blankness of never having lived. She'd never imagined that the Go Green Academy Science Fair would be her watershed moment, but something was broken in Will and Esther—something that Hal needed to fix.

For the next few days Hal tried to come up with a strategy to make Will and Esther remember. Even if they never traveled to the future again, they had a right to access their own pasts. The emptiness in Will's eyes haunted Hal; taking his memories was the cruelest form of theft she could imagine. She knew she needed help, but Rebekah had made her feelings on the subject clear. Hal never realized how much she counted on her best friend for advice. Rebekah's refusal to help left Hal totally on her own.

Knowing Rebekah was busy with SAT prep, Hal proposed a trip to the planetarium, hoping that maybe looking at the stars would trigger some deeply buried memory trace in Esther and Will. Saturday morning, they hopped on the subway to Central Park West and watched *Our Future in Space* under the dark planetarium dome. In resonant tones, the narrator described all the possible ways their children's children's children's children might travel to distant star systems and what they might find when they got there. Hal sat between Will and Esther, but since it was too dark to see their faces she had no idea how they were responding. Halfway through the program the narrator switched from the future to the present, describing how research at the International Space Station is helping scientists study proteins in the human body.

Hal leaned over to Will and whispered, "Wow. Maybe someday they'll figure out how to control human DNA." Will didn't respond, but Hal kept at it. "Maybe people will be able to change their physical appearance." Still no response from Will. "Maybe they'll even be able to manipulate human memories."

"Maybe you'll shut up so we can hear this," Esther growled, and that was that.

Hal attempted to jar their memories again during the subway ride home, but the thundering and screeching of the 7 Train made conversation difficult. She shouted over the noise until Will finally lost his patience.

"Hal, give it a rest," he said. "Since when are you so obsessed with a role-playing game?" Hal stewed in silent frustration for the rest of the ride. They emerged from the subway to find the bus waiting. Hal chose a seat as far away from Will and Esther as possible. She needed to think, but as her body shifted with the short stops and wide turns of the bus, she only felt more helpless and alone.

"What's with her?" she heard Esther ask.

"Dunno," Will said. Hal saw an uncharacteristic look of

concern cross his face, but she was too upset to care.

When they arrived home, Hal went straight to her room and threw herself across her bed. She wanted to text Rebekah, but she recognized something brand new in her feelings toward her best friend—anger. Why couldn't Rebekah understand that they had to help Esther and Will? Why was she so content to let them lose part of themselves, just to maintain the status quo? Why was this all on Hal? It wasn't fair. For the first time, Hal began to wish that Snorok had messed with her memory, too. It would have been so much easier to forget the future. She never wanted to go there in the first place. Why did Robbie send her back before Snorok could get to her? What a wimp he was, not even brave enough for an all-out betrayal. She should never have gone anywhere with Robbie. If only she'd refused his stupid invitations and his idiot, crystal blue eyes. If only she could go back in time to before any of this had happened. Hal buried her head under her pillow.

She didn't know how long she'd been asleep when she heard a soft knock at her door.

"Can I come in?" Mom asked, peeking her head inside.

"If I say no, will you go away?" Hal said from under her pillow.

"Not a chance," Mom said, sitting down at the edge of the bed. "Will tells me that something is bothering you," she said in her best caring mom voice, "something about a role-playing game with the Yims. Do you want to talk about it?"

Will had spoken to Mom about *her*? Now that was rich.

"No," Hal answered gruffly, but pushed the pillow aside. She'd never been intentionally mean to Mom before and she wasn't very good at it. "You wouldn't understand," she said more kindly, but realized that wasn't true. Hal sat up straight. If anyone should understand, it would be Mom. After all, she was the one who'd started this mess by traveling back in time. Other than Rebek, Mom was the only person on the planet who even knew time travel was real. What was the point of keeping her time travel secrets from Mom? She'd always shared her problems with Mom—why was this any different?

"Okay," she began, "I do need to tell you something. You might be surprised, you might be worried, but promise you won't be angry, okay?"

"Halia," Mom replied, "you know you can tell me anything. I'm here to help. What is it? What's bothering you?"

"It's a long story," Hal said.

"Why don't you start at the beginning?"

"Okay, here goes." Hal launched into an account of the last several months, starting with their discovery of the TTD. She talked fast and barely took a breath between sentences. She told Mom how they'd followed her back in time and how Will and Esther had gone to the future with Chester's help. She told Mom that she knew all about Fost and Tuley. She described how Will had set up the trip to MIT hoping to meet someone from the future, but how he'd found Chester instead. Hal talked on and on while Mom listened, nodding calmly. Finally, after what seemed like forever, Hal got to the events of Halloween night and described how the future had changed and how Robbie had betrayed her.

"Robbie is a boy at school?" Mom asked.

"No! Robbie is a guy in the future. I know it's complicated, but I'm almost at the end." Hal finished her tale with Snorok's theft of Will and Esther's memories. The only detail she left out was Will's plan to wipe himself from Mom's memory. No use hurting Mom's feelings for no reason.

"Rebek thinks it's better this way," Hal said. "But it's just, Will was so different there. He was happy. I can't let them take that away from him. I have to find a way to help him remember. Can you contact Fost and Tuley? Maybe they can help."

"Oh, Halia," Mom said, a tear escaping her eye. "This is my fault." She reached for Hal's hand and held it firmly.

"It's okay, Mom." Hal felt relief wash over her. "You were just doing your best. You couldn't have known going back in time would lead to all this."

Mom frowned. "Halia, listen. This is my fault because I let you think you had to fix our family. I let you feel responsible for your brother's happiness. You were always such a good sister. But I should have seen what was happening, and now you've constructed this, this fiction, this fantasy, to make sense of it all." Mom put her arm around Hal. "It's okay, Sweetie. You can stop worrying."

Hal pulled away with so much force that Mom almost fell off the bed. "Stop making believe!" she said. "Stop lying! We know about time travel! You can stop trying to protect us!"

"Hal, please, you're scaring me," Mom said. "There's no such thing as time travel. You've been playing a game with your brother, that's all it is. Honey, please." Mom reached out to Hal again, but Hal turned away.

"Fine. Whatever." She ignored Mom's pleas until Mom finally left a few minutes later. Hal picked up her pillow and threw it across the room. Why couldn't Mom come clean for once? Why did she have to keep up this act? Hal was sick of being treated like a little kid. She needed Mom's help, and for the first time, Mom wasn't there for her.

That night at dinner Hal sat in a sullen silence. She refused any overtures of friendship from Mom or Dad and retreated to her room as soon as cleanup was done. Will knocked at her door and entered without an invitation. Hal glared at him in anger.

"Since when do you talk to Mom about me?" she demanded.

"Since you started acting crazy," Will answered calmly. "You see what you've driven me to? Heart-to-hearts with Mom are not my thing."

Hal smiled a little at that.

"Next she'll be wanting to drink tea with me." Will shuddered.

Hal smiled a little more. Same old sarcastic Will. Same old Will who cared but would never admit it. Mom was right about one thing—Hal had always taken care of her brother. She couldn't stop now.

"I'm not crazy," she said. "Isn't it possible that what I'm saying is true? You and Esther had your memories wiped. Rebek and I left earlier, before Snorok could get to us. Don't you remember?"

"I do remember. I remember those moves in the game we made up. We were role-playing, Hal. That's what I remember."

Hal sighed.

"You said we stood on some kind of magic carpet to time travel, right? Where is it?"

"Gone."

"Look," said Will. "Here's an easy way to see who's right. You say Rebek's memories of time travel are intact?"

"Yeah, but she's no help. She thinks it's better that you and Esther can't remember."

"Do you think you could get her to talk about it if we aren't around?"

"What do you mean?"

"If you could record her admitting that your story is true, that all this stuff really happened, then that would prove it, right?"

"You mean like when we recorded Mom using the TTD?"

"Like when we made believe we recorded Mom...hey, where are you going?"

Hal had flown past Will through the hallway and into his room. Maybe the recordings of Mom stepping in and out of the closet would still be on Will's computer. That would be her proof. She scanned Will's desktop, looking for the video folder, but it was gone.

"Where'd you put them?" she asked, frantic. "You didn't erase the video files, did you?"

"What video files?" Will asked, and Hal saw the worry in his eyes.

"They must have deleted the files. Look in trash. Maybe they forgot that."

Will patiently scanned through his trash folder. "There's nothing there."

"I don't know how, but they got to your computer," Hal said, more disappointed than she'd ever been. As much as she hated the idea of secretly recording her best friend, it seemed like her last chance of getting Will to believe her.

"Okay," she said. "I'll do it. But I'll try a text first. If that doesn't work, I'll record our conversation."

Hal tried texting Rebekah that night, but she answered with an angry face emoticon and Hal got the message. The next day at school she suggested they go to the library during study period and Rebekah agreed. She set her phone to record and left it halfway sticking out of her backpack.

"I know you don't want to talk about this," Hal began, "but just answer one question and I promise I won't bring it up again."

"Bring what up again?"

"You know what. Just answer this—what happens to the future if Snorok wins? Don't you care about the future? If every life is a watershed, that means yours is, too, Rebek. What you decide right now matters."

Rebekah rolled her eyes impatiently. "Hal, stop. I don't want to play this game anymore. We came in here to study."

"It's not a game and you know it. Don't make me feel like I'm going crazy. You know what happened in the future. You were there for most of it."

Rebekah frowned. "Hal, are you saying you really believe all this? You're not just pretending anymore?"

"You know I believe it, and you know it's true. You were there," Hal insisted, her voice rising. Ms. Bowman, the librarian, shushed them as she walked by.

Rebekah touched Hal's hand gently. "It was a game, Hal. I think we need to talk with your mom about this."

Hal jerked her hand back and stood. "You have a lot in common with my mom," she said. "You're both traitors." She stormed out of the library and sat by herself for the rest of the day, seething at her friend's betrayal.

Later that night, alone in her room, Hal was still ruminating over her conversation with Rebek. It was one thing for Rebekah to refuse her help, but pretending that she didn't remember all they'd been through since last summer was quite another. Why would she do that? What did she have to gain?

Unless...what if Rebek wasn't pretending? What if she really didn't remember? For that matter, what if Mom no longer remembered her own travels through time? Hal stopped breathing for a minute. Someone from the future had deleted Will's computer files, and that same someone had altered Mom and Rebek's memories. They weren't pretending. They really didn't remember.

For the first time in her life, Hal felt absolutely, totally alone. She reached for a tissue to dry her tears as Chester slid into her room and jumped onto her bed. Hal put her arms around him and cried into his fur. "Why didn't they take my memories, too?" she asked. "Why do I have to remember?"

Chester didn't answer, but he stayed in Hal's room that night, purring softly next to his friend as she tossed and turned.

O—O—O

In the coming days, Hal tried her best to forget about traveling through time. She tried to forget flying through the sky in a crystal sphere. She tried to forget racing down a snowy hill with Robbie. She didn't want to remember the cozy satisfaction of walking beside him that moonlit night when she'd taught him to dance and ended up tangled in his arms—all before he'd stabbed her in the back, of course. Most of all, she tried to forget the excitement that had lit Will's face the whole time they were there. But the more she tried to forget, the more miserable she was. She stayed away from her friends and only left the house for school, preferring to spend her time in her room with Chester, who had always been more Will's cat. Now he followed Hal like her shadow until Will got jealous and carried him away. But when Will wasn't looking, Chester always returned to Hal's side, circling her legs or nudging her hand with his head. Mom and Dad were leaving her alone temporarily, but Hal heard them whispering, trying to figure out what to do with their delusional daughter.

"It's like she's changed overnight," Mom said. "We need to get her help."

"Let's give her some time," Dad answered. "She'll come around."

Mom looked more worried every day. She sneaked around the house, standing outside Hal's bedroom or the bathroom with her ear pressed to the door to make sure Hal was okay. Not that Hal blamed Mom for worrying; sometimes she was overwhelmed with the temptation to do something, anything, to relieve the ache of her lonely memories.

Once, Hal overhead Mom and Will discussing her mental state. Incredibly, Will was giving Mom advice about how to handle his troubled sister. Will talked more at dinner now, too, filling in the gap left by Hal's silence. Hal wondered if any of them noticed the slow but steady role reversal happening in their family.

School would be over in a month, but Hal had no plans for gainful summer employment. She couldn't sleep, she barely ate, and she'd lost all interest in her hair or the makeup she'd fought so hard for permission to wear. Even on those rare occasions that Hal could escape her memories, she couldn't shake her sadness. She gathered it around her like a cloak on a stormy night, and as much as she wanted to, she couldn't loosen her grip. Weeks had gone by without seeing Rebekah outside of school, and finally they stopped texting. For days at a time Hal barely touched her phone. Then, one dreary afternoon, Hal looked out the window to see Ami Coble jump out of her car and run up the steps to Hal's (former) best friend's door. Hal had seen them sitting together during homeroom and giggling in the corner at lunch. She guessed Rebekah had moved on, and she guessed she didn't blame her.

That night, Will watched as Hal passed a mirror in the hallway.

"Well, that's a relief," he said.

"What is?"

"You still have a reflection. The transformation is not yet complete."

Hal backtracked to take a good look at herself. Her skin was blotchy and she had circles under her eyes.

"More zombie than vampire, I think," she said.

"Listen," Will said, "I heard Mom and Dad talking today. If you don't snap out of it, they're going to stick you in a hospital. The kind for crazy people. Is that what you want?"

"I'm not crazy," Hal said.

"Then stop acting like it."

"I'm not sure I can."

"Then fake it," Will said. "Do what you have to do to keep

them off your back. I do it all the time, and so can you."

Hal couldn't deny that her brother was the faking it master. She wanted to tell Will about the one place where he hadn't been faking it, the future, where he'd been happy for the first time. But what was the point? He wouldn't believe her.

"Okay," Hal said, "I'll try."

The next day, a Saturday, Hal got up early to help Mom in the garden. Will and Dad would be asleep for hours, but Hal expected to find Mom outside, fertilizing or mulching away out in the fresh spring air. Instead, Mom was staring into her coffee mug at the kitchen counter. She was wearing her old flannel pajamas even though it was May, and she had a serious case of bed head.

"I thought you'd be outside," Hal said.

"I've decided not to plant this year. I've been too worried..." Mom stopped mid-sentence. "I mean, it takes up too much of my time and energy. I want to be able to spend more time with you. And your brother, of course."

"Oh."

"How are you this morning?"

"I'm—better. At least I'm going to try to be better. I thought maybe we could do something today."

"That's great, honey. I'm so happy to hear that. I'm yours, all day. What would you like to do?" Mom's voice was peppy but her posture was slumped. Her smile was overtaken by a yawn.

"Uh, I don't know. We can decide later. Maybe you should go back to bed for a while."

"Good idea." Mom stood and wrapped Hal in a tight hug.

"It's okay, Mom," Hal said. "I'm okay. Go back to sleep."

"I will. Just for an hour." She put her mug in the sink and smiled at Hal again as she left the kitchen. "Oh, one more thing," she said, turning back. "I've decided to give up my job at the farm. I'm here for you—whatever you need, okay?"

"Okay." Hal watched Mom walk up the stairs, holding onto the banister as if she'd aged fifty years. That's my fault, Hal thought with a sigh. Because of me, Mom looks like a washed-out dish towel. Hal couldn't remember a time Mom didn't have a garden, and now she's stopped working at the farm, as well. Mom was giving up everything she loved because of her problem child.

Hal glanced at the kitchen clock. In another hour she could walk up to Luv-n-the-Air Flower Shop and buy a bouquet for Mom. It was the least she could do, especially since tomorrow was Mother's Day and Hal had planned nothing this year. She took her time getting dressed and ate a bowl of organic cereal with almond milk. She organized her backpack and set her homework on the table to be tackled later. Then she grabbed $20 from her stash and shoved it into her pocket. That should be enough. She left a note on the kitchen table: Went for a walk to the store. Be back soon. Don't call the police. As an afterthought, she added, Yes, I'll be careful. Mom wasn't crazy about Hal walking anywhere alone, but with any luck she'd be back before Mom knew she was gone.

Hal headed up Steward Street, past the familiar mix of old and new houses in her neighborhood. She wished she'd grabbed a hoodie because, not two blocks into her half mile trek, the sky turned dark and a cold breeze lifted. She quickened her pace but when she reached the corner of

Steward and Chestnut she stopped, like she always did, to look at the old house with the red-brown shingles and green roof. It was the only house Hal had ever seen with a spire above the porch, and a younger Hal had always imagined a witch lived there. Hal had never seen anyone go in or out of that house, but today she saw someone standing in the yard, in the shadow of the spire. Judging from the shape and size, the someone looked like a guy, but Hal couldn't tell anything else about him. His hood was pulled forward covering his face, but his body was angled toward Hal as if he were looking at her. It's nothing, Hal thought, but in her peripheral vision she saw the figure step onto the sidewalk and move in her direction.

All Mom's warnings lit up in Hal's brain. She kept walking, careful to stay on the main road where there were plenty of people coming and going, dragging groceries or kids with them. I'm completely safe, Hal told herself. Look at all these people. Surely someone would help me if I needed it. She turned left at the intersection before the elementary school, glancing over her shoulder nervously. Maybe she'd imagined him. Maybe she was delusional, like everyone wanted her to believe. But there he was, the guy in the hood, keeping a steady distance between them but definitely following her. He was holding something, a phone Hal thought, looking down at it as he walked. Hal had forgotten her own phone. For a minute she imagined facing her pursuer to get a better look, but Mom's voice in her head shouted a definite "No." Sheesh. Why did she have to hear that voice all the time? She was probably imagining things. It's a free country, and maybe this guy just happened to be out for a little Saturday morning shopping, like she was. Even as Hal obeyed Mom's voice, she blamed her mother for filling her head with the fear of strangers.

Although Hal was on the same side of the street as the flower shop, she crossed the road as a test and moved into a slow jog. The stranger crossed, too. Hal felt adrenaline pump into her chest. Maybe she'd been too quick to blame Mom. Maybe Mom was right and Hal was in danger. Soon the houses and apartments were replaced by stores, some open for business but others still hiding behind graffiti covered metal barriers. One more block. As she jogged past the Korean restaurant, Hal caught a glimpse of herself in the window. The wind had expanded her hair like a pan of fried noodles and she looked as frenzied as she felt. She spotted the flower shop—the owner was just opening up. Hal checked for cars and stepped off the curb into a pothole that sent her sprawling, banging her knees and elbows against the rough asphalt. She looked around, but no one seemed to have witnessed her klutzy spill, which was a good thing. Slowly, she brushed herself off and surveyed the damage. Her knees hurt and she saw they were bleeding under her ripped jeans. The jolt of pain had made her forget about her pursuer for a minute. To her surprise, she heard a familiar voice behind her ask, "Hal, are you all right?"

Robbie.

Chapter 17
THE PLAN

All Will wanted to do was sleep in on a Saturday morning. Was that so much to ask? Ever since Hal started acting crazy last fall, Will had done his best to stay out of trouble, figuring Mom and Dad could only handle one problem child at a time (and not so well, at that). He'd done okay at school, and had even won the stupid science award that Mom went so gaga over. As much as he hated it, he'd allowed Mom to confide in him about Hal. But last night Hal had promised to snap out of it and Will figured he'd done his part for family bliss. He'd stayed up late playing video games and he was looking forward to the void of uninterrupted sleep.

No such luck. Though he tried to fight it, loud, irritating voices dragged him toward consciousness. If that weren't enough, Chester had planted himself on Will's chest and was purring into his ear with no mercy.

"Okay, okay," Will said. "I'm up. Didn't anyone feed you yet?" He stumbled out of bed, almost slipping on the *Inhumans* comic at his feet. When he reached the top of the stairs, he stopped and listened. There was an unfamiliar voice—a guy's voice. He went back to his room, threw on some sweatpants and a T-shirt, and headed down to see what was going on.

Hal and a dark-haired teenaged dude were sitting on the couch while Mom fussed over some cuts on Hal's legs. Dad stood off to the side, eyeing the stranger suspiciously.

"Are you sure you're okay?" Mom asked, applying enough Band-Aids to cover a gaping chest wound. "Do we need to go to the emergency room?"

"I'm fine," Hal said. "Just scraped up. And embarrassed."

"Well, thank you so much for seeing Halia home," Mom said. "She shouldn't have been out alone."

"It's my pleasure, Mrs. Horace," said the dude with a big, fake-polite smile. Who was this guy, anyway?

"And you say you know Hal from school?" Dad asked. "Robbie, is it? I don't think I've ever heard her mention you."

The name rang a bell. As Will tried to place it, Mom said, "Oh yes, I've heard all about Robbie. Nice to meet the real you." She stuck out her hand and Robbie stared at it for a second as if he didn't know what to do. Then he shook Mom's hand with another toothy grin.

"The pleasure is mine, Mrs. Horace."

Robbie. Will couldn't claim to know everyone from school, but he'd never seen this guy before. Robbie. Wait— Robbie from their role-playing game? Robbie, the guy from the future that Hal had made up on her turn? Two possibilities flashed through Will's mind. First, Hal had this guy in mind when she'd created the character, or second, Hal found some psycho guy and got him to play Robbie so that she could continue her fantasy. Will hoped with all his might that the first was true because otherwise Hal was worse off than he'd thought.

"I was just about to make some tea. Would you like some?" Mom asked. That was Mom, all right—one minute afraid to let you leave the house, and the next minute offering tea to a potential axe murderer who happened to have a nice smile.

Once again Robbie hesitated before answering. "Yes," he said finally. "I would like some tea."

Mom bustled away and Dad headed for the coffee pot. Will remained in the room, shocked that Mom and Dad would leave Hal alone with this character. He sat down without taking his eyes off Robbie.

"How come I've never seen you at school?" he asked. "You new or something?"

"Will, this is him," Hal whispered excitedly. "This is Robbie, from the future."

Will groaned. His worst fear had come true. Hal was loony and this guy was taking advantage of her lunacy.

"I think you should leave right now," Will said. Unfortunately, just when he was trying to sound tough, his voice cracked.

"I understand your suspicion," Robbie said. "Your memory of me has been wiped. If you watch this brief recording you will see that what your sister says is true." He offered a small plastic rectangular box to Will.

"I'm not watching any sicko video," Will said, pushing Robbie's hand away.

"Will, please," Hal pleaded. "Just watch it before they come back in. Trust me."

Will had always trusted Hal. He took the box from Robbie, but there was no picture, no display, and no controls. "This is nothing but a piece of plastic," he said.

"Wave your hand over it to activate the display," Robbie instructed.

Will looked skeptical. "Not very secure," he said.

"On the contrary, it is very secure. There are only three people currently on the planet the device will respond to."

"Yeah, right," Will said. This guy was as crazy as Hal.

"Only three of us have the implantations needed to activate it," Robbie explained.

Will studied his palm carefully. It looked the same as it always did, except for the marker from yesterday he hadn't washed off. "You're saying I have implantations? Real implantations?"

"Will, please," Hal begged again. "Mom will be back any second."

Will sighed and waved his hand over the plastic thing. He needed to show his sister that this guy was a phony so they could get him out of their house. Immediately a screen lit up with a video of a big greenish ball rolling along a grassy field. The ball picked up speed and then spiraled into the air.

"Nice special effects," Will said.

"Look closer," said Robbie. He waved his hand over the video and the picture zoomed in on the people inside the ball.

Will gulped back his shock. "It's us! How did you do that?"

"It's a simple recording. All our craft are equipped with recording devices," Robbie said.

Still suspicious, Will looked closely for signs of digital editing, but the images moved smoothly and the interactions seemed real. When he saw his signature move—sticking out his foot to trip Esther, and Esther's signature response, stepping over his foot without a word—Will knew this wasn't faked.

"Text Rebekah," Will said. "Tell them we're coming over."

○─○─○

"Have you punched him in the eye yet?" Esther asked Will. They sat at the table in her yard facing off with the guy from the future. For two hours they'd listened to his crazy story, grilling him with questions until the reality of what had happened to them finally began to sink in.

Will didn't answer. He was in one of his impossible to read moods, staring blankly at his hands.

"Good idea," said Rebekah. She stood, ready to pounce.

"Whoa, Tiger Girl, I was only kidding," Esther said, holding her sister back. Esther had never seen Rebekah in this state. Her usually calm sibling was seething. Not that Esther blamed her. Robbie told quite a story, all backed up with video from this little gadget he'd brought from hundreds of years in the future. As Esther watched the images, shock turned to awe, but awe quickly gave way to rage when she realized how deeply they'd been violated. Betraying them to this crazy uncle of his was bad enough, but taking their memories, that was unforgivable. If you can't remember something, did it really even happen?

"It's okay, it's all good," Hal said.

"It's not all good," said Rebekah. "He made us think you

were crazy. He took our memories and left you isolated."

Esther had been so busy nursing her own wounds she hadn't given much thought to Hal's. But how was it that the person with the most cause for anger was positively beaming?

"Technically, it was Snorok who did those things," Robbie said. "Had I known his plan, I would never have betrayed you."

This guy was either a liar or an idiot. "You must have known," Esther said. "What did you think he'd do?"

Smiling-boy stopped smiling. "Many of us who helped Snorok come to power now regret it," he said. "He made promises."

"What promises?" Will asked. "From the videos, it looks like things are pretty good in the future."

"Snorok promised order, lawfulness, and personal prosperity, but I realized too late that his true interest was power." Robbie bowed his head. "I ask your forgiveness." His words were meant for all of them, but he was looking at Hal from under his long eyelashes and she was looking back. Ugh.

"Is that supposed to make it all right?" Esther asked. "Because it doesn't."

"That's what I'm trying to tell you," said Hal. "Robbie has a plan."

"Why should we trust him?" said Esther, ready to engage in all-out battle, but Will interrupted.

"Let's hear it," he said, "this plan."

"Although it is strictly forbidden, we must do what Snorok did. We must change the timeline. You must send a message to yourselves in the future. Tell yourselves not to trust me. If you stop my betrayal, you will remain in my time and perhaps help us find a way to undo Snorok's damage to the timeline."

"How?" asked Will.

"Snorok's goal has always been to stifle your mother's role in saving our environment. He has attempted to do that in two ways: first, through Will's waywardness. When that didn't work, he allowed only Hal to retain her memories of time travel, knowing the emotional distress it would cause her and your family."

"It almost worked," Hal said. "Mom gave up her garden, and she told me yesterday she was quitting her job at the farm for me."

"But now Hal is fine and her mother can go back to normal. Isn't that enough?" Rebekah said.

"This will not be Snorok's last attempt," Robbie warned. "He has many resources at his disposal. We need your help."

"I meant, how do we send the message?" Will said. "I'm in."

"Of course you are," Esther said. Betrayal or no betrayal, Esther knew that Will would never give up a chance to see the future, no matter how crazy or dangerous the plan. "I am too," she said, just as her mother stuck her head out the door.

"Would anyone like a soda?" she asked.

"No thanks, Omma, we're good," Esther replied. Her mom exchanged glances with Rebekah, waited for a second, and then disappeared inside. Message sent. Omma might not have the facts, but she could smell trouble a mile away.

"Maybe we should leave things as they are. We're not meant for this," Rebekah said.

"We've had this conversation before. You just don't remember," said Hal.

Rebekah nodded. "I'm sorry I didn't believe you."

"It's okay. I wouldn't have believed me either. But trust me now, okay?"

"Yeah, because I'm going. With or without you," Esther said.

"That's a recurring theme," said Hal, but didn't bother to explain. Clearly, thought Esther, something had transpired among them that only Hal remembered. It was weird, this altered memory thing. Esther didn't like it at all.

"Can we get on with it now?" Will asked. "What's the plan?"

"I say we start with you giving us our memories back," Esther said.

"I don't have the ability to grant that request," Robbie answered. "But if we are successful, none of this will have happened and your memories will remain intact."

Okay, that was even weirder.

Robbie continued. "In my time, Will and Esther will study radiation waves leaked from a nuclear reactor you have access to in your time. We've learned that messages can be encoded on those waves and read centuries later. We simply need to get to the reactor and encode the message."

Will and Esther bolted upright. Here was something they did remember. "MIT!" they shouted together, and Esther thought, what are the chances?

o—o—o

Will wasn't sure how "simple" Robbie's plan was. He could see plenty of problems with it. First, how to get to MIT. After his failed runaway attempt last fall, he couldn't ask Dad to take him again. He remembered planning to hop on a bus to anywhere, but he couldn't remember why, or how he'd been stupid enough to think they'd sell him, a minor, a ticket. Anyway, Dad had showed up with a cop and that was that. The memory was clear and fuzzy at the same time, if that made sense, which it didn't.

Last weekend's conversation with Robbie had ended abruptly when Esther and Rebek were called in for lunch. Will's mom had plans for them, too. She dragged them to a movie and dinner, and if that weren't enough, she declared "family game night" when they got home. Will looked to Dad for help, but it was no use arguing with Mom when she went on one of her togetherness rampages. Esther and Rebek were busy at church the next day, so there was no talking to them. Hal spent Sunday looking out the window, but Robbie kept his distance. Will still didn't trust that guy, but he had to let Robbie take the lead, for now.

Will was surprised to see Robbie at 8:00 on Monday morning, waiting with the swarm to get into the school building. He watched Robbie cozy up to Hal as they went to homeroom together. Somehow Robbie had gotten himself enrolled at Go Green Academy, but hey, when you come from a time where people alter DNA and wipe memory, Will guessed registering for high school wouldn't be too hard. He and Esther went to homeroom together, as usual, and Will was about to go into his usual back-of-the-room slump when Esther poked his arm.

"Look," she said, pointing at the board. Will read the announcement: "The science faculty is sponsoring a trip to MIT to tour the nuclear reactor lab. Get your permission slip today."

"Wow," Esther said. "That was easy."

"He must have popped back in time to set this up," Will replied. Apparently, there was a brain behind the smile. "Now we just need to figure out how to get alone with a nuclear reactor and hope that future guy knows how to encode the message, because we sure don't."

At lunchtime Robbie led them to a classroom where they could talk in private. Mr. Getachew, who was now a long-term sub, sat at the teacher's desk ignoring them behind piles of books and papers. Will had to admit that the field trip idea was impressive, although he would never say so to Robbie. But what about the rest?

"Once we get there," Will said, "what then? How do we embed this message?"

"How do we even get away from the group?" Esther asked. "They watch you like hawks on these field trips."

Before Robbie could answer, a boy and a girl—ninth graders—barged into the classroom talking so loudly that Mr. Getachew looked up from his work.

"Hey Mr. G!" said the boy from under his shaggy, dyed black hair. He waved his hands around as he spoke so that everyone could see the silver rings he wore.

"That kid thinks he's a rock star," Esther said under her breath.

"Can we grab permission slips for the MIT trip from you?" the boy continued, still half yelling.

"Certainly," Mr. Getachew said quietly, picking up some papers from his desk. "I'm glad you plan to attend." He glanced over at Will and company. "Let's step outside to discuss it," he said, leading the rock star and his friend out into the hall and closing the door behind him.

"That was weird," Hal said.

"It was like he knew we needed privacy," Rebekah added.

"He is an ally," Robbie said. "He arranged the trip."

"You told a teacher about all this?" Esther asked. "And he believed you?"

"Not exactly," Robbie said. "Mr. Getachew, as you call him, is not from here."

"He's from Ethiopia," said Esther.

Will threw her an impatient look.

"What?" Esther said. "That's what he told us."

Will turned to Robbie. "You're saying he's from the future—from your time?"

"Yes and no."

"I still might punch you in the eye," Esther said. "What does that mean?"

"He is from the future, but this version of him is not from my time. You have all met him before, although only Hal will remember. He is Gyasi. It was he who placed the note in Will's locker that sent him to the bus station."

"Oh!" Hal said, smiling.

Will was not smiling. He didn't remember any note and, of course, he didn't remember meeting anyone in the future. He searched around in his brain, but it was no use. A swell of anger threatened to overflow, but Will paddled through it. There was only one way to get those memories back and that was to get the job done. He glanced down at his watch.

"We have ten minutes left. Once we get to MIT, what then? How do we embed this message?"

"For that we will need help from another ally," Robbie

answered.

"Don't tell me there are more teachers from the future," Esther said. "It's Ms. Moag, isn't it? I always thought she was weird."

"No," said Robbie. "Only Gyasi and I are from your future. Your other teachers are just naturally weird." Robbie chuckled at his own joke but no one else laughed. "We need to implant the message in the containment dome through the airlocks," he continued. "It will remain there until the leak, which will not happen for a century. No human is able to do that."

"Will the aliens help?" asked Hal.

"I have never met an alien," Robbie said. "We still have not understood that part of your story. No, not an alien. We must bring Chester with us."

"Chester? Their cat?" Esther asked.

"Chester isn't a regular cat," said Hal. "I didn't have time to tell you that part. He's from the future, too. But how do we get him to MIT?"

"Chester will travel as Hal's emotional support animal," Robbie said. "I believe the registration process is quite easy."

"I don't need an emotional support animal," Hal said quietly. "I'm not crazy."

"Of course, you aren't," said Rebekah. "You've always been the strong one." She looked in Will's direction, but he was too deep into scheming mode to notice.

"It makes sense," he said. "I saw a kid walking around school with a hamster in a cage the other day. He said it was his support companion. Once you register, they can't say no to you."

Robbie was right—his plan seemed simple. Once they got

to MIT, Chester would escape his carrier and do whatever a sentient cat from the future did to embed a message into a nuclear reactor. Will would have loved to have known the details, but he knew this wasn't the time.

Chapter 18
MIT

By the time they boarded the bus to MIT a week later, Hal and Robbie had been noticed by all but the most uninterested at school. Hal still wasn't sure of her standing on the unofficial *Do You Have a Boyfriend and How Cute Is He?* scorecard. Was Robbie her boyfriend? If so, he was the first real boyfriend she'd ever had, but did a guy from the future count? Judging by the knowing smiles and envious stares coming her way, Hal was starting to believe it did. She leaned in next to him on the bus, enjoying the closeness between them. Robbie gazed off into space for a second before putting his arm around her. Hal had noticed that move before, whenever Robbie encountered a new situation. Esther called it the android stare.

"Checking the database?" Hal asked.

"Yes. Your customs are very different. I want to be sure to behave appropriately, to avoid suspicion."

Hal sat up. "Is that what this is?" she asked. "The way you're acting? Avoiding suspicion?"

Robbie looked concerned. "Have I done something wrong?" he asked, staring into space again.

"No, and cut it out," Hal said. "Forget the database—just answer. What I mean is, the way you're acting toward me, like you like me. Is that real, or are you making believe to avoid suspicion?"

"I'm sorry," said Robbie, "I should have known from your movies and books how unsure relationships were in this time period. I'm not pretending to 'like' you, as you put it. My feelings for you are sincere, and have been since the first time we met. For this reason, I could not live with my betrayal."

Hal leaned in again, turning away from Esther's smirk across the aisle. They rode in silence for a while, looking out the window as they crossed the bridge and entered the concrete landscape of the Bronx.

"Your time period is so interesting," Robbie said. "There are so many crossroads, so many 'watershed moments,' as you say."

"Actually, it's as you say. According to Esther, you're the ones who came up with that mantra."

"Not in my timeline," Robbie said. "Anyway, I will miss being here."

"You sound sad."

"I am sad. Mostly I am sad that our relationship will end today."

"What? Why?" Hal asked, sitting up straight at the edge of her seat. "Can't we see each other in the future, in your time?" The bus changed lanes and jolted forward, but in a quick move Robbie held on to Hal to stop her from sliding to the floor.

"If our plan works, you will be warned not to trust me, and I will be apprehended before I have the chance to betray you. I will never have come here to redeem myself, and all this will never have happened. I doubt very much you would want to be close to me under those circumstances."

"Oh. I see what you mean. Sometimes I forget how this timeline stuff works."

"Understandable," said Robbie.

"So, none of this will have happened, and we won't be... close, like we are now?"

"I can't predict all possible futures, but that is my conjecture."

"Can't we send another message? One that says, 'don't trust Robbie but forgive him,' or something like that?"

"There is no time for such complexities," Robbie said. "Every change in the timeline comes with a cost. In this instance, I'm afraid that cost is our relationship."

Wouldn't you know it. Hal had finally found someone, and it was all going to end because of some stupid time shift. She put her head on Robbie's shoulder and sighed.

"I'll miss you," Robbie said.

"You can't miss what you never knew," Hal responded bitterly.

O—O—O

Three hours on a school bus might seem like a long time to some people, but to Hal the minutes flew by. She was quiet for most of the trip, letting Robbie's words sink in. She'd been so busy thinking about how to undo the pain of the last months that she hadn't thought of anything else. Everything would change after today. Sure, the others would get their memories back—or more correctly, as Robbie pointed out, they'd never have lost their memories—and she'd never experience the frustration of having people think she was crazy. The trade-off? Robbie, the guy she was currently holding hands with, would become her enemy. There was a cost to every shift in the timeline, she got that. But why did she have to be the one to pay the price? What if she did nothing? Robbie could stay here and they could forget about the future and just be present, together, doing the things that regular teenagers did. What was so bad about that?

But then there was Will. If Hal did nothing, Will would be stuck here, stripped of his memories of the future he'd loved so much. The light Hal had seen in her brother's eyes would be gone for good and she didn't know if he'd ever forgive her. What's worse, she might never forgive herself.

The air was nippy when they left the bus and headed to the dome for the tour. Still groggy from their early departure, the pack of teenagers plodded through the parking lot quietly. Mr. Getachew (Hal couldn't think of him as Gyasi in this form—a teacher was a teacher) must have notified the tour leader about Chester, because no one questioned the pet carrier. Hal never realized how heavy Chester was. Her arm was getting tired fast. Robbie offered to help, but Hal declined. She needed to feel the weight of what she was about to do.

According to Robbie's plan, once inside the thick, green, steel doors, Hal was to free Chester. The cat could find his way through the airlocks, but he needed time. Hal's job was to find an inconspicuous spot, open the crate, and hope no one would notice Chester's escape. Easier said than done— apparently the tour guide was a cat person and wouldn't stop commenting on how cute Chester was. For the first time Hal realized the indignities Chester had suffered at the hands of well-meaning humans. She bent down to the carrier and whispered a quick "thank you." Chester licked her face with his sandpaper tongue.

Hal looked around at the complicated maze of green and blue painted metal steps, ladders, and walkways. She saw what she thought looked like air vents, but they were far too small for Chester to fit through, even if he squeezed. How would Chester manage? She wanted to ask Robbie, but she was afraid to attract attention. Instead, she stayed at the back of the group and let Robbie and the others surround her, keeping her out of the tour guide's view. Mr. Getachew stood at the other end of the group, asking questions to create a distraction. The more questions Mr. Getachew asked, the more pleased the tour guide seemed to be.

"Are they flirting?" Esther whispered.

"Whatever," Will said. "Now! Let him out."

But Hal let the opportunity slip away and the group moved on.

"What's wrong with you?" Will asked. "Why didn't you open the crate?"

"It's just," Hal looked at Robbie, "everything will change."

"That's the point," Will hissed.

They stopped again at a control panel the size of the wall. What with the red and green buttons and flashing digital numbers, the room felt to Hal like a futuristic Santa's workshop.

"Fascinating," Robbie said a little too loudly. "So much power in such primitive surroundings."

"Excuse me?" the tour guide asked, frowning. "Did you have a question?"

Mr. Getachew coughed loudly. "Can you explain the color designations to us?" he asked. "How are green and red used to designate function?"

"Way to go, genius," Esther muttered at Robbie once the tour guide had turned away.

"This is it," Will whispered. "Open. The. Crate."

Hal hesitated, balanced on a tightrope with Robbie on one side and Will on the other. A fall was inevitable—the only question was, on which side would she land? She pictured long walks and movie dates and holding hands with Robbie. Then she envisioned Will, eyes bright, working on a holographic display or piloting a vehicle through the open sky. Suddenly, the choice wasn't so hard after all.

Hal opened the door of the carrier and set Chester free. She thought she saw the cat shrink a little as he slipped out of sight.

PART IV– WATERSHED

Chapter 19

TAKE TWO

Hal watched her holographic image in the bubble that Okoko had conjured from thin air. She remembered Will's words—"It isn't magic"—but the way these people manipulated time and matter sure seemed like magic to her. She and Rebekah were spending the day with Mr. Salazar and the Time Guard while Will and Esther were off in the field, studying radiation waves with the Science Sentinels.

"I remember that jacket. That's when we were in first grade," Hal said. She was still basking in the knowledge of her secret tryst with Robbie, and watching herself swing at the park with Rebekah added to her dreaminess. The little girls in the bubble soared higher and higher, laughing and pumping, ponytails rising and falling behind them. "We used to have a contest, remember? To see who could swing the highest. You always won." Hal smiled, lost in happy memories.

Mr. Salazar waved his hand and the image abruptly disappeared. "The interference we see involved your brother," he said.

"Yeah," Hal said, "Esther told us you showed Will some kind of alternate reality where he was a bad kid. You said you gave Mom time travel so she could fix it."

"Yes," Gyasi said, calling up another hologram. "Here we are, the first time we met your mother." There was Mom talking with Gyasi and Okoko out in the yard. Nearby, Hal and Will dunked a mini-basketball through a plastic, kid-sized hoop.

"Look! You saw us when we were kids!" Hal exclaimed to Robbie.

"No, I joined the Time Guard later, after these events."

"Oh," said Hal, disappointed. "Anyway, technically, in our timeline that scene never happened, because you didn't give Mom time travel. The aliens did."

"Yes, the aliens," said Mr. Salazar. "Interesting."

"Can you tell us more about Will and Esther's first visit here?" asked Okoko.

Rebekah answered, "Esther said that some great planetary disaster had been avoided because of Hal's mom and all her green gardening stuff. She saw horrible events going by in fast motion—floods, destruction, civilizations wiped out."

"Yes," said Gyasi, "by giving Alexis the ability to travel back in time, we avoided environmental ruin. Her quiet influence on others who later became prominent was crucial. Even so, our present timeline differs from what Will and Esther experienced the first time they were here. We believe that someone interfered to cause smaller scale climatic catastrophes centuries ago. Thus, our scientific advances were slowed, but not stopped." As Gyasi waved his hand, rain poured down in heavy sheets and swirling winds ripped trees out by their roots. Hal looked for cover, but there was nowhere to go in the small bubble room. The water rose until it almost reached Hal's chin, then suddenly receded. The temperature plummeted and Hal felt the sting of icy snow on her face.

"We get it," she shouted over the howling gale.

Gyasi waved his hand again and the storm subsided, replaced with a broiling sun. All around them vegetation sprang up, then shriveled and died in the intense heat. "The extreme changes in climate threatened the food supply. The economy weakened, and disaster loomed." Just when Hal felt she would melt in the burning heat, Gyasi ended the simulation. To her surprise, she was completely cool and dry.

"But, with the help of Servant Leader Snorok, we have been in recovery for the last hundred years," Robbie explained. "He helped develop the green technology that provided the foundation for all our advancement."

"You're saying Snorok is over a hundred years old?" Hal asked.

"Yes, lifespans are longer here," Robbie said.

"I've always found it quite interesting that Snorok had all the solutions to our society's problems at his fingertips," Mr. Salazar said. "His timing was impeccable."

"He is a great leader," Robbie said. He waved his hand and Snorok appeared in a bubble, floating above a sea of cheering people in gray overalls. Hal looked closely—there was Robbie in the front row with a look of total adoration on his face. She was almost jealous.

"Perhaps," Mr. Salazar said. "But Snorok has not been satisfied with his position on council. He's gained power and gained it quickly. I suspect our servant leader has altered the timeline to his own advantage."

"That would explain why our present is different—less joyful, more guarded, it seems—than the one Will and Esther first experienced," said Okoko.

Mr. Salazar's face became grave. "Jikon, a new aperture, please—one that is shielded and transmission free." Jikon sprang into action, pressing his hand against the jellylike surface of the wall to create a new, circular room. They stepped inside, but just as Jikon was about to close up the entrance, Will and Esther rushed in, red-faced and out of breath. With them was a tall, thin girl with bright red hair pulled back in a tight braid. Esther stepped directly up to Robbie and knocked him down with a punch to the eye.

"Esther, what are you doing!" Rebekah exclaimed, pulling her sister away. Hal took Robbie's arm to help him up.

"He's a spy!" Esther shouted. "We found a message in the radiation waves that said not to trust him. Frona did some digging and sure enough, this slimeball has been spying for Snorok all along."

Hal let go of Robbie's arm and stepped away.

"Snorok knows we're here and he has the Council's okay to arrest Mr. Salazar at dinner tonight," Will said. "Frona found the arrest orders and the official document giving him permission to wipe our memories."

"Transmitting the data now," said Frona. A few seconds later, the Time Guard gasped in shock.

"If Snorok goes through with this, we'll never know we've been here," said Will.

"Not all of you," Robbie said. "He allowed me to spare Halia. I planned to send her back tonight, before the arrest."

"You're awfully honest, for a spy," Esther said.

"There is no reason to hide the truth now. My only goal has been to protect the timeline." Robbie turned to Hal. "I would never do anything to hurt you."

"Save it for someone who cares," Esther said, and Hal nodded in agreement even though she hadn't stopped caring yet.

"Frona must return to the Science Institute in order to avoid suspicion. Jikon, flight please, to these coordinates," said Mr. Salazar, waving a navigational panel into existence.

"Where are you taking me?" Robbie asked.

"To a torture chamber, I hope," Esther said.

"No," said Mr. Salazar. "We need some answers. We're going to the Altvume."

○─○─○

Great, the Altvume, Will thought. He tried to make his heart stop pounding. He wasn't the subject this time. He wouldn't be handcuffed and shoved into the back of a police car in some sinister alternate timeline.

They landed at the base of the hill where the entrance to the Altvume was hidden.

"Why the Altvume?" Esther asked with a sideways glance at Will. "Couldn't you just use one of the hologram bubble things?"

"Only the Altvume can show us alternate realities. And

we'll be sheltered inside it," Mr. Salazar answered. "Snorok knows nothing of this place and no one can enter without my permission." Will's breathing got a little easier. This was Mr. Salazar's turf. They were safe, for now.

"Come." Mr. Salazar placed his hand on a boulder and the entrance to the Altvume appeared. "Jikon, Okoko, and Gyasi will remain here. Robbie will accompany us."

They stepped into the bright white tunnel that burned in Will's memory.

"We will start with what we know for sure," Mr. Salazar said. "Snorok's first plan was to use Will to distract your mother from her environmental activities.

"Wait," Esther said. "You're not going to do that to Will again." It was not a question.

"There is no need," said Mr. Salazar, looking at Will kindly. "The Time Guard discovered the interference, although we were not sure who was responsible until now. We countered by giving Alexis time travel, which allowed her to restore the correct timeline. When Snorok failed in that attempt, he altered the timeline in a smaller way. Isn't that correct, Robbie?"

Robbie didn't answer.

"Can we beat it out of him?" Esther asked hopefully.

"Again, no need," Mr. Salazar answered. He took Robbie's hand and pressed it against the white wall of the Altvume. "As Snorok's spy, Robbie has access to the data we need. Observe."

The walls of the Altvume fell away to reveal workers bustling around a large hall filled with holographic images and computer-like screens. In the center of the room sat a short, round man with a balding head and a stubby, dark beard.

He worked steadily, punching away at a screen, stopping once in a while to rub his eyes or rest his head in his hands. When a very official looking woman approached him, he sat up straight in a hurry.

"Did you receive the data I transmitted?" she asked.

"Yes. I will analyze during the next quadrant."

"Very well. In the future, please respond with a receiving message."

"Yes, of course," the man said, bowing slightly.

"Who's he?" Will asked. "What does this have to do with anything?"

"The man before you is Snorok as he would have remained had he not tampered with the timeline," Mr. Salazar said.

"What?" Esther exclaimed. "That's Snorok? Where's the snowy mane? Where are those beady eyes? This guy looks nothing like him."

"The DNA altering serum," Rebekah said. "He's used it to change his appearance, hasn't he?"

"I'm afraid so," Mr. Salazar responded.

"I like him better this way," Esther said.

"Agreed," said Mr. Salazar, "but I suppose he felt his natural state was not sufficiently imposing."

They continued to watch as person after person stopped by Snorok's workstation to remind him of work needed or reprimand him for work not done. Each time Snorok apologized he sank a little lower into his seat.

"He's just a regular old grunt," Will said. "I feel kind of sorry for him." Just goes to show, thought Will with a bit of satisfaction, every bad guy has a backstory.

The room grew dark and people faded from view. Snorok

remained at his console, looking around furtively. Sure he was alone, he took a tiny hypodermic needle from his pocket and jabbed it into his thumb. Instantly, his screen was replaced by a holographic bubble. Images sped up and slowed down inside the bubble as Snorok manipulated them.

"The timeline!" Robbie said.

"Yes, we are witnessing the beginnings of Snorok's interference," said Mr. Salazar.

The time bubble expanded and displayed an image of Mom in Mrs. Bumbly's office, slumped in her seat like a kid who got caught cheating.

"Snorok saw to it that Alexis eased up on her gardening pursuits in small ways. Here, she missed an important meeting because of Will's difficulties in school. That's all it took to ensure our current timeline."

"Wow," Esther said. "It's that watershed thing all over again."

Mr. Salazar continued. "But these smaller changes wouldn't be enough for someone whose goal is absolute power. Only a total collapse of society would provide him that opportunity, especially if he had all the solutions for recovery at hand—solutions he could easily pass off as his own." Mr. Salazar's dark eyes lit with understanding. "Snorok needed to completely stop Alexis from her work. When his plan to stop your mother through Will didn't work, he conceived of another way." Mr. Salazar fixed his attention on Robbie. "He planned to use Robbie's loyalty."

"By turning us in, you mean," said Will.

"Snorok is more cunning than that," Mr. Salazar answered. "Observe."

Will spun into the kitchen at home, where he sat at the table eating Halloween candy. He could taste the chocolate in his mouth, but he was both in the scene and watching the scene, like sometimes happened in his dreams. A sad looking jack-o'-lantern sat in the window and Hal was crying, begging them to remember that they'd just returned from the future. Feeling irritated and annoyed, Will disappeared upstairs with a pocketful of candy and closed his door on the ruckus.

The scene shifted and Will became an audience member, watching from the sidelines. The pumpkin was gone and now Mom and Hal were talking in the kitchen, where the morning light fell across the counter. Mom looked tired and Hal seemed thin and pale, like she'd been sick or something. He heard Mom say she'd given up gardening and she was quitting her job, too. Then Mom left and Hal sat there, all alone, with a blankness on her face that reminded Will of himself. In the next instant the scene dissipated and they stood in the starkness of the Altvume again.

"So, in that timeline Snorok used me to get to Mom," Hal said.

"Yes," Mr. Salazar said, "and Robbie inadvertently helped him."

Robbie hung his head in shame. "I didn't know fully what he'd planned." He set his blue eyes on Hal. "I sent you home to spare you his wrath, but instead I almost doomed you to a lonely and isolated existence."

"Yeah, you're a real hero," Esther said.

"But who sent the message through the radiation waves?" Rebekah asked.

"I think I know," said Will. He pressed his hand to the wall

242

and they whirled into a sequence of settings: the four of them with Robbie, discussing their plan at school, then sitting on a school bus, and finally, entering the lab at MIT with Chester in a pet carrier.

"How'd you do that?" Esther asked when the last scene faded, but no one paid attention.

"I think we have enough information to bring Snorok down," Mr. Salazar said. "The council will not take lightly to his interference."

They walked out of the bright light of the Altvume into the orange dusk, where Jikon, Okoko, and Gyasi were waiting. Will remembered them as they were on his first trip to the future, the Time Team instead of the Time Guard, geeking out with their chant and their brightly colored clothes. He'd thought they were goofy then, but now he wished he could help them get back to that reality, somehow.

"Greetings," Jikon said when they approached. "Did the repairs go well?"

Mr. Salazar stopped abruptly but said nothing.

"Repairs?" Will asked. "What are you talking about?"

"The repairs to the Altvume you were sent to make," said Okoko. "Did you succeed?"

Before anyone could answer, Mr. Salazar motioned for silence.

"All is well," he said. "We need information for one final adjustment. Please transmit a report of the events of the last two days."

The Time Guard stood completely still except for their eyes, which were flashing like strobe lights.

"Very good," Mr. Salazar said after a moment. "You may

return to your other duties. We will signal when we are finished."

"We don't mind waiting for you," Okoko said.

"We may be longer than expected. You may go."

"As you wish," said Jikon. They entered the bubble and waved goodbye through the transparent walls.

Will watched them ascend and shoot through the sky. "So cool," he sighed as they disappeared into the clouds.

"What was that about?" Esther asked. "What repairs?"

Mr. Salazar and Robbie exchanged knowing glances. "I'm afraid our friend Snorok has not quite given up." Mr. Salazar said.

"What does that mean?" asked Hal, but Will's stomach churned. He knew what it meant.

"Perhaps he's altered their memories," Robbie said. "They think you're someone else, someone from our time."

"Why? What would be the point of that?" Hal asked.

"This is not a simple memory wipe," said Mr. Salazar. "Something else has happened—or not happened."

"I still don't get it," Esther said.

"He means they never met us," Will said, voice shaking. "They never traveled back in time and gave Mom time travel. Snorok's original plan will work."

"Then why are we still here?" Rebekah asked.

"The Altvume protected you from the effects of Snorok's tampering," Mr. Salazar said. "I suggest we return there immediately before the time wave catches up with us."

"Which I believe will happen in less than ten seconds," Robbie said.

Will didn't need a countdown to spring him into action. He ran as fast as he could to the safety of the Altvume, hoping against hope that he would make it there in time.

Chapter 20

THE FUTURE IS GRAY

Something gripped Will as he stepped into the Altvume. A power he couldn't resist pulled him toward a tunnel of harsh, deafening wind. The force of the timeline reached for him, and Will knew once it took hold there would be no escape. He fell to the floor and rolled into a tight ball just as the Altvume sealed shut. After a few seconds of total silence, he reached out his hand and felt the cool, smooth surface of the Altvume floor. He was still here.

"We made it!" Will said, breathless, clutching his middle with his eyes still squeezed shut.

"Not all of us," said Hal.

Will sat up and looked around. Esther and Rebekah were gone. "What happened to them?" he asked, although he already knew the answer.

"They were just a few steps too late," Mr. Salazar answered. "Their reality has shifted to a timeline in which they were never here."

"But the Altvume will protect us, right?" Will concentrated on keeping his voice even.

"Yes," Mr. Salazar said. "You will remain in this time period as long as you don't leave the Altvume." Will nodded and let out a deep breath.

"What good is that?" Hal practically shouted. "Do you plan on spending the rest of your life inside this, this whatever it is?"

Will had to admit she had a point.

"Maybe you should spend eternity playing at different realities," Hal continued. "You'd rather do anything than go home and live your real life, right? The one with your family who loves you?"

Another good point, although not the one Hal was trying to make. Will was stuck, no matter what, either here, in a world of false realities, or back there, in a life that would never satisfy. He put his head in his hands.

"I don't know what to do."

"I believe I may have an answer to your dilemma," Mr. Salazar said gently. "With your permission, I can take us further into the future. Once there, I think we may find a way to undo Snorok's tampering."

"Travel to the future is strictly forbidden," Robbie said.

"We know that, spymaster," said Will. Where was Esther when you needed her?

"I am aware of the Time Travel Dictates," Mr. Salazar said, "since I helped write them. However, in the words of an ancient philosopher, 'A strong disease requires strong medicine.' Snorok is a disease and we must do our best to stop him."

"Okay," Hal said. "But how will going to your future help?"

"Will we be able to stay there?" Will asked.

"No, not permanently. But the technology we need is there."

"How can you know that?" Robbie asked.

"Because he's from there, or then," said Will. "He's from the future—further into the future, I mean. Isn't that right?"

Mr. Salazar nodded. "You are correct."

"When exactly are you from?" Hal asked.

"That's not important now. But we must all be agreed if our plan is to work."

"I'm in," Will said.

But Hal needed a minute to think. "If we go home now, to a world where my mother never travels in time, my brother turns into Bad Will, right? The one that gets arrested?"

"That is likely," Mr. Salazar replied.

"Then I'm in, too," said Hal. "I can't let that happen." Rebekah was right, Will thought. Hal really is the strong one.

Mr. Salazar looked to Robbie. "It is up to you now. You need only step outside the Altvume to return to a timeline in which none of this has happened. You will not be Snorok's spy and will have nothing to atone for."

Robbie hesitated, and for a second Will thought the creep was going to ruin everything (again). But he turned toward Hal and spoke quietly. "I see now the harm that my uncle has caused. I'll help." He kept his eyes fixed on Hal. "Besides, it turns out I'm not a very good spy," he added, and as Will almost heaved, his ever-forgiving sister returned Robbie's smile.

"Move closer together," Mr. Salazar instructed as he arched his arms above them. Will felt a slight tingling, far more muted than his previous travels through time. Nothing around him changed—no flashing lights, no chimes, no

247

spinning, no grinding gears. He guessed time travel worked differently here, inside the Altvume.

"Now what?" Will said. He was anxious to get on with it. "How far have we come?"

"Thirty years, by your temporal reckoning," Mr. Salazar said.

"That's it?" Will said, not trying to hide his disappointment. He thought they'd go a hundred, maybe a thousand more years into the future. The further, the better, as far as he was concerned.

"That is all that is required."

"Can we see what it looks like?" Will asked. "I mean, if this thing can show us alternate realities, can't you at least open a window?"

Mr. Salazar chuckled. "I'll see what I can do while we wait for help from a colleague." With a touch of his hand, the blankness of the Altvume was replaced by endless rows of long, flat, rectangular, structures, all the same size and the same murky brown color. The buildings were windowless, not that there was much of a view, anyway. This future looked like an overgrown preschooler had lined up a bunch of giant blocks in the middle of a dirt pit that stretched as far as the eye could see.

"This is...boring," Will said.

"What happened to the green bubbles?" Hal asked.

"Yes," said Robbie, "and where is the foliage? Where are the energy synthesizing shafts? How is the city powered?"

"What we are seeing is much changed from last I was here," Mr. Salazar said. "It appears that Snorok has done his worst."

Although still within the safety of the Altvume, they walked along a path in between buildings, jostling through a crowd of people wearing the same bulky, grayish clothing. This world seemed devoid of color. Even the sky was gray.

"Look at their heads," Hal whispered. Every head was shorn close to the scalp.

"That's one way to save time in the morning," Will muttered, brushing his own unkempt hair out of his eyes.

They reached a wider thoroughfare that ran in front of the buildings—not a street exactly, since there were no cars in sight. Just more people trudging along silently in front of prison-like block buildings with no windows.

Then Will noticed the most striking difference between this world and the future he'd come to know.

"They're all old, like you," he said, "uh, older, I mean. Where are the kids, the people our age?"

"That is not clear," Mr. Salazar replied. "But apparently Snorok has arranged for their separation from adults in everyday life."

"Maybe in schools, as in your time," Robbie suggested.

"Oh. That's not so bad," Hal said.

"Yeah," Will said, "sitting in a boring classroom is so much better than flying around, traveling through time, altering DNA."

Before Hal could argue, a square metal block appeared from nowhere and landed in the middle of the crowd. Will realized it was a vehicle when the side dematerialized and four adults in white uniforms jumped out. They made their way through the crowd who scattered before them like bugs about to be stepped on. A minute later the people fell back into step and the white uniforms aimed their palms randomly at the haggard souls dragging heavily on, heads bowed.

"What's going on?" Hal asked. "Shouldn't we hide?"

"It's not real," Will said. "We're in the Altvume,

remember?"

"It is real," said Mr. Salazar, "but we are not really here. No one can see us or sense our presence."

"They're some kind of police force scanning the crowd. They must be looking for something," Robbie said.

"Or someone," said Mr. Salazar.

"I don't see any guns," Will said.

"They don't need guns," replied Robbie, "look."

One of the guards approached a pedestrian, encased her in a square plastic shell that materialized spontaneously, and levitated her into the block vehicle, all with the wave of a hand. The other guards jumped in and the last thing Will saw before they disappeared was the look of horror frozen on the woman's face. No one in the crowd stopped or even seemed to notice.

"I've seen enough," Hal said.

Mr. Salazar waved and the image faded to white.

Hal took Will's hand. "We can do this," she said. "At least we have to try. The worst that can happen is that they'll send us home." She looked to Mr. Salazar. "Right?"

"I can't say that for sure," Mr. Salazar said. "But we can put certain safeguards in place to protect you. I'll explain. But now, our help has arrived." He created an opening at the end of the Altvume and in walked that sub from school, Mr. Getachew. Will almost didn't recognize him, with his shaved head and dreary outfit, but his eyes looked just the same.

"What's he doing here?" Will asked.

"This is Gyasi," said Mr. Salazar, "as he appears in this time period."

"Gyasi!" Hal exclaimed, throwing her arms around him.

"Uh, yes, it is very nice to meet you, Halia. You also, Will," Gyasi said.

Hal stepped away. "Oh. I forgot. You don't remember us," she said.

Gyasi smiled kindly. "I'm sorry, I don't. But Salazar has transmitted your story and I am here to help." He took three vials from his pocket. "This serum will allow you to remain in this time period for exactly one hour. After that the time shield will dissipate."

"This is the safeguard I spoke of," said Mr. Salazar. "If you have not accomplished your task within an hour, the change in the timeline will catch up to you and you will simply return to your own time. None of this will have happened. You will be safe."

"And stuck," Will muttered. He gulped down the serum and Hal and Robbie followed.

"Now that you can leave the Altvume you must go to the Science Institute to retrieve the DNA altering formula," said Mr. Salazar.

"The Science Block," Gyasi corrected. "There are no research institutes, as you call them, in this timeline—only organizations designed to control and contain information for Snorok's purposes."

"I see," said Mr. Salazar. "All the more reason to act quickly."

"But why do we have to go to the institute, or block, or whatever it's called?" Hal asked. "Why do we need to alter our DNA?"

"So that you can return to your own time and give your mother time travel technology," Gyasi explained. "We must alter your DNA so that you don't return to your own bodies in that time. In that state you would be unable to activate the Past Finder device for your mother."

"But the aliens gave Mom time travel," Hal said, puzzled.

The aliens...

Will exploded into a full, joyful laugh. He laughed so hard that he doubled over, holding his stomach. Mr. Salazar looked on and smiled.

"Oh," said Hal. "Oh! I get it!"

"Welcome to Aliens R Us!" Will said. His laughter subsided but he couldn't stop from beaming. He was an eagle, ready for flight.

"Wouldn't it be simpler if I traveled to Alexis' time with the technology?" Robbie asked.

"Way to kill the moment," Will said. "And like we would trust you to get it right."

"I assure you, I am quite capable," Robbie answered.

"Regardless, you would be easily tracked and stopped by Snorok's forces," said Mr. Salazar. "In Will and Halia's new forms, they will be untraceable."

"Okay, what are we waiting for? Let's go," said Will.

"Wait," said Hal, and Will was afraid she was about to chicken out. "One more question. Why couldn't Gyasi just bring the DNA altering stuff here? Why do we have to go out there to get it?"

Gyasi replied, "I do not have access to the Science Block, where the DNA serums are kept. That is why Frona will meet you there."

"But Frona won't remember us," Hal said.

"Yeah—for her, there's nothing to remember," said Will. "We were never here."

"She will not remember you, but she has been informed. I'm transmitting the coordinates of the Science Block to Robbie now," Gyasi said. "The megalopolis is a grid. You should have no trouble finding it."

"Okay," Hal said. "I'm ready. The worst that can happen

is that the time shield wears off and we go home in an hour."

"Assuming we are alive in an hour," Robbie said, and once again, Will wished with all his heart that Esther were here.

Chapter 21

LAST CHANCE

Even though they'd changed clothes to blend in, Hal was terrified when she stepped out of Gyasi's transport in a small alleyway near the Science Block. She pictured herself being stopped on the street, imprisoned in a chunk of plastic, and carted off to Snorok to be sent back to a version of the timeline that held nothing but pain for her family. She pushed the panic away as best she could, determined to do her best.

"I must leave you here," Gyasi said. "It's safer if you walk the rest of the way. Frona will meet you at the entrance." There was the possibility they'd be stopped for a random street check, but they'd have to take that chance.

Hal, Will, and Robbie shuffled along with their heads down and shoulders slumped, like the people of that time. Although no visible chains bound them, these people were enslaved; hopelessness hung on them like iron shackles. Hal tried to stop herself from imagining the horror of their lives. Just get to the lab and everything will be fine. And if all else fails, just stay out of sight for the next forty-five minutes. That's all she had to do.

They plodded on for a short distance, when suddenly a moving block like the one they'd seen in the Altvume appeared directly behind them.

"Keep walking," Robbie whispered. "Do not turn around."

Hal heard the guards spill out into the street. It took every ounce of courage she had to resist the urge to run or duck into some corner and hide. She reached for Will's hand, but Robbie saw and shook his head.

"Do nothing to draw attention to yourself. Just walk. We are almost there."

They turned the corner and approached a building indistinguishable from the others except for a large symbol on its front of a vulture with razor sharp teeth and an arrow sticking out of its mouth. Hal didn't know what it meant, but she trembled as they stood in front of the building, waiting for Frona.

"Where is she?" Will hissed.

"I just received a transmission from Gyasi," Robbie said. "Frona is delayed. We are to wait here."

A square opening in the building appeared and a group of people streamed out without taking notice of Hal and the others. A woman, dressed in the same white uniform as the guards on the street, looked them over suspiciously.

"Why do you linger here?" she barked. "And why haven't you been shorn? Reveal your designations."

Hal felt as frozen as the woman she'd watched being hauled away. Robbie stepped up to the guard and spoke in a soft, reassuring tone.

"Our designations are in need of upgrade," he said. "We have come for that purpose."

"These are not the droids you're looking for," Will mumbled.

"Designation upgrades are automatic," the woman said, "as you well know. Why aren't you at your indoctrination center?"

"We only know that we were sent here," Robbie said sweetly. He looked into the woman's eyes, which were the same shade of blue as his own. They both seemed to have a moment of recognition and then, inexplicably, the guard stood to the side.

"You may enter," she said, and as they did Frona appeared, hurrying down the corridor toward them. She was older and thinner and walked with the same hunch as everyone else. In place of her long, fiery red hair was a pale, bald scalp.

"These are with me," she said, showing the guard her forearm, where a series of symbols appeared vertically just above her wrist. The guard nodded and they hurried off, walking quickly and quietly until Frona stopped and turned to face the wall.

"This will take us to my lab," she said. She waved her wrist at the wall and a section dematerialized. Hal looked into an empty space. She hung back, but when Frona and the others entered she had no choice but to follow, closing her eyes as she stepped onto nothingness. She found herself ascending quickly in an elevator with no floor. After a few seconds they rotated ninety degrees and swooshed head first, sideways through the building. This was no elevator—this was more like the vacuum tube at the bank's drive through window.

They stopped and swiveled upright again. Will faced Robbie and asked, "What was that, out there? Don't tell me you charmed that guard with your baby blue eyes." Hal had almost forgotten about Robbie's betrayal, but her brother, of course, had not.

Robbie was quiet for a moment as a look of deep sadness overtook him. "No," he answered finally. "I almost didn't know her, because she looks so different. She is my mother."

Hal hadn't seen that coming. "Did she recognize you?" she asked.

"I don't believe so," said Robbie.

"She could not have," Frona said. "You do not exist in this timeline. That is why you have been allowed to participate in this mission. There is no chance of you running into your future self."

Robbie nodded. "I'm glad, in a way. I don't think I would want to exist in a world that could do that to my mother."

As sappy as it was, Hal felt her heart sink for Robbie. A guy who loved his mom couldn't be all bad, could he?

"But if he doesn't exist, why would she let him pass?" Will asked.

Frona replied, "It's possible that the guard sensed something familiar in Robbie—a time echo, perhaps. It could explain why she didn't arrest you all immediately."

They came to a stop and stepped out into the corridor. Frona opened a doorway to her lab, which looked like nothing more than an empty room. Once she'd sealed them in, a holographic display appeared in the space above Frona's head. Lights and symbols flashed faster than Hal could follow.

"I've adjusted the surveillance mechanisms," Frona said, "but in a short time the changes will be noticed. We must move quickly." She touched the wall and a small drawer opened containing two plain metal cylinders about four inches long.

"Here is the serum we've developed for you," Frona said,

handing the vials to Will and Hal. "It will take a few minutes to read your DNA from the skin of your hands. When the serum turns green, simply drink it and go."

Simple, right. Hal was getting tired of simple plans that backfired in the end. She needed more information. "How does the serum know what to change us into? What if it makes me a monster? Or a hornworm? And once it's done, then what?" Her brother might be willing to jump in feet first, but Hal needed to test the water. "How do we get back home? How do we even get back to the Altvume? We can't exactly walk around looking like, like whatever we'll be."

"We'll be Fost and Tuley, from Mom's journal," Will said. "We could fly back to the Altvume. Mr. Salazar will send us back to Mom's time."

Hal frowned. "You mean our time, right?"

"Whatever."

"You will need to take this with you," Frona said. She reached back into the draw and retrieved the TTD. "It's programmed for your mother's use."

"So that's why she didn't need Chester's help," Will said. He studied the device, turning it over carefully. His eyes brightened and with the edge of the metal cylinder he scratched the words, "just one day" on the back of the device.

"All set," Will said. "Now, as soon as the serum does its magic, we'll fly."

"This is not magic, and that would be dangerous," Frona said. "Our sensors would detect you."

"And there is no need," Robbie said. "I can send you back to your own time."

"That means we have to trust you," Will answered, "and I don't."

"Will, stop," Hal pleaded. "He said he's sorry, and he's

proven himself. I trust him, and you should, too."

"Actually," Frona said, "I don't believe Robbie's implants can adequately draw from our energy sources. Watch." Abruptly the room dissolved and they stood under a metal tower the height of a skyscraper. In the center of the structure a massive earthworm was held upright with steel spikes and chains, squirming ferociously. Bolts of electricity prodded it every few seconds and Hal could see the bristles on its enormous rings flail about wildly with each zap. The giant worm curled its head up and opened its mouth as if to scream, but then burrowed into the ground with a powerful crunching sound. Hal ducked when, a few seconds later, a shower of dark, moist soil flew out of the tail end.

"What the heck?" Will shouted over the sound of the electric current blasting the earthworm's body.

"In our timeline, we derive energy from the earth's outer core," Frona said. "The DNA of these creatures has been altered to create an energy efficient workforce. They can burrow through the earth more effectively than any machinery while producing fertilizer at the same time."

The scene vanished as quickly as it had appeared.

"Isn't that animal abuse?" Hal asked.

"Judging by how they treat the people, I don't think they care much about the worms," Will answered.

"In any case," Frona continued as if they hadn't just witnessed the horrendous scene, "Robbie will not be able to glean energy from the atmosphere with his implants, but it is of no concern. Once you have ingested the serum, you will gain the ability to change your appearance and to travel through time. You need simply focus your mind, and the technology will do your bidding."

"How long will it last?" Will asked. "How long will we

have these abilities?"

Frona looked puzzled. "The effects will be permanent, of course," she said.

"So, you're saying we can send ourselves back, visit Mom, then return to the future?" Will asked. "The good future, I mean, not this one."

"Of course," Frona said again.

"And we can come and go whenever we want?"

"Theoretically, yes," Frona said. "Although you will be restricted to travel between your birth and this time period. I'm sorry, but Salazar was clear on that."

"Wahoo!" Will shouted.

Hal wanted to share her brother's joy, but her tether to home gave a tug. "Promise you won't leave forever," she said. "Promise you won't forget us."

"Promise. I'll always come back, even if it's for just one day. And we'll have to tell Mom and Dad. They'll freak out at first, but they'll get used to the idea." Will turned to Frona. "Can we bring others back here with us?"

"Yes, the technology will allow that on a limited basis."

"You want to bring Mom and Dad to the future?" Hal asked. She pictured her family living in a space-age home, like the Jetsons. She'd never thought of that, but it could work. Mom would love a world powered with green energy, and Dad...was there baseball in the future? Probably not, but Hal was sure Dad could get something started. Bubble ball, maybe.

"Are you crazy?" Will said. "I meant Esther. She should have the same chance we do. It's only fair."

Hal suspected that fairness wasn't the only reason her brother was thinking of Esther, but before she could say so the lights flickered.

"We have been discovered," Frona said. "But we need more time. The serum is not yet ready."

"What should we do?" Hal asked, her anxiety peaking.

"You must remain here and wait for the serum to adapt fully. Once it does, drink it and leave immediately."

"How can we be sure we'll hit the right time period?" Will asked.

"Hal knows the exact point in time you first appeared to your mother," Robbie said. "She read it in the journals. The technology will find that memory and lead you there. Hold on to each other through the journey."

Hal nodded. She squeezed the vial tightly, as if to hurry the process.

"One more thing," Robbie said, but before he could finish the wall opened and two guards stepped in. Neither of them was his mother.

"Don't move!" they commanded. Hal saw the computer above Frona's head flash. A clear tube materialized and encased her and her brother.

"Dismantle the shelter immediately!" one of the guards shouted. "That is an order!"

"Nevertheless, we resist," Frona replied calmly, and Hal realized that Frona was not acting alone. She wondered how many others had risked their lives to get the formula to them. The vial remained unchanged.

The guard sneered. "Your puny resistance, as you call it, will die with you this moment." He aimed his palm at Frona and she fell to the floor.

"You," the second guard shouted at Robbie, "stop them immediately or you won't be as lucky as your friend." He nodded toward Frona's lifeless body, curling his lip in a cruel smile.

"Of course," Robbie said calmly. He turned his back on the guard and placed his hand on the surface of the tube.

"Don't do it!" Will shouted, but it was too late. The tube dissolved and they were left unprotected, at the mercy of the guards. Hal couldn't believe Robbie had betrayed them again. Why had she trusted him?

"You must use a sneaker wave," Robbie said. "He will help."

"What? Who?" Hal screamed, but Robbie couldn't answer. He'd raised his arms above the guards, trying desperately to form a bubble around them. Sparks of green light flew from his fingers. The guards seemed confused, at least for the moment.

"He's trying to send them back in time," Will said, dragging Hal away. "Run!"

They sidestepped Robbie and leapt out of the lab, only to see another guard coming in their direction.

"We're running out of time," Will said. "Drink it!"

Hal looked back into the lab and saw that Robbie, too, had fallen. She popped open the lid of the cylinder and gulped down the warm, smooth liquid.

Nothing happened.

The guards approached carefully, palms forward. Hal took Will's hand.

"Is it an hour yet?" she whispered.

"Almost," Will said. "Stall."

"We have been instructed not to harm you," said the guard who had struck down Frona. "President Snorok wants to interrogate you personally."

"Okay," Hal said, her voice shaking. "But first, I have to go to the bathroom."

"What?"

"I have to pee. Unless you want a puddle on the floor, take me to the bathroom."

"She means it," Will said. "She's got the bladder control of a two-year-old."

"Enough!" the guard shouted so loudly that Hal jumped. "You will come with us!"

This is it, Hal thought. The serum wasn't working—they'd probably drunk it too soon. Their only hope was that the time shield would wear off and they'd be sent hurtling through the timeline toward home. How long had it been? Every moment since they'd left the Altvume had felt like an eternity. How long before they stood in Snorok's creepy presence? Maybe, if they were lucky, they'd disappear before they got there.

"The President will meet us at the rendezvous in five units," one of the guards said. "Let's get moving."

Hal didn't know what five units were, but it didn't sound good. She held on tight to Will's hand and moved a half-step closer to him.

The guards proceeded toward them slowly. An image of her parents flashed in Hal's mind. Maybe Snorok wouldn't send them home. Maybe he'd kill them on the spot or keep them prisoners in this time until they lost all hope, like the people here. Mom and Dad would live the rest of their lives not knowing what had happened to their children. A devastated Mom would give up on life and Snorok would have his way.

Across the corridor, a small circle opened midway up the wall.

"What's that?" Will asked, pointing.

"Reinforcements," the guard barked. "Hands behind your back."

Hal and Will didn't budge. The guard grabbed Will and yanked him hard.

"Leave him alone!" Hal screamed, but to her surprise, Will suddenly seemed the very epitome of calm. He smiled and nodded toward the opening in the wall. Before Hal could get a good look, a gray torpedo streaked toward them, claws out, and landed on the guard's face. The man screamed and pulled frantically at the mass of fur, teeth, and claws, but just as quickly as it had landed it launched again, this time heading for Hal's arms.

"Chester!" Hal exclaimed.

The warmth of the serum filled Hal's being and without warning they rose to the ceiling and through it, beyond the confines of cement walls and block buildings, and found themselves at the center of a time wave that washed above and across the timeline, with their very own cat at the helm.

Will tingled from his head to his toes. He held on tight to Hal, fighting the impulse to throw open his arms and allow his transformation the freedom it deserved. His body was growing, expanding, reworking itself from the inside out, and the best part was that he controlled the metamorphosis. He thought, "feathers" and feathers sprouted, covering his upper body while his human legs became thick and muscular. He kept his arms and hands human, but from his sides he grew wings—wide, powerful, glorious wings. Now, what to do with his face? He didn't want to appear too scary; after all, his mom would have to see him this way. He tried the full eagle look, complete with sharp beak and bright yellow eyes, but in the end, he decided on a human face surrounded by a thick tuft of stark white feathers. The final touch was his clothing. He wasn't sure how this worked since his clothes weren't part of his body. Carefully, he manipulated the molecules of his plain